THE SHATTERPROOF MAGICIAN

THE SHATTERPROOF MAGICIAN

THE INSCRUTABLE PARIS BEAUFONT™ BOOK 4

SARAH NOFFKE

MICHAEL ANDERLE

This book is a work of fiction. All of the characters, organizations, and events portrayed in this novel are either products of the author's imagination or are used fictitiously. Sometimes both.

Copyright © 2021 LMBPN Publishing
Cover copyright © LMBPN Publishing
A Michael Anderle Production

LMBPN Publishing supports the right to free expression and the value of copyright. The purpose of copyright is to encourage writers and artists to produce the creative works that enrich our culture.

The distribution of this book without permission is a theft of the author's intellectual property. If you would like permission to use material from the book (other than for review purposes), please contact support@lmbpn.com. Thank you for your support of the author's rights.

LMBPN Publishing
PMB 196, 2540 South Maryland Pkwy
Las Vegas, NV 89109

Version 1.00, June 2021
eBook ISBN: 978-1-64971-839-6
Print ISBN: 978-1-64971-840-2

THE SHATTERPROOF MAGICIAN TEAM

Thanks to the JIT Readers

Deb Mader
Dave Hicks
Diane L. Smith
Micky Cocker
Veronica Stephan-Miller
Dorothy Lloyd
Jackey Hankard-Brodie
Zacc Pelter
Debi Sateren

If I've missed anyone, please let me know!

Editor
The Skyhunter Editing Team

To Rob for being a fantastic supporter, good friend and pillar of strength.

— Sarah

*To Family, Friends and
Those Who Love
to Read.
May We All Enjoy Grace
to Live the Life We Are
Called.*

— Michael

CHAPTER ONE

Creating love in the modern world was going to involve destroying it first. That's what Agent Ruby had concluded after watching the debacle that was happening worldwide.

Matchmaking was a joke. Divorce was on the rise. Love simply didn't last in the modern world.

It was all the current Saint Valentine's fault.

The love meter had never been lower, and the reason was the avant-garde ways taking over. Traditions were lost. Men and women forgot etiquette. So much of it stemmed from technology, loss of gender roles, and of course, the fairy godmothers weren't doing their job like they should—as they used to.

Agent Ruby strode right by the security desk in the lobby of FriendNet. The guard jerked to a standing position and darted around the desk.

"Sir, I'm going to need to see some ID." The man's hand went to the gun in his holster since Agent Ruby hadn't made any attempt to slow as he trespassed into the corporation.

Agent Ruby paused and sighed, realizing that he would have to use magic to bypass this gatekeeper, although he could show identification. However, it was best if no one knew that the director for Fairy Godmother Agency, also known as FGA, was there.

He nodded as if he was complying, his eyes shaded by the black bowler hat he wore. Instead of pulling an ID from the inside pocket of his black suit, Agent Ruby withdrew a silver ballpoint pen that had a red heart-shaped gem on its end.

The security guard tilted his head, obviously confused by the sight of the pen instead of identification.

In a hypnotizing fashion, Agent Ruby slowly waved the pen back and forth. "You're going to let me pass without a problem. Then you're going to forget you saw me. Are we clear?" he said in a melodic voice.

The guard's eyes glazed over, a white sheen covering them briefly as he nodded robotically. Then his eyes cleared once more, and he pivoted and marched back to his station.

Agent Ruby pursed his lips, keeping his pen—a wand of sorts—out in case he needed it again. Fairies often needed magical objects to direct or store their powers—a minor limitation for their superior skills in matchmaking.

Brainwashing was Agent Ruby's specialty, but few knew that. If they did, it wouldn't be his secret weapon. Of course, it wasn't foolproof and hadn't worked when he tried to get Saint Valentine to do certain things.

The current Saint Valentine—the highest position held at FGA—had recently changed the protocol for matchmaking, disregarding age-old customs. He started subscribing to the notion that practices should evolve for the modern world. It was absurd and would be the downfall for matchmaking, abolishing centuries of efforts.

The current Saint Valentine started to allow fairy godmothers to rely on dating websites, social media, and other modern ways to create love. It wasn't going to work. It was only a matter of time before all traditions passed down from Saint Valentines of the past would be gone forever, and the world would be full of trashy relationships.

As Agent Ruby had suspected, these new approaches to matchmaking weren't creating lasting love. It was all superficial. The modern world, with its desire for instant gratification, didn't know how to stick around in relationships, staying when it got hard.

The problem was widespread, but it started at Saint Valentine's office, Matters of the Heart. It had spread to the governing agency for the fairy godmothers—FGA. Soon it would demolish the curriculum at Happily Ever After College.

Already, word had spread that Headmistress Willow Starr was reviewing the curriculum at the college and making changes. The course study for fairy godmothers was steeped in traditions that had worked for centuries—creating love and romance for those worthy of such things. Now, all that was changing.

Agent Ruby couldn't believe it when the rumor spread that the college was training a half-magician as a fairy godmother. These were precisely the types of things that were destroying tradition and the sanctity that once was true love. Soon all that remained would be superficial relationships created by fairy godmothers who had forgotten the mission.

True love was a product of two disciplined people of poise and good stock coming together. It was about matching princesses to princes. It was about pairing royalty. The notion that Plain Janes could marry kings—that commoners should be matched and encouraged to breed, that love was for everyone— had defiled that.

The current administration believed that love was about emotions and feelings. This Saint Valentine was wrong. Love had and would always be about practicality. That's what made the strongest matches. That was what kept them together.

People didn't divorce a century ago as they did presently. That was because fairy godmothers weren't pairing the right people anymore. The modern world said it was okay to abandon your vows. A high-speed world of instant gratification and social media that created constant dopamine hits was destroying the traditions of a family. Many decried arranged marriages as outdated practices…but that was wrong and Agent Ruby's grandfather, the predecessor to the current

Saint Valentine, knew that. These new practices were demolishing his work in this modern world.

Agent Ruby used his ballpoint pen several more times as he cruised to the top story of FriendNet, ensuring that no one stopped him as he made his way to the person he'd come to see. Unfortunately, he wouldn't be able to use brainwashing to get this guy to help. When someone forced people to do something, the results weren't always favorable with tasks of this complexity. Brainwashing tampered with the required skills.

No, Agent Ruby simply had to convince this executive programmer—the highest in the social media company—to do what he needed. Persuasion was another one of Agent Ruby's top-level skills though. It also didn't hurt that he had deep pockets, having come from a family of old money.

The skyscraper's top floor lacked any class or elegant design. The exposed bricks and polished concrete floor gave it an industrial look. Agent Ruby grimaced as he strode across the open space that had large bean bags and pool tables. Several people he'd learned identified as hipsters were sitting on large inflated yoga balls, their shiny laptops on their legs as they worked—apparently against such practical things as desks.

One particularly repugnant-looking guy with a handlebar mustache was typing on a typewriter.

Agent Ruby snapped at him. "Where is the senior programmer for FriendNet?"

The guy looked up, unrushed, sending the typewriter back to the reset point. "You mean Dash? Oh, we don't go by titles here, man. Don't let anyone hear you call Dash the senior. We call him our Yoda Programmer."

"Whatever, where is this...Dash?" He scowled at the awful name. What was this guy, a Dalmatian or a programmer?

"He's over there putting on some tunes for us." The guy pointed over his shoulder toward a guy wearing jeans rolled up past his ankles, a bow tie, and a vest next to the far wall. Although Dash was probably only about thirty, he had a monocle.

He held up a vinyl record and glanced over his shoulder. "How about some Gregory Alan Isakov?" The question made many of the hipsters stationed around the open space look up.

A girl wearing a t-shirt that said, "You've gotta risk it to get the biscuit," shook her head. "No, he exceeded half a million listeners on Spotify. He's very popular."

Dash's mouth popped open, his expression of offense evident even with his thick beard. "I had no idea he'd sold out to the man. I'll find someone obscure for us to jam to."

Agent Ruby rolled his eyes and strode in Dash's direction.

The guy looked him over, mild distaste on his face as he took in Agent Ruby's appearance. "Whoa, why do you look like you walked out of a Sherlock Holmes' novel?"

Agent Ruby arched an eyebrow at the guy with a monocle. "I work for a very powerful organization and need to enlist your help. Do you have someplace we can meet privately?"

Dash held out his arms wide. "We're all friends here."

Agent Ruby glanced over his shoulder at the hipsters playing chess or typing on their laptops and shook his head, turning back around. "Someplace private," he insisted.

"Yeah, I guess we can use my office, but I can't stay confined in that space for too long. It inhibits my creativity." Dash led the way to a set of offices on the far side of the large room. On the outside of the space that Dash led the agent into was a placard that read: "Yoda Programmer—raz8.dash."

Agent Ruby paused outside the office and pointed. "Is this your name?"

"Yeah, but most call me by my last name, Dash," the hipster explained. "Although I'd prefer it to be lowercase so I don't insist upon my self-importance."

Agent Ruby let out a breath, willing his patience not to evaporate. This plan was bold and seemingly against everything he stood for, but if he was going to overthrow the current Saint Valentine, he had to take the risk. He had to ruin modern love and the only way to do that was to accelerate things already in motion.

When all the technology and avant-garde ways brought the love meter to zero, the magical world would see the truth. They'd get rid of the current Saint Valentine. Agent Ruby would replace him. The world would return to what it was supposed to be—love only created for the rich and refined using traditional ways.

The office was contemporary like the other spaces, but at least it had a desk and chairs. Without being invited, Agent Ruby took a seat, crossing his legs and folding his hands over his knee in a dignified manner.

"I'm Agent Ruby, a director for the Fairy Godmother Agency. I'm enlisting your help to break up relationships worldwide."

CHAPTER TWO

"Why would someone who works for the Fairy Godmother Agency want to destroy relationships?" Dash stroked his dark brown beard.

Agent Ruby sighed. "It's complicated."

"I graduated valedictorian from MIT," Dash countered. "Try me. I can do complicated."

It wasn't that Agent Ruby had to explain his motives, but he knew that by doing so, he had a better chance of getting Dash to do what he wanted. The guy hadn't dismissed the plan. He'd seemed interested. Now he wanted to know the "why," which would hopefully seal the deal rather than take it off the table.

"You see, technology is ruining relationships—"

"You don't have to tell me that," Dash interrupted. "Less is more. I got rid of television a decade ago."

"Good for you," Agent Ruby said dryly. "If I sit back and do nothing, the degradation of relationships would be gradual. By the time it was evident that technology and progressive ideas were the culprits, it would be too late. So instead, I propose we accelerate things linking the cause directly to social media, technology, and liberalism. Then the board of FGA will see the error of our ways, promote me to Saint Valentine, and I'll be in a position to reinstate the values that we've abandoned and turn things back to how they used to be."

"I'll be out of a job," Dash argued.

"I'm willing to make it worth your while," Agent Ruby said plainly.

Dash arched a bushy eyebrow at him with an expression that said, "Do tell."

"I'm willing to pay you handsomely to do this," Agent Ruby continued. "How about your full year's salary here at FriendNet to start? Then another year's salary once we've been successful. Does that seem fair?"

The guy's face didn't change. Instead, he simply nodded, unimpressed by the offer. "I'd do it anyway, but that will help to ensure I land on my feet after this."

"You would?" Agent Ruby was surprised.

"I only took this job as a thought experiment," Dash explained. "I was curious how social media algorithms could change and shape human behavior. I've played out the experiment. It turns out that we're simply rats in a maze and any small high can direct behavior. Most have no idea that they're simply puppets and companies like FriendNet control everything from their mood, shopping, and health. It really is sad, and I'm happy to demolish this system and allow you and love to benefit."

Well, that was easier than I realized it would be. Agent Ruby hid the victorious grin on his clean-shaven face. "Very good then. I'm glad we share a common goal in all of this."

"I have some ideas for how to accomplish what you've outlined." Dash indicated the folder that Agent Ruby had provided with project details. "FriendNet is hooked into everything from shopping to restaurant reviews to digital music. The possibilities of ways to break up couples are huge."

"The data on how to find out what will create relationship problems between two people is at your disposal?" Agent Ruby asked.

Dash nodded triumphantly. "I can tell you everything about someone. Their likes, dislikes, phobias, turn-ons, turn-offs, relationship history." He pointed at the sleek laptop and his phone on his desk. "It's all in there and there and every day more is recorded."

Agent Ruby nearly shuddered with disgust. That's what the modern world had come to. They'd given up privacy for convenience, and the price was that they'd become easily manipulated. That's precisely what Dash and Agent Ruby were going to do. Take the information that millions had volunteered and use it to make them angry, jealous, paranoid, and inevitably distrustful about their boyfriends, girlfriends, wives, husbands, and partners. It was only a matter of time before lawyers and law enforcement were up to their eyebrows in crimes and lawsuits. That was because passion led to irrational behavior and that usually resulted in illegal acts, divorce, and violence.

"It's important that no one knows about this," Agent Ruby stated with authority.

Dash held up his hands. "Not to worry, man. No one at FriendNet will have any clue. It simply doesn't behoove me to share this with anyone."

"Good." Agent Ruby nodded proudly, surprised at the strange hipster with whom he'd formed an unlikely alliance. "More importantly, no one can come between this project and our success. If they do, we'll need to go to any lengths to ensure they aren't a problem."

That piqued Dash's interest, judging by the keen expression on his face. "You know someone who could be a problem?"

"FGA has various agents, always monitoring love and relationships," Agent Ruby explained. "Fairy Godmothers are sent on jobs and usually do them without question. Agents have an interest in the whole picture and report to Saint Valentine. He has various ways of keeping an eye on things. When love starts to plummet, someone will investigate. If they link it to you and FriendNet, I need you to do whatever it takes to ensure they don't stop us, and more importantly, that they don't know I'm behind it."

Dash smiled wickedly. "I can do that. The beauty is that I run things with a few simple programs and no one knows I'm the guy behind the curtain. I can hack into everything from prescription medication systems to traffic lights. Funny how a little tweak and someone's life is poof...gone." He snapped his fingers, a glint of crazy in his eyes.

Agent Ruby narrowed his gaze at the guy but nodded, making note that he'd aligned himself with a very powerful person—one he needed to keep close and dispose of when the right time came.

CHAPTER THREE

Paris Beaufont's hands shook as she pulled the brush through her tangled blonde hair. Faraday the talking squirrel watched from her dresser, catching sight of her in the mirror over the small bedside table.

"Does brushing your hair make you that nervous?" Faraday flicked his tail.

She rolled her eyes and spun to face him directly. "No, you know why I'm nervous."

He nodded understandingly. "Because you're starting transformative magic today, and you're worried that you're going to turn the blue bird into a paper airplane rather than a hot air balloon."

Paris dropped the brush on the bedside table, abandoning the efforts. "I'm considering turning you into a pair of fur-lined slippers."

The squirrel grimaced. "I wouldn't. I hear that squirrel's fur causes athlete's foot."

"What a strange thing to hear." Paris hid her amusement.

He shrugged. "I didn't say it's true. I've heard that...can't remember where."

"Probably Lies Radio, a program that you don't subscribe to, but you're the host and producer for."

His tail flicked again at his back. "Why would I subscribe to a radio program that I host? That's like buying your own product. What's the point?"

Paris shook her head, threading her arms over her chest. "I can't help but think that you missed the point, dear *friend*." She added extra inflection on the last word.

"Are you still upset about that thing?" he asked.

"That thing where you said you'd tell me your secrets after I defeated the Deathly Shadow, but then all of a sudden you can't?" she challenged.

His eyes darted to the side. "I'm sorry. I really am. I thought I could tell you about my past, but I found out afterward that I can't."

She sighed. "Again, how did you find this out?"

"Someone told me," he said nervously. "Similar to how Papa Creola had to be the one who told you about your past, I'm not allowed, in so many ways, to tell my secrets."

"What does 'so many ways' mean?"

"It means that I'll break a deal if I do."

Seven days. It had been a long seven days since Paris defeated the Deathly Shadow, recovered her parents from the parallel universe, and returned to Happily Ever After College. Liv and Stefan were still recovering, according to Papa Creola, and Paris hadn't seen them since that night when they were too exhausted to say much. The reunion hadn't been the one she envisioned, but also, nothing in her life had happened the way anyone would guess.

The father of time had said that sleep was important for Liv and Stefan to reacclimate. They'd only been gone a day in the other universe, but Paris' parents had missed fifteen years in this world. Although they'd been able to return, their bodies were having trouble adjusting. To avoid rapid aging and all sorts of problems with mental schisms, Papa Creola had put them into a deep sleep and wasn't waking them up until he was sure it was safe.

So, after everything and risking so much to save her parents, Paris still hadn't seen them. Each day that passed made her feel like it wasn't real—that they weren't really back. Or she worried that maybe they would never wake up.

Faraday going back on his promise to share his secrets had been a good distraction for Paris, giving her something tangible to be upset about. Because in reality, how could she be upset that her mother and father were in a coma of sorts to prevent them from degenerating after coming through a vortex, something that Papa Creola said almost none in this universe or any other would attempt. It was simply too dangerous with too many potentials that could go wrong.

Paris sighed again and sat on the edge of her bed as the shaking returned. "You know why I'm so nervous."

The squirrel hopped off the dresser, landed next to her on the soft pink comforter, and looked up at her with a thoughtful expression. "They'll wake up soon, I'm sure."

Paris gulped. "Then there are the other worries when my parents do wake up."

"Why wouldn't they like you?" He'd been through this with her every night that week.

"Because I'm a rebel and weird and always getting myself into trouble."

"Your mother was a rebel who challenged the House of Fourteen when no one else would," Faraday reminded her. Much of her parents' history had come out since they returned. It seemed that since the family couldn't yet reunite with Liv and Stefan, they'd settled for telling their stories in the meantime. Uncle John was the one who had the most sentimental look on his face when he recounted memories.

"Your father hunted demons," Faraday continued. "So if that doesn't make someone weird, I'm not sure what does."

Paris stared off without really seeing, grateful that her friend didn't mind repeating these reasons over and over to her, although they hadn't sunk in yet. She worried that after fifteen years, she'd be a disappointment to her parents. They had expected to find a little child when they returned, and she was far from that. Maybe if they'd raised her, she'd be like them, and they'd have something in common. What if they didn't like rock music or didn't laugh at her jokes or they disagreed on core beliefs?

"I think hunting demons makes my father courageous," Paris argued. "I'm becoming a fairy godmother. The biggest thing I risk is getting a paper cut when licking wedding invites."

"I don't think you're the one who sends those," Faraday countered.

She scoffed at him. "Again, you miss the point, squirrel. When my parents had nearly passed out, they seemed fine with the notion I was attending Happily Ever After College. When they come to... Well, Uncle Clark is a Councilor, Aunt Sophia is a dragonrider, Uncle John is a detective—and I'm a fairy godmother in training."

"Which I contend is an essential job," Faraday stated. "Maybe as you help to evolve the college, it will become dangerous. Perhaps you'll have to fight trolls who break into the Enchanted Grounds or witches who pollute the water supply with anti-love potions."

Paris perked up. "You think? That would be fantastic!"

He shook his head at her. "And you call *me* weird."

"You are the weirdest." She stood and checked her appearance in the mirror. She looked like her parents—more so like her mother. Her true concern was if she was like them internally, in a way that made the last fifteen years not feel like a wedge. "I hope they like me," Paris said to her image, mostly talking to herself.

"Well, if it makes you feel any better," Faraday began, "your parents will probably be asleep for several more days, so you have time to worry through all the different scenarios."

Paris lowered her chin and regarded him with hooded eyes. "Not cool, Slippers."

The squirrel laughed at this. "Your threats only make me like you more."

"Then get ready to be my best friend," she chirped and headed for the door to her room. "What will you do today?"

Faraday had hopped from the bed to the window sill, looking out at the Enchanted Grounds as the sun rose over Happily Ever After College. "I have to talk to a guy about a thing."

Paris nodded. "More secrets. You're a real bestie."

"After that," he continued, ignoring her statement, "I'm going to make you a friendship bracelet."

"Out of twigs and leaves, as a real squirrel would?" she teased.

"I was thinking out of some thermoplastic insulated wires with high heat resistance since you'll need something that withstands all your dangerous endeavors," he explained. "Maybe something nylon-coated with a synthetic polymer."

She nodded. "Yep, that's the type of bracelet I'd expect a woodland creature to make for me." Paris opened the door, smelling breakfast aromas wafting up from the downstairs of the mansion. "Try and stay out of trouble, squirrel."

"Same to you, troll-hunter." He bounced out the window and along the roof of FGE.

Paris sighed and pulled the door shut behind her, curious about the squirrel but also feeling like he'd tell her the truth as soon as he could. She understood better than most that sometimes things didn't go the way you thought. You believed you had to bring some people back for everything to be okay and that simply wasn't the way things went. People didn't live happily ever after, it seemed.

Faraday had promised to tell her his secrets, but something was preventing him. She simply hoped that one day things changed and he could. Until then, she wasn't kicking him out. He was the best friend she had—and that was saying a lot because Paris finally had real friends.

CHAPTER FOUR

Since Paris' return to Happily Ever After College after defeating the Deathly Shadow, even her friends had been walking on eggshells around her. She knew they meant well and didn't want to pressure her for details, especially because they sensed that things hadn't gone perfectly. Well, she'd survived, and that was key. Her parents had returned. However, they weren't really part of her life yet, and the stress of it all was evident on Paris' face.

Sitting at the long dining room table, Paris pushed the creamy scrambled eggs around on her plate, conscious that many around her were staring. Most of them were friends. Some a few seats down weren't so much, and their scrutinizing gazes weren't going unnoticed.

The whispers about Paris had grown louder lately—hardly considered a secret anymore. The growing scrutiny over the fact that Paris was half-magician, a rebel with a rap sheet, and an outcast who refused to wear the blue gown or eat desserts most of the time was on the rise.

"Starship, I hear someone saw your mother buying a beauty potion from a freshwater nymph." Christine leaned over and slapped the table between her and another student named Starship, who was gawking and gossiping with the girls clustered around her.

Starship's face instantly flushed red as her brows knitted together. "How dare you? She would never. Everyone knows their potions don't work."

"Well," Christine drew out the word. "I didn't know that, but it sounds like you've had extensive practice testing them out."

Starship gasped, jumped to her feet, and charged off.

Christine grinned triumphantly. "One down, a ton of busybodies to go." She glanced up and down the table. "Who's next? I know dirt on all of you hippies, so keep talking about Paris, and I'll spill your business."

Paris pushed her plate away, offering a well-meaning smile to her friend. "You don't have to do that. I don't care and can defend myself."

"I know that," Christine replied next to her. "You could have everyone in the room hogtied and begging for mercy."

"Don't give her any ideas," Hemingway cut in, winking at Paris. "I sometimes fear what she might do if she gets bored."

Chef Ash, Penny, and Christine all laughed.

"I don't mean to overstep," Christine said to Paris. "It's just that it's so annoying that you're the constant topic of conversation."

Paris regarded her uneaten food. "I don't care."

"Well, I do," Christine replied. "I mean, Chef Ash and I helped to break up Grayson McGregor from his fiancé. Then we sent the chocolates that broke up Amelia Rose with that lame-o. That led to Grayson and Amelia falling in love. People should be talking about that."

The group all laughed again.

"I should have realized this was never about defending my honor," Paris remarked, thoroughly entertained by her friend.

"You should get more attention for it around the school," Penny supplied. "It's amazing how their union quickly helped the love meter to recover."

Chef Ash nodded. "It goes to show love breeds love. It's a very tricky thing with the pendulum constantly swinging back and forth. Still, the new corporation the two lovers quickly formed and their instant goodwill instead of spite at each other, shifted so many different things."

"A definite ripple effect," Hemingway added.

"I think you'd rather not have everyone talk about that." Becky Montgomery leaned in from a few empty seats away, obviously having been eavesdropping.

"Oh, good, someone whose opinion means less than a pile of horse manure is chiming in on this," Christine said dryly.

The other woman narrowed her eyes at her, but then they lit up with evil delight. "For starters, I hear that although there was an uptick on the love meter, your efforts didn't have as big of an impact as you might have initially thought."

Christine's grin disappeared. She glanced at Paris and Chef Ash, but they did their best to cover their nervous expressions. None of them wanted to believe that Becky the Bully was right.

"Second," she continued, growing with confidence. "Second and especially first-year students aren't allowed to go on cases of that magnitude. There are several agents at FGA who are looking into this matter."

"The case originated at Happily Ever After College with one of our instructors," Chef Ash argued. "That's why it fell under our jurisdiction to resolve how we saw fit."

Becky shook her head. "Cases are still under the final authority of FGA."

"Cases are still under the final authority of Saint Valentine," Hemingway countered.

Tossing her grayish-blue hair over her shoulder, Becky scoffed. "I don't think the current Saint Valentine holds much authority. Throwing out laws and age-old practices isn't putting him in a good light with the board." Her gaze darted to Paris. "Many don't like that he's allowing the headmistress to do so many things that go directly against our curriculum and supreme standards."

"You mean, allowing her to teach a half-magician," Paris said boldly.

Becky shrugged as though indifferent. "There's that. Let's just say that Saint Valentine is under scrutiny for many reasons."

"Let's also say that no one gives a damn what you or your snotty family thinks," Christine fired back.

Becky shot her a defiant expression. "I think you'll find that there are many who care what the Montgomerys think and not only that, but we can make a lot of things happen."

Christine took a large gulp of water and nodded. "I know what you mean. You make me sick and seemingly without trying."

Becky, like Starship, shot to a standing position as she fumed and marched from the dining hall.

Christine pulled her plate closer. "Finally, my appetite can return."

Hemingway leaned over on the other side of Paris. "I know that having everyone talk about you isn't easy, but I think it's because you're different and there's nothing wrong with that."

Paris regarded him with a speculative stare for a moment. They both knew she knew his secret. He was a magician, masquerading as a fairy. The last thing he wanted was for anyone to know. He'd be the one talked about, but more importantly, under rules that the headmistress couldn't change, Hemingway would be thrown out of Happily Ever After College. A half-magician who was also half-fairy was more than enough for everyone to digest, but a magician in the faculty, well, the fairy godmothers weren't ready for that type of progressive move yet…or maybe ever.

After a long moment, Paris nodded. "It's fine. I know I'm making things harder for myself by not talking about what happened with the Deathly Shadow and my parents, which makes everyone gossip and speculate."

Christine nodded. "Finally! You get it. So end the rumors and come out with it. We know you survived, obviously, unless you're one hell of a ghost. But what's going on with your parents? What happened in the showdown?"

Paris pursed her lips, knowing that her friends meant well. The truth was, coming clean about it all was mostly about her not wanting to admit all that had happened. It had been her demon blood that saved her. Afterward, the father of time cut their reunion short because her parents had passed through back into their universe. She wasn't with them, and now, although the Deathly Shadow was gone, there was a hole in her heart.

"I faced the Deathly Shadow," Paris began, her voice slow. "And I was able to put him in the container and open the portal."

"Wow, you're horrible at storytelling," Christine teased. "A bit of suspense and lead up goes a long way in keeping your audience's attention."

Paris laughed, grateful for her friend making light of all this and easing the tension. "My parents are back, and they are…well, that's yet to be seen. They're adjusting."

"So you haven't seen them?" Chef Ash asked.

"I have," Paris answered. "Briefly and it was weird, and well, we'll see…"

"I think this situation will take time to mend," Hemingway offered sympathetically.

Paris nodded. "Yeah, they've been through a lot, and Papa Creola says they have to acclimate, so I'm waiting and hoping to see them soon."

Chef Ash offered her a thoughtful expression. "I know they can't wait to see you."

"So that was it?" Christine asked. "You faced a deadly villain that's been hunting you all your life, opened a vortex, and rescued your parents? That's what you couldn't tell us a week ago?"

Hemingway gave her a look that said, "Don't be so insensitive."

Paris lowered her chin. "My parents, although gone from this timeline for fifteen years, were only in the other universe for a single day."

Christine's mouth popped open. "Okay, mind totally blown. Now I get why you haven't wanted to pony up the details. You're more like your mom's sister at this point."

Paris nodded. "It's complicated. The time gap is the main reason Papa Creola wants to give them time to recover before putting them back in the real world. So I've been hanging out and waiting."

"That has to be difficult," Penny offered, her expression thoughtful.

"I'm glad that they're back and hopefully things can return to normal. I don't have to look over my shoulder anymore. My family, who redesigned their entire life for me, can hopefully return to the way they were. I don't know what that means for my Uncle John and the rest, but it sparks a new era for the Beaufonts."

"Your family hasn't had it easy, but they loved you very much to sacrifice so much," Chef Ash imparted.

"She's the only halfling magician and fairy in the world," Christine insisted. "She's a big deal."

"I'm not," Paris argued.

"Father Time has been working to keep you alive," Christine countered. "I don't think he gives two licks about the rest of us."

"He does," Paris said, then added, "Well, Mama Jamba does, and she probably makes him care."

"Mama who?" Christine asked.

"That's Mother Nature's name to those she knows well," Chef Ash explained.

"Oh, like our resident royalty here." Christine held out a presenting hand to her friend.

"I've only met her once," Paris demurred as if needing to defend against the idea she was royalty. She was though, by House of Fourteen standards, and she was from a founding family of magic, making her more powerful and considered elite.

"She's the one who created the fairy godmothers," Chef Ash explained while pulling the pencil he always kept there from behind his ear.

"Well, she created everything, now didn't she?" Hemingway countered with a sideways grin.

Chef Ash nodded, tapping the pencil on the table and conjuring his notebook where he kept sketches of his various designs for recipes. "That's right. Specifically, she founded Happily Ever After College, which then created the foundation for FGA and she put Saint Valentine over it all."

"Because love is what makes the world go 'round," Christine sang.

"And Mother Nature needs the world to keep spinning," Hemingway added.

"However, the FGA that she created is different than what it came to be, and it's evolving even now," Chef Ash explained.

"I heard rumors," Hemingway began, "That Mother Nature wanted something that created love worldwide, but she often has gone into hiding throughout the centuries. She's only just returned. It was a dragonrider who brought her back this time. Someone with a blue dragon—"

"That would be my Aunt Sophia," Paris interrupted.

Christine laughed. "Of course it would be."

The others joined as many of the other students finished up and moved out of the dining hall.

Chef Ash patted his notebook. "All this talk about Mother Nature gives me an idea for some meals—things with lots of spring and summertime vegetables to celebrate the seasons. I'm going to go work on it." He glanced at Paris. "I'm glad your parents are back, and you're safe. I'm sure things will continue to get easier with time."

She smiled in reply as he moved off.

"I better follow him out," Hemingway stated. "I have things to get ready for today's lessons. You all are in for a treat."

"Can't wait," Christine muttered, not sounding at all excited. "I won't clean under my fingernails."

Hemingway wagged a finger at her. "Just you wait and see."

The two stood and made their way for the entrance, leaving Paris and Penny alone at the table while many bustled around them. Paris turned to her friend and smiled.

"I wanted to say thank you for your words of wisdom before I faced the Deathly Shadow," she began, thinking back to that moment. "Although simple advice, remembering to believe in myself really helped when it came time…well, and also my demon blood." She laughed, thinking of how strange that had come to help her so much.

Penny's eyes went wide. "You have demon blood?"

"Apparently," Paris stated. "I mean, it's why my parents asked a genie to help me, and I became half-fairy. However, I still have the blood of a demon, which I guess is counteracted by being a fairy. Let's hope it's mostly dormant in me." She laughed again.

However, her friend was deadly serious but still nodded. "That makes sense. Demons don't mess with fairies. We're too loving and emotional for their tastes, I think. They mostly go after magicians and mortals, from what I've heard. Wow, that's fascinating about how you became a fairy. I had no idea."

Paris shrugged and stood. "No one does, really. Only my family. Well, regardless, thanks for your help. It meant a lot."

Penny beamed and joined her friend. "I'm glad I could help."

The two moved off for their first classes, not seeing that hiding in the crowd close by and eavesdropping once more was none other than Becky Montgomery.

She released a wicked smile as she stepped forward, glancing at the spot where the halfling had been moments prior. "If the board didn't like it before that a magician was at the college, they are going to hate to find out there's a demon in our midst."

CHAPTER FIVE

A figure who Paris didn't recognize stood in the middle of the classroom where she normally attended Art of Love. Backing up, she glanced outside the room, checking that it was the right place. It was.

It was so strange to see a man standing at the front of the classroom. Unlike Wilfred, Chef Ash, and Hemingway—the only other men at the college—this one stood out in a bizarre way that Paris couldn't pinpoint.

The man wore an all-black suit, but unlike Wilfred, who wore the very tailored butler's uniform, there was an element of superiority to this stranger's appearance. He had a chiseled jaw and slicked-back black hair. When he glanced up at Paris, there was a scrutinizing glint in his brown eyes. He ran his gaze over her, obvious disapproval on his face that she wasn't wearing the fairy godmother blue gown.

"You must be Miss Paris Beaufont," he said in a refined tone, very much like Wilfred but with actual distaste audible.

"And you are?" She took her seat at the front of the class as usual.

He pursed his lips. "I'm Agent Topaz, and I'm taking over for Headmistress Starr, teaching Art of Love."

"Why?" Paris' question earned many conspiratorial whispers behind her. "Where is Headmistress Starr?"

Agent Topaz sighed, his eyes shifting to the side as if he was trying to decide whether to answer her or not. "She's been replaced as the instructor for this class. The FGA wants to be more involved with the college's curriculum, and therefore they've assigned me to teach this class as well as a few others."

So this was one of the agents at the FGA who supervised fairy godmothers. She'd heard about these guys. Only men were part of the FGA, the way only women could be fairy godmothers. It was a strange hierarchy, but Paris had tried to maintain an open mind about the rather archaic-seeming organization. Maybe that was how Mama Jamba had set it up, or it hadn't evolved, or it had devolved through the years.

"Now, today, we're going to be studying historical events where fairy godmothers were critical to important unions," Agent Topaz continued, an air of dominance in his tone, his chin held high as he glanced around the classroom of students. "Many have no idea that the FGA was responsible for the most important matches in history. If it wasn't for the work led by many Saint Valentines of the past, we wouldn't have had such influential couples as Katherine Hepburn and Spencer Tracy, Pierre and Marie Curie, Jackson Pollock and Lee Krasner, as well as many other notable couples who advanced everything from economics to art and science."

Paris crossed her arms over her chest and sat back. "So we have the FGA to hold responsible for the absurd popularity of abstract expressionism paintings?"

Agent Topaz's eyes widened suddenly, obviously not used to being interrupted or having a student challenge him in such a way. "Miss Beaufont, Krasner's support of Pollock's career was crucial to creating an artistic movement."

"I believe that she put her career on hold to support his," Paris countered. She'd been devouring books on every subject over the last week to take her mind off her problems.

"That was foretold and critical for Pollock's artwork to break out and make millions of dollars," Agent Topaz countered.

"So it was about money?"

"Let's get one thing quite clear, Miss Beaufont," Agent Topaz began in a sharp-edged voice as his face flushed red. "Matchmaking by fairy godmothers has always been about pairing the rich, influential, and those of high status together. It isn't our job at FGA to worry about how commoners match up. History proves that when important people create a union, critical things come out of it."

"So this isn't really about creating true love for two people then? It's about deals and money and border agreements?"

"It's never been about true love," Agent Topaz nearly stuttered, spit flicking from his lips. "That's exactly why I'm here. This romantic notion has been spreading across Happily Ever After College and our fairy godmothers at FGA for too long, and the consequences are becoming more apparent."

Paris couldn't help but laugh. "Yeah, how absurd to think that a place called Happily Ever After would be about creating love for Cinderellas and Prince Charmings. Of course, this has always been about trade negotiations and unions that benefit society rather than about a product of true love."

"Miss Beaufont, what we do spreads love, but that's a result of matching the right people. How many relationships do you think were sparked because of John F. Kennedy's devotion to Jacqueline Kennedy Onassis or Johnny Cash and June Carter Cash's relationship on stage?"

"Good point," Paris said. "Is FGA also responsible for matching up Jay-Z and Beyonce, John Lennon and Yoko Ono, or how about David and Victoria Beckham?"

He narrowed his eyes at her but didn't answer, which was answer enough for her.

"So we can thank FGA for putting together alliances for career benefits? Or power couples who popularize unhealthy images? Or splitting up the—"

"That is quite enough," Agent Topaz interrupted, his eyes bulging.

The students around Paris all fell deadly silent.

"My point is that I don't know that our focus should be to pair up the wealthy and self-inflated at the expense of ignoring creating true love for real people," Paris argued, not standing down. "Who are we to judge what will increase the love meter? Maybe some famous couples like Wesley and Buttercup from The Princess Bride inspire love."

"They aren't a real couple," he cut in.

"That's my point," Paris stated with confidence. "If our motivation is to pair up two people who inspire love worldwide, then we don't have to sling together two famous people. In this class, when Headmistress Starr taught it, we learned about poetry, music, and movies that have inspired romance. Shouldn't our focus be on creating love for all people? Not only the rich and annoying?"

"No!" Agent Topaz boomed, throwing his fist down on the desk in front of him. "That is a waste of our time. Before you derail this conversation any longer, I'll prove how important our jobs are because we focus on pairing up the right people."

He pulled a silver pocket watch from his suit. On the front was a large flat topaz gem. Pointing it at the wall beside him, Agent Topaz muttered an incantation and an image projected onto the space—displaying a movie of sorts.

"Now watch and learn how FGA is responsible for the most important unions in history. This is one of our most significant accomplishments."

CHAPTER SIX

"Cleopatra and Marc Antony?" Paris announced when two figures materialized on the projected movie screen.

Agent Topaz rolled his eyes. "Oh, good, you do know your history."

"I do," she affirmed, watching images of the ruler of Egypt as she rode through an elaborate procession on the screen. "I know that the two influential leaders during the Egyptian empire made some advancements. Cleopatra was the first female pharaoh, was educated and created much change for Egypt. "

"Exactly!" Agent Topaz exclaimed. "Now, as you can see, Cleopatra protected Egypt from Rome—"

"She also lost the throne to Rome," Paris argued. "Not to mention that Marc Antony left her and his children with her for years to marry another woman. In the end, she orchestrated her husband's death and committed suicide out of guilt."

"That is irrelevant," Agent Topaz fired, pausing the movie playing with his pocket watch.

"I think that it's very relevant," Paris countered. "There might have been benefits from the union, but the indulgences of two people might have also been the downfall of the Egyptian empire. How are we to know?"

"We know," Agent Topaz said through clenched teeth, restarting the movie. "Here we see Cleopatra entering Tarsus where Antony was. It was fairy godmothers who orchestrated this elaborate entrance, knowing that it would attract the indulgent tastes of Marc Antony."

Paris watched as Cleopatra was carried through the city on a canopy bed by boys dressed as Cupids. The pharaoh fanned herself, dressed as Venus. All around them were a great entourage, all in costumes as well. Paris couldn't help but think of how many impoverished and hungry they could have fed if they'd spent the pageantry's money in other ways instead.

"How romantic," a girl at the back of the class gushed.

"It was," Agent Topaz affirmed. "And it worked to get Marc Antony's favor. He was instantly smitten with our pharaoh, and their union has been famous throughout history, a model of romance and power."

"Again, the two love birds pretty much committed suicide," Paris said dryly, feeling like the only person really thinking about this critically.

"They were in love and had chemistry, according to history," Becky Montgomery argued.

Paris spun to face her. "Antony left Cleopatra when she was pregnant to marry another woman. Wow, if that's love, then never ever sign me up."

"As if anyone would fall for you like Antony did for Cleopatra," Becky fired back, her freckled nose drifting into the air.

"Yeah, I think I dodged a bullet there," Paris stated.

"Thank you for your thoughtful input Becky." A smile flicked to Agent Topaz's mouth. "The Montgomerys always know their history well."

"I think they know it selectively, it seems." Paris turned back to the front.

"I will urge you not to talk about an influential family at FGA in such a way," Agent Topaz scolded.

Paris held up her hands as if in surrender. "I won't talk about Bec's family if she stops talking about mine."

"The Beaufonts don't have a reputation among fairies," Agent Topaz said coldly, looking down at her.

"I believe you're the one who needs to brush up on your history, Agent Topaz. My parents saved magic so that we can all be here right now. My aunt has saved this planet numerous times. And—"

Agent Topaz narrowed his eyes at her. "If you're so proud of your magician family, maybe you'd be better suited with them than here at Happily Ever After College."

There it was. FGA didn't want a magician here. How long would Headmistress Starr be able to protect Paris? Things weren't getting better since her parents were back. They were somehow getting worse. She desperately wanted them to wake up and help her, but instinctively, she knew she had to help herself. Beaufonts saved themselves.

Instead of answering, Paris' eyes flickered to the screen where the indulgent display by Cleopatra was still playing. She would have disregarded it, but as the pharaoh approached Marc Antony, Paris caught the image of a slender black cat with unique markings in the background. She thought she had to be really overstressed because she could have sworn the cat from Cleopatra's time looked right at her and winked.

CHAPTER SEVEN

Paris had to be losing her mind. She was pretty confident about that once she entered Transformative Magic class. It was on the Enchanted Grounds, out beside the Bewilder Forest.

The class was all gathered around none other than the slender black cat from the video of Cleopatra and Marc Antony. Paris knew it was the one who had winked at her because of the unique markings. It was all black and small but had white on each of its paws and a spot under its chin. There was also something special in the feline's eyes that made her think it had to be the same cat from the video clip. *But how?*

She shook her head as she joined the class, trying to shake away the strangeness of seeing the cat right after the video from 60 BC or whenever they took it or however they took it. Magic was weird, and she was increasingly learning that time was even weirder.

When she questioned Papa Creola about how her parents could have only been gone twenty-four hours in the other world, but fifteen years had passed here, he had explained that time didn't move linearly. He said the absolute best explanation of how time progressed was from an episode of *Doctor Who* where the tenth Doctor explained time as, "a big ball of wibbly-wobbly, timey-wimey stuff."

When she questioned him on the legitimacy of using a science fiction show to explain something that was his job, the father of time said the show had him figured out in many regards.

Events in time didn't happen in sequences as many expected. It moved differently depending on the person and place. It was volatile, and others could mess with it at will. That had been Liv's job for Papa Creola, policing those who messed with time, which often created holes in the fabric of the universe.

A chill ran down Paris' back as she thought about all this and regarded the cat. Everyone in the class was staring at the black cat with white markings in the middle of the circle with curiosity. However, none of them seemed as unnerved by it as Paris. Had she been the only one to see it in the video? The animal did look straight at her, and she could have sworn it winked. Plus, it was in the background of a scene with many things happening with Cleopatra and her entourage.

Maybe she'd imagined it, Paris reasoned, blinking at the cat.

As if the act had cleared her vision, the cat suddenly transformed, rising through the air until it took the shape of none other than Mae Ling, the fairy godmother. She glanced around at the class, wearing a neutral expression and her usual plain black clothes. Most all of the students let out gasps of surprise and awe.

"Welcome to Transformative Magic, where you will learn not only how to transform objects for your jobs as fairy godmothers, but you'll learn how to transform yourself."

She turned and looked directly at Paris, then did something that made another chill run down her spine. The fairy godmother winked like the cat from the video.

CHAPTER EIGHT

Yep, I've lost my mind, Paris concluded as Mae Ling refocused on the class.

It was bizarre to think that the fairy godmother had been there when Cleopatra and Marc Antony had been courting. However, Agent Topaz had said that FGA had been behind it, so a fairy godmother would have been involved and maybe more than one.

Even stranger was how Mae Ling had known to look at the "camera" of sorts and wink, then did it just now. More importantly, why? It always seemed that Mae Ling was trying to orchestrate something for Paris or communicate something but without doing it directly. It had been the fairy godmother who urged Paris to rebel from the beginning. She suspected the other woman was the reason she got so many opportunities that most wouldn't at the college.

"As you all know, fairies can't easily do magic without having an object to focus our powers," Mae Ling began, pacing the circle and glancing at the students. "Many of you have wands or tools you use when doing spells that require a lot of energy. That's very helpful, but I'm going to teach you how to turn objects into things. Transform them, if you will, so you can create the right environment for your

Cinderella and Prince Charming. Ambiance is everything when trying to set a romantic scene."

"Is this like when Cinderella's fairy godmother turned the pumpkin into a coach and the mice into coachmen?" Paris questioned.

"Well, the story comes from somewhere, I'm sure you realize," Mae Ling answered.

Something from the Art of Love class before was still fuming inside Paris. She couldn't get over this notion that fairy godmothers orchestrated matches for only the elite and wealthy. It seemed discriminatory and restrictive when others deserved to find love.

Usually, Paris wouldn't have cared, but she was becoming a fairy godmother and didn't want to be a part of something so selective. She didn't wish love and romance for herself, but she knew it was difficult for many to find it. If fairy godmothers could spread love and bring people together, they should—no matter who they were or how much they had in their bank account.

"The pumpkin is a good example for our studies," Mae Ling continued, striding over to a tree outside the circle of students. She plucked a shiny red apple from a low-hanging branch and held it up. "Fruit is good for creating music." She tapped the apple with her finger, and it disappeared. A melodic tune filled the air from an unseen source. It was instantly captivating. Again, this met with impressed noises from the students.

"Flowers created ideal weather," Mae Ling added over the music. "Vegetables change lighting, which is crucial for setting the mood in romantic situations. Objects like books, furniture, and clothes can become whatever you need in your matchmaking situation."

Most of the students were quickly jotting down notes as they stood around. Paris had found that she didn't need to take notes in her classes. Headmistress Starr had explained this was because of her magician blood. They were naturally the smarter of the magical races and excelled in learning where it was normally more difficult for fairies to retain information.

"How do we transform ourselves?" a student by the name of Moon Sparkle asked.

"You don't," Mae Ling answered at once, a serious expression on her face. "Transforming yourself is very advanced magic and requires a great deal of power. If anything goes wrong, you risk getting stuck in that form for good. As an animal, you will be unable to talk or do any magic so it's unlikely you'd be able to reverse the effects. There are also cases where people didn't transform all the way, and you can imagine the results."

Many around the class shuddered, probably picturing a half-cat, half-person.

"You transformed yourself," a student called Poppy pointed out.

"I've been doing magic for a very long time," Mae Ling countered. "A time will come for some of you when you're ready, and I'll teach you. First, you must master transforming objects for your match-making missions."

"How do we know what to transform when trying to get two people to fall in love?" a student named Petal asked.

"Good question," Mae Ling answered. "Bringing two people together is an art form that requires creativity. That's part of what you're learning here, but as we saw recently with the Amelia Rose and Grayson McGregor case, it's about strategy too, which I think we've ignored for too long." She gave Paris a very pointed look, making her slightly embarrassed. "You see, it's all about creating an opportunity two people need to fall for each other. Sometimes that's simply throwing them together. Sometimes that means making them stranded in a rainstorm. Or it might be as traditional as ensuring their date is full of romantic elements. That will always depend on the two people you're matching. The key is to know your Cinderellas and Prince Charmings, to understand what will work for them."

"Like with Cleopatra," Poppy offered. "The FGA knew that Marc Antony liked elaborate displays so she made a grand entrance when she met him."

Mae Ling nodded. "That's a good example."

"Were you the fairy godmother who worked on that mission?" Paris asked, earning many scrutinizing gazes.

Becky Montgomery laughed rudely. "Fairies live a long time but not that long."

"Fairy godmothers live longer though," Petal argued.

"Not that long," Becky fired back.

"I wasn't assigned to that case," Mae Ling stated, returning her attention to Paris. "I don't know that I approve of that union, but of course, I'm not an agent and don't assign cases."

Paris studied the fairy godmother. There was something she wasn't saying. She didn't refute that she could have been there at the union of Cleopatra and Marc Antony. There was something very mysterious about Mae Ling, and her power wasn't to be underestimated.

"Now," Mae Ling pressed her hands together in front of her, "please find an object and practice transforming it into something else. I'll come around to help you but do keep in mind, it is unlikely that you'll be successful today or any time soon. The art of transformation, even on objects, is incredibly difficult. Pick a small object to start with and remember what it has the potential to become. It's important to remember there are limits for what you can transform specific items into. A piece of fruit can't become anything but a piece of art. Likewise, a living creature can only become another living creature."

For the third instance recently, a chill ran down Paris' spine, but this time, she wasn't entirely sure why. It seemed that this piece of information was important.

CHAPTER NINE

"Now that's unfair," Christine complained when Paris turned a small rock into a spoon. "You did that after only a few times of trying."

Paris, feeling everyone's eyes on her rather than transformative magic, lowered her chin and blushed. "It was luck."

"Magic is never about luck." Mae Ling arrived at her side and appraised the shiny metal spoon. "It was smart to choose to turn the stone into a utensil. That's the lesson I was trying to convey about potentials. A piece of wood has more of a chance of becoming a table than a car."

Christine nudged the twig she was trying to transform and muttered, "Become a coaster already."

It simply remained a twig.

Mae Ling pointed at the edge of the Bewilder Forest, where many students were foraging for things they could try and transform. They'd been at it for over an hour, and many had gone through several objects, hoping to find one that changed. No one had any "luck" until Paris. "Go and find some bark. I think that makes for a better coaster than a twig. Turning something slender into something flat takes more skill than you possess yet."

Christine rolled her eyes. "Not all of us were born with a silver spoon in our mouth in terms of magic." She glanced at Paris while pointing at her spoon. However, a sly grin graced her mouth as she strode for the Bewilder Forest to fetch a piece of bark.

Mae Ling turned to Paris with a proud look in her eyes. "Good work successfully transforming your item."

"It's because I'm a magician, isn't it?" Paris picked up her spoon and checked it.

"It's because you're you," Mae Ling stated. "I know many magicians who can't change the way they think, let alone turn an object into something else."

Paris shrugged, not willing to abandon her search for the reason she'd been successful with transformations in her first lesson. "I do have founders' blood as a Royal for the House of Fourteen."

"You also have a lot on your mind and weighing on your heart," Mae Ling argued. "Under that stress, you were still able to do something incredibly complex."

"I work better under pressure," Paris admitted.

Mae Ling nodded. "I do as well."

"Can I ask you something?" Paris glanced around, ensuring none of the other students were close to them. Most had scattered around the Enchanted Grounds or Bewilder Forest, foraging for objects or deep in concentration trying to transform something.

"Yes, that was me," Mae Ling said as if Paris had already asked her burning question.

"The cat in the video of Cleopatra and Marc Antony?" Paris asked, needing to ensure they were talking about the same thing.

The fairy godmother nodded.

"Okay, well, that brings up a lot of questions," Paris began, suddenly overwhelmed. "Like, how did you know I was going to ask that? Why were you looking directly at me in the video? Why did you wink? Why did you choose to be in cat form directly after that lesson? What exactly are you trying to tell me?"

"To begin, I'm blessed with certain insights," Mae Ling stated. "Furthermore, as fairy godmothers—as I mentioned to the class—it's about creatively choosing how you deal with charges. The little things we do can help those on their paths."

"Are you fairy godmothering me?" Paris knew that Mae Ling guided her Aunt Sophia. Apparently, the fairy godmother also worked outside the boundaries of matchmaking.

"I'm simply helping you on your path."

Paris scratched her head. "I'm not sure I understand how. I mean, when I saw you in the video, it got my attention, and it felt like an endorsement."

"Of what?" Mae Ling challenged.

"Of my idea that our job shouldn't only be about pairing up the wealthy and powerful."

The fairy godmother nodded. "I agree. I've never been much for the idea myself."

"Then why don't you challenge it?" Paris asked. "Why, again, do you encourage me to rebel, but you don't?"

Mae Ling pointed at her plain clothes, different than all the other fairy godmothers and students. "I believe I do. I also work outside the area of matchmaking because that's my choice. However, as I've told you before, I'm not a change agent. That role is reserved for very rare and few people."

Paris pointed at herself. "Me? You think I'm a change agent?"

Mae Ling didn't answer, but the glint in her eyes was enough.

"Well, then how were you in the past? That would be a very long time for a fairy godmother to live."

A rare smile flickered to Mae Ling's mouth. "Therein lies the other reason behind it all. I needed you to ask that question so I could provide you with this important answer. It is much easier for animals, or those transformed into animals, to time travel. Papa Creola doesn't allow it normally, but it doesn't affect the fabric of time as much when an animal travels through history."

"What?" Paris hadn't at all expected that answer. "You time-traveled to be in the video? All so I'd ask that question, and you could provide me with that information. I'm really confused now."

Mae Ling nodded. "Which means you won't stop until you understand this and use the information for what it's intended."

"Will you please fill in the gaps?" Paris begged. "I have a lot going on, and I'm not looking to solve another riddle."

"Think about what you've learned today, and I'm sure it will lead you in the right direction." Mae Ling walked away at once, off to assist other students.

Paris wanted to yell, argue, and run after her, but she knew it would do no good. Instead, she did as Mae Ling suggested and thought about what she'd learned, the parts that had chilled her coming to mind.

She knew that living creatures could only be transformed into other living creatures. Now she knew that animals could time travel more easily. Finally, she'd learned that when transformations went wrong, the creature got stuck.

Her eyes widened at the realization. It all made so much sense, and yet it didn't add up. It explained so much about Faraday, except for the fact that he could talk.

CHAPTER TEN

Straight away, Paris sped for her room, hoping to catch Faraday taking a nap or completing a chemistry lab experiment or whatever he did while she was in classes. However, there was no sign of the talking squirrel in her room.

Deciding to skip lunch to hunt around the Enchanted Grounds for Faraday, Paris made her way back down to the mansion's first floor. She had to have her questions answered. He might have some reason that prevented him from telling her things, but now that she knew questions to ask, she thought she could pull the information out of him—even if it was a simple game of twenty questions.

The smells from the dining hall sought to lure Paris to the other side of the fairy godmother estate, but she sped toward the entrance, thinking she might find Faraday on the front lawn. She was almost to the front door when Headmistress Starr's open office door caught her attention.

Paris wanted to find Faraday, but her curiosity over this new instructor, Agent Topaz, was also begging for answers. She paused at the open door to peek around the frame.

To her relief, the headmistress was hunched over her desk, scribbling on a thick piece of pink parchment with her feather quill. She didn't look deep in concentration but rather frustrated as she crossed out one word and sat back to reread what she'd written.

Knocking on the doorframe, Paris called, "Headmistress Starr? I'm sorry to interrupt you but…"

Willow glanced up, her long grayish-blue hair framing her face. A welcoming smile replaced her prior expression of stress.

"Oh, Paris. You're never interrupting me. That's what I'm here for." She waved a hand at the poufy armchair on the other side of her desk. "Please come in."

"Thanks." Paris slid into the office as she checked over her shoulder, hoping no one would overhear them in the hallway.

Maybe spying her gesture or perhaps that intuitive, Willow said, "Would you like privacy for this discussion?"

"Well," Paris drew out the word, hesitating. "It's about Agent Topaz."

Understandingly, Headmistress Starr nodded and twirled the feather quill in her hand, creating a silencing spell. "Well, I'd say a little discretion wouldn't hurt."

Paris took the seat on the other side of the desk that looked like something out of an old study. There was no computer on the top, but rather notebooks and a quill, a strange device, and an old rotary telephone. Other than the last two items, there wasn't anything technical in the office. It appeared to be a place stuck in time.

"So you would have met Agent Topaz already," Headmistress Starr stated with an edge of reluctance to her tone.

"Why are agents teaching here?" Paris asked. "Has that happened before?"

"It's not that there isn't a precedent for it," Willow began, laying down her feather quill. "However, FGA is changing in new ways. It's always about the influences, and currently, there are a few agents who are challenging Saint Valentine."

"He's supportive of Happily Ever After College evolving into the modern world, isn't he?"

Willow nodded. "The current Saint Valentine is progressive, which I can't say is a common trait among those who have held his position in the past. However, he can't control everything, so when the changes to the college became known, the board put pressure on him to allow an agent to teach here to monitor the curriculum and changes."

"Like the fact that you're allowing a half-magician to be taught here," Paris grumbled.

"A half-fairy too," Willow added. "FGA can't deny that enrollment is down at the college and I believe that's because our practices are out-of-date. That's the reason I agreed to allow you entry. So far, I've been happy with that decision, making me consider other recruitment strategies, but first, we have to update the curriculum. I dare say, it's the image of Happily Ever After as an archaic institution that's caused a ripple effect such as low enrollment."

"About these practices," Paris began. "I knew that Professor Shannon Butcher was in favor of creating love for only the refined and wealthy, but I didn't realize that was a widespread belief across the college. Do fairy godmothers only focus on matchmaking for the elite?" She thought about Amelia Rose and Grayson McGregor and their status, and therefore their reach, realizing that she'd been a part of that union.

Willow gave her a regretful look. "There are different schools of thought for FGA that have constantly served to divide. Currently, our board believes our focus should be on pairing up influential matches. It's gone back and forth through the centuries, but many of us have wanted love for everyone. Honestly, I don't know what I believe. I can see the rationale on both sides. Powerful couples do serve as an inspiration."

"But who are we to say who can become powerful?" Paris challenged. "Maybe if we focus on matching up those with chemistry, creating opportunities and bridges for them to connect when they wouldn't otherwise, they'll go on to do amazing things that they wouldn't have."

"I do understand that perspective." A torn expression radiated from Willow's eyes.

"It's just that pairing up people based on their W-2s and education or social status feels…wrong…" Paris let the sentence trail off, not wanting to be overly critical of the headmistress. She knew that Willow was open to change, but it was still difficult for her. Many of the fairy godmothers' ingrained practices were tough to set aside.

The headmistress drew in a breath, obvious tension on her face. "I don't entirely disagree. Progress was the goal of Happily Ever After College in light of changes we've seen recently. However, there's new pressure from the board and some agents. It seems as soon as we were ready to take a few steps forward, then those more conservative-minded stepped forward encouraging us to retreat once more."

The two were quiet for a moment. "Progress is difficult."

"Change is the culprit here and old ways of thinking," Willow replied. "Saint Valentine sees that we need to evolve with the modern world, but he's being fought more and more with opposition, so we have to play by the rules a little more to appease the board."

"Which is why Stuffy McStuffison is teaching Art of Love and perpetuating the idea of reserving matchmaking for the elite rather than those who have chemistry," Paris muttered.

A small, rebellious smile graced the headmistress' lips. "I think Agent Topaz wants to keep a closer eye on things. The Rose and McGregor union was successful and brought us some accolades, but we quickly met with speculation. The board doesn't like us using untraditional methods."

"It worked," Paris argued.

Willow tipped her head back and forth. "It did, but strangely enough we appear to have a new problem robbing the love meter."

Paris' head jerked to the side, gauging the meter on the sidewall. She wasn't sure how she hadn't noticed it straight away. The love meter, which had recovered after matching the two tycoons, was back to being seriously low again.

Her eyes widened. "What happened?"

Headmistress Starr reached forward and straightened the long piece of paper from the small device on the corner of her desk. It resembled a telegram machine in that it had a wheel and gears and churned out a narrow message of sorts. She ripped off the paper and guided it through her hand, reading silently. Finally, she lowered it and sighed.

"What's that?" Paris pointed at the machine.

"It's a tele-eventor," Willow answered. "It tells us about potential matches, break-ups, and other events that are directly affecting the love meter."

"What events has it been detailing?" Paris read the tension on the headmistress' face.

"I don't know much about social media," Willow began, squinting at the message. "So you'll have to excuse me in that I'm not sure I can make too much sense of this. Apparently, globally, there's a rise in turmoil in romantic relationships, resulting in a myriad of problems and inevitably break-ups."

"Hence the drop on the love meter?" Paris guessed.

Willow nodded. "And apparently, through Saint Valentine's office, Matters of the Heart, which is where the communications of the tele-eventor come from, the problems are being linked to social media."

"Well, it can be a source of drama," Paris related. She wasn't much for socializing through such means, mostly because she didn't socialize. She wasn't turning down any friend requests because she didn't get many—only from that one gnome who wanted to show her a good time, and she was going to show him a fist if he didn't stop messaging her.

"Matters of the Heart is conflicted about this problem," Willow continued. "They think social media isn't the ultimate culprit and could be a tool used for good as much as bad."

"That makes sense," Paris reasoned. "I mean, you can kill a man with a knife, or it can be his very survival depending on the situation."

Willow laid down the paper from the tele-eventor. "I can see that and things like FriendNet being a way to connect couples or help them to court, but in recent instances, it appears the medium is instigating feuds. Infidelity, arguments, and breakups are on the rise, and Saint Valentine believes that FriendNet is responsible, although he's not sure how."

She sighed, looking at a loss. "This is where we are coming up short because we don't have enough expertise in such matters. It shouldn't have come across my desk, but it has, which makes me think..."

"Saint Valentine doesn't know how to attack the situation," Paris guessed, filling in Willow's sentence.

The headmistress glanced at the open door before redirecting her gaze at Paris. "There's that, but I also sense that Saint Valentine is getting a lot of scrutiny and pressure from FGA. The board is increasingly criticizing his progressive ways. Problems linked to love only serve to make Matters of the Heart look worse for endorsing such methods for matchmaking."

Paris pulled her lips to the side, thinking. "Well, it sounds like if we're going to keep evolving and not give them a reason to go back into the Dark Ages of romance and tradition than we have to get to the bottom of all this."

Willow nodded. "Yes, but as I said, I'm not as well-versed on these technical things."

Paris grinned. "Lucky for you, there's a new generation at the college."

"Paris, you have a lot on your plate," Willow stated. "Although I appreciated your help with the last mission—"

"Because I have so much on my plate that I don't want to think about is exactly why you should let me help," Paris argued.

She considered this for a moment. "I was evaluated harshly for allowing a first- and second-year student to handle a case."

"Which turned out successful," Paris countered.

"That's true," Willow affirmed. "However—"

"This problem with the conservatives at FGA and the board is only going to get worse," Paris cut in once more. "I sense you know that the only way for fairy godmothers to be successful is to evolve and learn how to create love in the modern world. Those who are married to the old ways of thinking will continue to serve as the opposition, especially if they're monitoring the current administration and putting supervisors here at the college. So the way to get ahead of them is to figure out this problem and fix it using our new, unorthodox methods. Then they won't be able to deny that adapting to the modern age is necessary."

"What you say makes sense." Willow chewed on her lip, not looking totally convinced.

"I like that the current Saint Valentine is open to change," Paris continued. "I also like that he doesn't have a problem with a half-magician being educated here at the college. Still, I sense that he's going to lose power unless he can put those old crusty families who have no desire to take FGA to the next level in their place."

"You may underestimate what we're up against here," the headmistress stated.

"Well, I didn't much care for being a fairy godmother when circumstances forced me to come here," Paris said boldly. "At first, I'll admit, I was doing things for the wrong reasons. Now, I see the importance of love in creating a more peaceful world for all. So now I want to do this, and hopefully for the right reasons. However, I don't want to do it 'the way we've always done it.' I want to challenge that and do it better. Do it in the way that makes sense for this world, not the one that came before."

Headmistress Starr smiled at this. "You sound like Mae Ling."

"Well, maybe she's set a good example for me," Paris offered.

"She does things her way, but that's never had much of a change on how everyone else does," Willow replied.

Something sparked inside of Paris, and her eyes lit up with excitement. "Well, maybe there's someone who can change that. Or maybe, we can at least keep things from slipping back into the Dark Ages."

Willow glanced at the message from the tele-eventor. "I'm going to give you a chance to work on this, but not publicly if that's all right with you."

"Yes," Paris nearly exclaimed. "Why are you giving me this?" She had to ask, not thinking that as a newbie she'd get this chance again, especially after getting criticized the last time.

The headmistress leaned forward. "Honestly, if someone overthrows Saint Valentine, things will change dramatically. They will go back to the more conservative ways we've tried to change. The rules will be much stricter, I fear." Willow's eyes were suddenly intense. "Those who the board doesn't think should be here will be expelled."

Paris nodded, gulped, and sat back, fully understanding the implications. "Then do I have your permission to pull in a few resourceful people who might be able to help me investigate this FriendNet business?"

"As long as they use discretion." Willow picked up her quill, probably realizing that she meant Christine, who was savvy on modern things, unlike many of Happily Ever After's students. "I'll send a message to Saint Valentine telling him that we'll help how we can and to expect more information in the future."

Paris pushed up to a standing position. "Thank you for the discussion and the opportunity."

"The pleasure is mine. Not many have come to me to inquire about changes. Actually, no one ever does. Fairies, particularly students, usually accept things the way they are."

"I think being a rebel runs in my blood," Paris said proudly, thinking of her parents and already missing them.

"Well, I've sensed that a rebel was what we've needed for a long time," the headmistress admitted. "I hope I'm right. If I am, I dare say that Saint Valentine will be indebted to the person or people who help him with this situation."

Paris left the headmistress' office at once with only a slight nod, feeling both ecstatic and overwhelmed by what she'd signed on for.

CHAPTER ELEVEN

Since the last time that Hemingway had requested the class meet him by the stables, Paris thought this lesson would have to do with something at Mirror Lake like mermaids or other special creatures. That's why she was instantly on guard when a large horse trotted in her direction as she approached the large red building. No one else was around, and it was unbridled, picking up speed as it neared her.

Paris paused, knowing better than to put her back to the animal. She didn't see a tree in the vicinity that she could magically climb either, like the last time when she escaped the deranged stallion that nearly ran her down on her first day at Happily Ever After College.

"Slow your roll, Horsey," Paris encouraged the spotted brown and white Arabian now galloping toward her with its head down and attention focused on her.

She glanced over her shoulder, wondering if there was something nearby provoking it. Since she was early to class, having skipped lunch, there was no one else around.

She was what was provoking the beast—who was almost upon her.

"Whoa now, Zar!" Hemingway yelled from the stables, running out and seeing what was about to happen. He held up his hand and shot out a force from his palm that spiraled forward like an invisible wall and sped until it was right in front of the horse.

The strange barrier halted in front of the racing animal and froze with a loud *bong* like a weird drum. The horse reared back to avoid colliding with the see-through divider, whinnying before its front hooves slammed back onto the ground. Its eyes were wild and still focused on Paris as it pawed the earth.

However, although the barrier that Hemingway had shot from his hands was see-through, there was a reflective quality to it in the afternoon sunlight that let Paris, and the horse, know that it was solid. Zar wouldn't be able to pass through it without injury or worse.

The horse charged back and forth along the invisible wall with obvious angst in its every movement, its gaze on Paris. She remained frozen, watching the creature as Hemingway raced in their direction.

"Zar!" Hemingway yelled. "Back to the stables!" He circled his finger, and as if suddenly robotically controlled, the deranged horse turned at once. It dutifully trotted back for the stable with its tail swishing back and forth as if moments before it hadn't been about to murder Paris with its hooves.

When it was back inside the stableyard, Hemingway sighed, put his hands on his knees, and leaned over as though he was the one nearly trampled.

Needing the laugh, Paris said, "You okay? Looks like that was quite the ordeal for you."

An abrupt laugh burst out of Hemingway's mouth as he straightened. "Very funny. I'm surprised you're standing there so calmly."

She motioned around. "Well, there wasn't any tree to climb so I decided to close my eyes and pretend this whole thing was a dream. That works in the movies."

He continued to chuckle. "I'm sure if I hadn't arrived, you would have come up with a way of rescuing yourself."

"For sure," she joked. "I was about to pee on myself. That would work, right?"

He nodded. "Totally. Or you could try portaling, shielding, or any of the other combat spells in your arsenal."

"Well, I've gotten out of the habit of throwing combat spells at animals since that's frowned upon."

"Reconsider it then," he advised, holding up his hand and pulling down the invisible barrier separating them. Unlike fairies, since he wasn't one, the secret magician didn't need an instrument to channel his power. The shield had been a powerful spell that he'd thrown up instantly, which was impressive.

"Why?" She studied him. "Why is that the second time a horse has charged at me on the grounds of Happily Ever After College?"

"I'm not completely sure." He ran his hands through his short brown hair. "I mean, none of the usual reasons that horses don't like people fit. You're not carrying anything they dislike, such as plastic bags, traffic cones, or balloons."

Paris looked around as though checking. "Yeah, I left all that stuff in my room earlier."

He laughed. "You're not a chicken, miniature horse, or a butterfly."

"Wait. Horses hate those kinds of things?"

He nodded. "Yeah, vehemently. Oh, and also demons."

She lowered her chin, the realization dawning on her. "There we have it. Mystery solved."

"You're a chicken?" he asked. "I mean, I knew you were full of surprises, but I wasn't expecting that one."

She laughed. "No, remember when I told you I became half-fairy because of a wish my parents made to a genie?"

He nodded.

"Well, I forgot to supply the reason that my parents asked the genie for the wish."

"I'm guessing it wasn't because they wanted you to get into Happily Ever After College."

She shook her head. "It was because my father was a demon hunter and one had bitten him. They were worried that I'd be part demon."

"But you were born half-magician and half-fairy," he argued.

"With demon blood," she explained.

He understood at once. "The fairy part of you counteracts that, but you still have the blood of the demon. Smart genie."

"Or conniving little jerk who was messing with my parents," she imparted. "They simply asked the genie to make me not a demon."

"You're not. Not really because the fairy part of you overpowers it," he reasoned. "Although you still have the blood of the demon."

"So is that why horses loathe me?" She looked at the stables.

Hemingway followed her gaze. "I'm afraid so. Even if the blood doesn't do anything to you, they still sense it. But hey, if it makes you feel any better, your blood also gets you into any rave in lower Manhattan and into the underworld."

She couldn't help but laugh. "It doesn't make me feel better, but thanks."

"Come on now. You never know when you'll need to go down there and fetch someone," he teased.

"I've met enough evil spirits for one lifetime. My demon blood was how I was able to overpower the Deathly Shadow, but it also almost ruined me."

He nodded, suddenly serious. "I could see it being something hard to wrestle with if you let it loose."

"Says the guy who is a magician pretending to be a fairy," she joked, grateful to be able to throw it back at him.

To her relief, he grinned, pressing his hands into his jean pockets. "Well, we all have secrets. Yours is safe with me. I'm guessing you don't want it out that you have demon blood."

She shook her head. "No, I have enough problems being part-magician. You know, and so do Penny and the talking squirrel. Which, have you seen that rascal?"

Hemingway pursed his lips. "No, can't say I have. You'll have time to look for him because I'm going to give you a free pass for equestrian lessons today and oh, yeah, for the rest of your life."

Paris laughed. "Oh, so you don't want me to learn how to ride horses for the ridiculous purposes of creating true love?"

"Well, in all honesty, there is a takeaway for those learning to be fairy godmothers to master equestrian studies," he explained. "Learning to tame and work with horses is an artform that transfers to crafting romances for some. However, I think you should skip this part of the curriculum."

"Because I'm going to get stampeded if I try?"

"Exactly," he affirmed with a wink. "I dare say you can skip a few lessons here at Happily Ever After College and be fine."

"Why?" She asked but immediately felt like she was fishing. Still, after everything and all the new responsibility, she needed someone objective like Hemingway to tell her why she could skip lessons to be a fairy godmother when so many others had their doubts.

"Because you understand that love is more than an emotion," he explained, looking out on the Enchanted Grounds with a dreamy expression in his eyes. "Don't get me wrong, I appreciate the fairy godmothers, but they're short-sighted in many ways. They believe that it all boils down to creating a feeling for two people, but they forget that people also think. Too often, people 'think' themselves out of love. However, when someone—well, perhaps like you, who takes a more holistic approach—matchmakes, well, maybe, just maybe, you consider how to get two people to 'feel' and 'think' about each other so that true love blossoms."

He held up his hands suddenly. "Of course, that's merely a suspicion from my observations with you, and I realize you're new to this whole business. So only time will tell."

"Yeah, only time will tell." Paris smiled back at him, appreciating the look of pride in his eyes as he regarded her and the Enchanted Grounds that she knew he loved so much. "Well, I better get out of here before I anger your horses. Besides, I have to find my squirrel."

He nodded while backing toward the stables. "If I had a dollar for every time a student here said that to me."

"Yeah?" She stepped back toward the mansion.

"Yeah, I'd have a dollar."

CHAPTER TWELVE

After an hour of searching for Faraday, Paris gave up and headed to Magical Cooking and Baking class. She was thinking of what kind of stew she would put the squirrel into when Chef Ash breezed into the classroom, sketching on his drawing pad. He looked up absentmindedly as if he'd forgotten he was supposed to be teaching a class.

"Oh, hello everyone." He lowered the pad, then glanced at it again. "I think the recipes I'm currently constructing will be perfect for today's lesson."

"You create recipes like you cook food," Becky corrected snobbishly from the back of the room. "There's no constructing involved."

Paris glanced back at Becky the Bully, having about as much of her mouth as she could take for a day. "Grab a thesaurus, genius. Constructing is defined as creating, building, forming, or making. You can use all of those words for making food."

"I quite like the idea of building flavors," Christine chimed in.

"It's simply incorrect terminology according to the FGA board," Becky complained, crossing her arms over her chest.

Paris was also getting really tired of hearing about FGA, the board, and these uptight agents.

"Hey, Bec, why don't you stuff it unless you want a pie on your head," Paris threatened.

The class laughed.

"I think it might improve her appearance dramatically," Christine joked.

"I appreciate that you two like the terminology that I use in my class to describe cooking and baking," Chef Ash said diplomatically from the front of the demo kitchen. "I assure you, any matters that the FGA board has with instructors go through our headmistress and shouldn't be the students' concerns."

Paris smirked at Becky before facing Chef Ash. She had a very confident feeling that the socialite was behind many of the problems that resulted in the agents scrutinizing the curriculum at Happily Ever After College.

"As I was saying," Chef Ash continued. "Inspired by a recent conversation, I've been crafting recipes that remind me of Mother Nature." His gaze connected with Paris momentarily before he directed it around the room again. "Now, although these heavily involve fruits and vegetables to celebrate spring, there's something else that Mother Nature brings to mind for me."

"Fertility," Christine supplied.

Chef Ash cracked a smile and nodded. "That's definitely true. I can't argue with that, and we will have a lesson on foods related to that at some point. However, I'm thinking of something else more specifically connected to your purposes as fairy godmothers."

"Love," Paris supplied.

Chef Ash's grin widened. "Bingo!"

"Oh, no fair," Christine mock-complained. "She's met Mother Nature."

"We *are* in the business of love," Paris reminded her. "It wasn't that hard to guess."

"You've met Mother Nature?" Poppy asked.

"That's incredible," Lilly Pad said.

"What's she like?" another student questioned.

"Shorter than you'd expect," Paris answered simply.

"She also hangs out with Father Time," Christine bragged.

"I don't," Paris stated. Then her phone buzzed in her jacket pocket, which shouldn't have happened since it was on silent. Plus, no one she knew except her got text messages at Happily Ever After College, and that was because Faraday had fixed up her phone with some special magitech.

Chef Ash, as surprised as everyone else in the classroom that she'd gotten a message, arched an eyebrow at her. "You need to get that?"

Paris realized that it might be important, so she retrieved her phone and glanced at it. The message said,

You do hang out with me, and I need you to come to the Fantastical Armory after that class. Subner says to bring cookies. –Papa Creola

Paris couldn't help but laugh at the message, its timing, and that Father Time signed his text messages.

"Who's it from?" Christine asked loudly.

Paris put her phone in her pocket, blushing slightly. "Father Time. He wants me to bring him cookies after this."

"Liar," Becky fired bitterly. "There's no way that the father of time eats cookies or hangs out with you, halfling."

Paris' phone buzzed again. Getting an encouraging look from Chef Ash, she checked it.

She read the message aloud for all to hear it. "Father Time says that his assistant 'wants the cookies to be chocolate fudge with chocolate chips.' And to 'tell Rebecca Montgomery that she could use better time management skills since she slept in late this morning, after forgetting to do her Cinderella Studies assignment until the last minute and therefore stayed up late last night finishing it.'"

Becky gasped. "How did you know about that? Were you spying on me?"

Paris held up her phone. "No, but apparently Papa was. And, as if. I have no interest in spying on you, Boring Montgomery."

Before Becky could reply, Chef Ash clapped enthusiastically. "All right, looks like we need to make a great batch of chocolate fudge, chocolate chip cookies for Father Time's assistant. The timing couldn't be any more perfect for today's lesson. It's as if Father Time knew."

"Sounds like he did," Christine offered.

"They don't have to be great cookies," Paris imparted. "Father Time's assistant is kind of a jerk."

Right on cue, Paris' phone buzzed in her hand. She glanced at it. The message read:

I think the same about you. –Subner

She sighed and glanced up. "And a peeping Tom."

Chef Ash chuckled. "Well, as I was saying, this works well for our purposes because today we're studying ingredients in food that are considered aphrodisiacs. One of the main ones happens to be chocolate—especially for women."

Many students around the room giggled nervously at the mention of aphrodisiacs.

Waving off the commotion, Chef Ash regained control of the class. "Now, the term aphrodisiacs comes from the Greek goddess of love, Aphrodite. She is often symbolized as a dove and depicted in artwork, literature, and religion throughout history. In other classes, you will study Aphrodite and how she'll help you to better understand love for matchmaking purposes." His usual casual smile dropped away. "Of course, I hope you do since I believe it's an important part of your education."

The stricter standards forced on Happily Ever After College from the agents at FGA were being felt by many—including Chef Ash, it seemed.

"Now, for you as fairy godmothers," Chef Ash continued, "it will be helpful to know what foods can encourage romance between your Cinderella and Prince Charming. It's all about setting the mood and food is one of the best ways to do that. Many cultures believe certain foods, drinks, herbs, and chemicals can increase the good feelings related to love and desire."

"You mean sex," Christine cut in.

"What I mean is that for whatever reason, there are certain things that put people in better moods, make them more open to romance, and have desires," Chef Ash explained. "Sometimes your jobs will be pairing up people, but sometimes it's about taking down boundaries related to inhibition that keep two people from pursuing each other. My job is to give you an arsenal, and your job is to figure out how to use it creatively."

Paris liked the idea more and more that being a fairy godmother was about creatively using strategy to bring two people together. Like how Mae Ling had set her up, there seemed like there was no one way to orchestrate things for people.

"Common known aphrodisiacs are chocolate," Chef Ash continued.

"There's not enough in the world to make Father Time's assistant loving," Paris joked, earning laughter from some of the students in the class.

"It sounds like you don't want that guy being all sexy anyway," Christine teased.

Chef Ash nodded. "Keep in mind that aphrodisiacs aren't limited to desire. They should create more of a euphoric feeling, which can lead to romance. Think about how you feel after you eat a piece of my double chocolate ganache cake."

"Angry because I'll never fit into my jeans." Christine chortled.

"Well, simply use some magic, and you'll be fine," Paris offered.

"It doesn't work quite the same for us fairies, lucky magician halfling," Christine replied.

Chef Ash nodded. "Fairies' reserves do come from food, but we use magic less readily so we have to use more for the calorie burn. However, my point about the chocolate cake remains. Hopefully, you feel good, albeit full."

"It's like a high," Poppy added.

"Good," Chef Ash affirmed. "The idea with these ingredients is to create that blissful state and therefore set the stage for love. Who knows some other foods besides chocolate that are considered aphrodisiacs?"

"Oysters," Lilly Pad offered.

"Ginseng," Moon Sparkle suggested.

"Asparagus," Star Ship imparted.

"Very good!" Chef Ash exclaimed, obviously excited that the class was getting into the subject. "Some lesser-known ones are supposedly more potent, although I'm not sure where to source them from. They include bufo toad, horny goat weed, yohimbine, and ambrien, which is the gut of sperm whales."

"Can we pour our charges some wine and call it a day?" Christine asked. "I'm not sure about gutting a sperm whale, even in the name of love."

Chef Ash nodded. "Wine works depending on your charges. That's the reason I'm giving you options. If you have a vegan, asparagus might be an option. Seafood is often associated with aphrodisiacs because Aphrodite was born from the sea. So it's going to depend on the situation. Today, I want you to construct a dish that's satisfying to the taste buds and also elicits feelings of love and desire. You'll find a full selection of ingredients at the back. Please get started, as you only have an hour to prepare your dish."

The students all took off like contestants on a cooking show, racing to get the best ingredients. Paris didn't though, noticing that Chef Ash headed her way. He offered her a thoughtful expression as Christine also strode over in her direction.

"Looks like you're making chocolate fudge, chocolate chip cookies," he said.

She nodded. "Where do you keep the arsenic?"

Both Christine and Chef Ash laughed. "I'm sure he's not all that bad," he offered.

She shrugged. "He apparently doesn't like that I was born."

"I feel the same about some people." Christine glanced over her shoulder to where Becky Montgomery was picking over ingredients, yanking them out of other students' hands.

"How about you help Paris with the cookies," Chef Ash suggested before trotting to the back of the demo kitchen to supervise the chaos ensuing as students fought over supplies.

Christine nodded. "Sure, I'll help you, but I also get to be the taste tester."

Paris nodded. "That's great because I have a new reconnaissance mission for us to discuss. Get ready to put your social media knowledge to the test."

CHAPTER THIRTEEN

Paris' hands shook many times when they were making the cookies for the ungrateful and grumpy Subner. She knew Christine noticed. However, she was glad for the help and that she had a recipe instead of devising one like the others in the class.

If Papa Creola wanted her to come to the Fantastical Armory, she hoped that meant her parents had awoken and she could finally see them—really see them. Talk to them. Get to know each other.

However, she didn't want to get her hopes up because it could be as likely that Papa Creola wanted to talk to her. She wouldn't say that she hung out with the father of time, but over the last week, he had wanted to spend time explaining things to her that she had been confused about. Maybe he felt sorry for her, knowing that she only wanted her parents to wake up.

On the few occasions she'd been in the Fantastical Armory, Papa Creola had explained how time moved differently depending on several factors. He'd also educated her about why her parents had to stay asleep until ready and some of the things she'd experience as a halfling. The last part was mostly conjecture since there was no example in history to draw from. On every such occasion, Subner had sat behind the counter in the shop and grumbled about various complaints.

Paris doubled back to her room with the tray of warm chocolate fudge, chocolate chip cookies, hoping to freshen up in case she was going to be able to see her parents. Christine, sensing that she was nervous about the meeting after class, had simply tried to put her at ease by telling jokes. It had helped, but Paris couldn't help but feel the jitters. She suspected it would be that way until after the initial real time with her parents. Until then, she had sufficient time to wonder and worry.

"Oh, you brought me some cookies," Faraday squealed when she entered her bedroom.

She slid the tray of chocolate fudge, chocolate chip cookies onto the dresser and wagged her finger at him. "Don't touch those. They aren't for you."

"Well, then where is my cheese sandwich?" He looked her over as if she was hiding it in her pocket or something.

"It's in the kitchen still." Paris rushed over to the vanity, picking up the hairbrush and going to work taming her locks.

"Oh, this is awkward then." Faraday looked over her shoulder at her image in the mirror. "You're getting ready by brushing your hair, and you forgot my sandwich. You must have an important meeting."

"I'm not sure," Paris answered, giving up on her hair and deciding to straighten her clothes instead. That was also a lost cause. There was only so much she could do to make her black-on-black ensemble look nice. "So quick question for you."

"If it's about the electrostatic field inside the Bewilder Forest, the answer won't be quick," he replied.

Paris turned to face him directly. "So this spell that made you a talking squirrel…" She watched as he tensed.

"Yes," he chirped, his tail flicking.

"Did it have to do with you transforming into a squirrel rather than being one to start with?"

He did that thing he did when nervous—his cheeks puffing out suddenly. "I wish I could say."

"So you can't flick your tail once for yes and twice for no?" she asked.

He flicked his tail three times.

"Does that mean maybe?"

He flicked his tail twice.

Paris rolled her eyes. "Oh, you're impossible."

"I told you I'm not allowed to say anything."

"Well, can you at least tell me if I'm close?" Paris questioned. "How will whoever you made this agreement with know?"

"They'll know," he said at once.

"Fine," Paris reasoned. "How about you hear my speculation and not make any reactions if I'm totally off base."

"I don't think this is a good idea." His eyes slid to the side with obvious nervousness.

"I don't know who you're worried about putting the smackdown on you, but I know some pretty important people who can keep you safe."

"Yeah, that's the thing." Faraday's eyes slid to the side again.

Paris tilted her head and regarded the squirrel. "Wait, are you saying the deal you made was with someone I know? Who? Is it Papa Creola?"

"I've never met Father Time, but I hear he has a horrible bedside manner."

So it wasn't Papa Creola. Paris needed to eliminate all the powerful people she knew. However, she realized that could be harder than she thought. Her connection with her parents made it so she now knew a lot of powerful people—like her aunt, a leader of the dragonriders, or her uncle, a Councilor for the House of Fourteen. Then there was King Rudolf Sweetwater—the leader of the fae. Not to mention Bermuda Laurens, the expert on all magical creatures. Lee, the assassin baker shouldn't be underestimated in all this too.

"If I find this person who has you bound not to tell, can I get them to allow you to share your secret?" Paris questioned, but the squirrel didn't answer. "You know, the secret of how you transformed yourself into a squirrel, time-traveled, and got stuck."

His cheeks puffed up again, but he didn't say a word.

Paris sighed. "Fine, let's continue to play the quiet game. I'm going to figure this out. I'll find out who can tell me and I'll put them in a headlock until they spill the secret or allow you to do so."

Faraday clicked his claws together nervously. "If anyone can figure this out, I'm sure it's you. If you do, well, that's the first step."

"The first step in what? A series of steps to do what?" Paris figuratively pounced on the clues Faraday was leaving for her.

"The first step in undoing the past." He hopped for the open window where he disappeared before she could question him any more.

CHAPTER FOURTEEN

Roya Lane always looked the same lately, but it felt different every time Paris entered it. She reasoned that she was the one who was different and not the magical lane full of shops and strange creatures.

The vibrating in Paris' chest returned as she strode down the cobbled road carrying the tray of chocolate fudge, chocolate chip cookies. Talking to Faraday had helped, although he gave her more puzzle pieces than answers.

"You see, here is the monument of where they signed the Gettysburg Address," a familiar voice said through a crowd of people.

Paris stopped short. Not only because she recognized the voice and knew what they were saying was ludicrous, but she also had to admit she was stalling. She was maybe about to see her parents after the long wait and ironically she was putting it off. However, she knew it wasn't because she didn't want to see them. It was because she was afraid they were going to reject her or that she'd built it all up in her mind, and they wouldn't have this beautiful relationship that she'd romanticized.

She cut through the crowd, found the speaker, and confirmed she was correct. It was none other than King Rudolf Sweetwater. He was standing next to a lamp post covered in ivy and regarding it like it was a beautiful statue. "I remember when Abby Lincoln signed the address, I was standing right here." The fae pointed at the stone where he stood.

Unable to stop herself, Paris shook her head. "That never happened."

King Rudolf gawked at her, a sound of offense falling from his mouth. "Well, of course, it did. I was right here. Abby was sitting on the bench, and he asked me for a pen because the one he'd brought had run out of ink. I was like, 'Oh, aren't you happy I'm here to save the day.'"

"Ummm…yeah, no, it didn't happen." Paris hid her laugh.

Many in the crowd pursed their lips at the king of the fae and moved off, apparently thinking the show was over.

"I told you," a young magician said to his companion as they retreated.

"It's funny to hear what he comes up with," another person said while trudging off.

"Where does he come up with this stuff?" Someone shook their head as they strode for a magical candle shop.

King Rudolf waved as the crowd dispersed. The only two people that stayed behind were Ramy Vance, the clerk from Heals Pills, and Paris. "The next tour will be tomorrow. Same place and time."

"You're giving tours?" Paris tilted her head, thinking that couldn't be a good idea.

King Rudolf nodded. "Yeah, since I've been allowed to return to Roya Lane, you know, since you know your secretive past and Papa Creola can't keep me out, as much as he'd like, I figured it would be good to offer my experience on the historical places here since I've seen them all."

"It's fascinating stuff." Ramy looked at the king with a dreamy expression.

"It is?" Paris had to remind herself that the clerk might not be all there since he regularly died and could come back to life thanks to a fall into the Fountain of Youth.

"Yeah, he was telling us about how the Gettysburg Address was signed here, right on Roya Lane. Can you believe that?" Ramy looked impressed.

"I can't," Paris remarked dryly. "Because for starters, the Gettysburg Address was a speech given by Abraham Lincoln and not a signed document."

King Rudolf nodded. "That's what they want you to believe."

"Who?" she questioned at once.

"Them," he said in reply. "He gave the speech here at this bench, then signed it."

"I'm so glad you're back to educate me on such things." Ramy batted his eyes at King Rudolf. "It's been hard not having you here for all those years."

King Rudolf nodded and pointed at Paris. "You can blame her for that. I mean, it wasn't her fault or anything, but if we are to blame someone for why I couldn't grace Roya Lane with my presence, it would be because of her."

"Second, the Gettysburg Address is part of American history, so why would the speech be given here in London on Roya Lane?" Paris decided it was best to address concrete facts with the fae.

King Rudolf shook his head and clicked his tongue. "Don't you know, it's always location, location, location."

"So the President of the United States gave an address after the Civil War here in London?" Paris questioned, hoping that some sense rang true.

"Now you're getting it!" King Rudolf sang delightedly.

She shook her head, concluding that reason was beyond the fae. *Thankfully he's handsome and charming.*

"You don't look like yourself." Rudolf gave her a compassionate look.

Paris remembered the weight on her heart about her parents and straightened, trying to force a normal expression on her face, which she realized probably showed lines of stress. She held up the tray. "It's because I'm holding cookies."

"That must be it," Ramy chirped, his eyes wide as he sniffed in the direction of the plate.

King Rudolf put a hand on his shoulder and urged him back. "I don't think it's the cookies, Ramy-Cans. My observation, which is never wrong, tells me that something is stressing Miss Beaufont."

"Oooooh." Ramy stepped back. "I see it now too."

"You do?" King Rudolf asked him.

Ramy shook his head. "No, but I wanted to sound cool."

"You did." King Rudolf returned his attention to Paris. "Now, tell Uncle Ru what's bothering you. Is it Clark? I find that if I hum a tune in my head when he talks to me, I don't fall asleep."

Paris shook her head, not wanting to go into what was bothering her. "I'm fine. How is Captain Morgan after the abduction? Has she recovered?"

"She's fine." King Rudolf waved her off. "The whole thing has given her a new lease on life."

"Oh, that's nice," Paris remarked.

"You'd think, but do you know how hard it is to source only organically raised mink coats?" King Rudolf asked. "Plus, she refuses to eat anything but pistachios, but they must be free-range. She has such a big heart, my lovely daughter. She doesn't want anything that goes into or onto her body to be harmed beforehand."

"A real saint," Paris muttered.

"Anyway, don't think that I've forgotten that you look like my wife Serena after she's looked at the calorie count on a box of bonbons." King Rudolf snapped his fingers at her. "Out with it. What's got you down?"

Realizing that she couldn't keep denying it, Paris slumped. "Papa Creola summoned me or whatever you want to call it. I've been waiting to hear when my parents awoke. It might not be now, but I don't know. Something in my gut tells me that it is. If I'm honest, I'm nervous because, well, I'm getting to meet my parents for the first time, really. The whole thing is nerve-wracking."

"Oh, I hope that Liv has awoken," King Rudolf cheered. "I need her to settle a bet between Serena and me. She insists that you can do a blood transfusion with a coconut because she saw it on a supposed reality show. I insist that it's impossible. We're going to attempt it and need an impartial judge. Liv is the only objective option."

"Please don't attempt this," Paris begged, realizing he was serious.

King Rudolf held up his hand. "Now, I understand about being worried about getting to know your father. That will undoubtedly involve long, boring conversations where he will fail to meet expectations, disappoint you with his lack of a sense of humor, and make you hope that you're the mailman's baby."

Paris blinked at the fae. "I don't think we had a mailman, being magicians and all."

King Rudolf shrugged. "Well, then you might have to face the fact that you're Stefan Ludwig's legitimate child. I mean, if it's any consolation, you're pretty, and therefore, there's a chance that Liv had a side thing with a fae."

"Did you forget that whole part where I became a fairy because I inherited my father's demon blood and the genie was trying to fix me?" Paris questioned.

"I always try to forget anything that includes your father. He truly is the worst. Clark is, of course, second to him."

"Well, I think this is our opportunity to make Paris feel better." Ramy stepped forward.

"Great idea, Ramy-Cans," King Rudolf remarked with a broad, toothy grin. "What do you have in mind? We can go bar-hopping. Tie a gnome to a giant's back and watch him do that turn around number, trying to get the rascal off. Or, of course, there's the old standard morale booster."

"Balancing things on our head and seeing how long we can go for?" Ramy questioned.

King Rudolf scowled at him. "I don't ever put anything on my head that will mess up my hair."

"Oh, well, then I'll go big to make up for it," Ramy said excitedly. "Paris, I have just the thing to make you smile and take your mind off your problems. Watch this." He waved his hand at a large metal trash receptacle that was full to the brim while muttering a spell. It wavered before lifting magically into the air, teetering back and forth, looking like it was close to spilling over at any moment.

"Really, that's not necessary," Paris urged, waving her hands back and forth. The stone-encased trashcan had to weigh a few hundred pounds by itself. Then with the trash, it was really heavy.

King Rudolf waved her off. "Oh, Ramy-Cans loves to do this kind of stuff. It gives his life purpose. He's like our resident clown."

"Watch as I balance this impossibly heavy structure on the top of my head," Ramy said proudly. "Don't try this at home, boys and girls. I have incredibly strong neck muscles and have been practicing this stunt for days."

Paris gulped, wanting to close her eyes but knowing that she couldn't since the show was on her behalf.

The large trashcan lowered onto the brown curls on Ramy's head, mashing them to his forehead before settling onto his head. He held his arms out wide, his face tentative at first before lighting up with a wide grin. "See there! It's an art form! I can—"

The trashcan tilted one way, then the other. His eyes went wide, and he stepped sideways, trying to correct his balance to keep it steady. Paris was about to spring into action, but King Rudolf pushed her back, away from the collateral damage. There was a lot. In an instant, the heavy trashcan crashed down and crushed the man underneath it. There was hardly time for a scream or much else.

Paris turned away, not wanting to see the sight. Thankfully when she turned back to check if there was a Ramy to rescue, trash covered the scene and she suspected he hadn't survived. Also thankfully, he'd recover and come back to life soon.

King Rudolf shook his head and clicked his tongue. "Such a senseless and totally avoidable death."

He held out his arm. "Well, let's not let him ruin your afternoon. Shall I accompany you to the Fantastical Armory?"

CHAPTER FIFTEEN

Paris declined King Rudolf's offer to escort her to the Fantastical Armory. Although Ramy intended to make her feel better, she was more on edge than before she'd arrived on Roya Lane. Witnessing a death usually did that to most people. She knew he'd come back to life and be fine...well, as fine as he ever was. However, she thought that some solo time might be what she needed before entering Subner's shop.

She had paused to ask King Rudolf if he knew anything about a talking squirrel. He explained that he didn't do hallucinatory drugs anymore, not since he realized the paperweight he'd carried around for a quarter of a century wasn't a talking duck. Paris reasoned he wasn't the one who knew Faraday's secret and decided she'd look more into it later when she wasn't potentially about to see her long-lost parents.

The tension was starting to feel overwhelming in her chest as she neared the Fantastical Armory.

"You know what I find to be the best thing to calm my nerves?" another familiar voice said close by her.

There weren't many people in that area of Roya Lane, and no one was nearby. Paris glanced around, looking for the source of the voice, and finally down to the cobblestones, where she found none other than the black and white cat known as her mother's familiar.

"Plato." Paris smiled, relieved to see him there. She glanced around and noticed that suddenly there was no one around and they were alone on that part of the road—toward the end of Roya Lane where the Fantastical Armory was.

Whereas seeing King Rudolf and Ramy had been weird, entertaining, and unnerving, something was relieving about seeing her mother's familiar.

"What calms your nerves?" Paris smiled down at the lynx.

"Being timeless and having no known predators," he remarked.

Paris pursed her lips. "Well, that helps *me* none."

"Yes, I guess it wouldn't since magicians become disarmed by emotions and relationships and all that stuff that goes on in your psyche."

"Were you this helpful to my mother as her sidekick?" Paris still held the tray of cookies.

"Even less so," he stated matter-of-factly.

"Thanks for your honesty." She paused and looked between the cat and the Fantastical Armory in the distance, realizing that once more she was stalling. "So what gives me the pleasure of your visit?"

"You're going to see Liv," he stated rather than asked, nodding in the direction of the Fantastical Armory.

She shrugged. "I don't know exactly. I'm not sure."

"You brought Subner cookies," he argued.

"So?"

"Well, the only reason that grump would want those is to cheer himself up because Liv has awoken."

"Oh, that makes sense. He's eating his feelings, then?"

"I guess so," Plato replied.

"So it's true then…I'll get to see my parents…They're finally awake." She didn't sound as excited as she thought she should.

He sensed her tension. "Don't be nervous. She will love you. She loves you. Nothing you could ever do will change that."

"I know but so much time has passed," Paris reasoned. "I've changed so much."

"Another hundred years can pass," he reassured her. "That's the thing about those you love. Time means nothing to two hearts that are connected."

Paris smiled. *Those* were the words she needed to hear.

"Thing is," he continued. "Papa Creola won't let me see her yet…"

"I thought rules didn't apply to you," she challenged.

"They do if it means that breaking them would harm Liv."

"Oh, that makes sense."

"I don't know when I'll be allowed to see her. I hoped that you'd give Liv a message for me."

"Of course."

"Tell her that I did as she asked," Plato continued. "I ensured that her daughter was never alone. And when Guinevere Paris Beaufont needed to go away on her own, I ensured she had a friend. Because he needed a friend too."

Paris' mouth popped open. "It was you. You're the one who sent Faraday to accompany me? He was sent then? Why?"

She suddenly felt like more of her life was a lie, but she couldn't force herself to be mad about this. Faraday had gone with her to Happily Ever After College because of a deal, but she also sensed that he wanted to. Apparently, he needed help and therefore agreed. That was life, Paris reasoned. Others did something to get something out of it, whether help or resources or knowledge or love.

"He was drafted because your mother never wanted you to be alone. I knew that. Faraday was perfect for the job because he's smart, resourceful, and good at his core. As I said, he needed a friend as much as you did. I'm not sure if you noticed, but he's strange."

Paris laughed. "I like that about him. But that means it's you, isn't it? You're the one who knows Faraday's secret and won't let him tell it, aren't you? What is it then?"

"Tell Liv that much like her familiar, her daughter's made a promise," Plato explained, not directly answering her question. "He has fulfilled his end of the deal, and I'm willing to make good on my end now."

Paris knew that he was telling her all this for her benefit and not so she'd communicate it to her mother. Faraday had made a deal with Plato, but now she needed to know why and what he got out of it for helping her. "What was his promise, Plato? Was it to assist me?" Paris thought of how Faraday had been by her side when she faced the Deathly Shadow. He'd been by her side all the time, she realized, even when she didn't know it.

"Indeed, he was to assist you, and he's done that, helping you to bring back your parents. I can't tell you his secret, but I can tell you where to look. I can also tell you that I've set up everything to help him undo the past if that's what he wants. I'll make good on my end of the bargain, as promised."

"I'm getting tired of this 'can't tell me' bullshit and puzzle pieces cloaked in mystery. Where am I supposed to look for this secret and undoing thing to help Faraday?"

"The one place you're never to go to at night at Happily Ever After College." Plato winked.

"The Bewilder Forest? It's haunted, and that's only going to cause more problems for Hemingway."

"Yet, that's where you must go if you want the truth," Plato said flatly.

"Does it have to be at night?"

"Yes, it *must*. Tell Faraday that it's all arranged. He can find the last two remaining puzzle pieces there. Once he recovers them, put it all together, and he'll be free."

"He still can't tell me anything, can he?"

"He can, but first, you must recover those puzzle pieces in the Bewilder Forest all cloaked in mystery that you don't like so much."

Paris sighed, realizing it was never going to be as easy as simply being told Faraday's secret. Still, it also sounded like there was maybe something to undo, to fix Faraday. Why had Plato said that he'd set everything up to undo Faraday's past "if that's what he wanted?" She needed more answers. Paris needed these puzzle pieces.

More confused than ever, Paris closed her eyes for half a beat. There were so many things weighing on her shoulders, but they didn't deter her.

Letting out another breath to loosen her chest, she opened her eyes and turned her attention to the Fantastical Armory, trying to figure out what other questions she had for the lynx. When she returned her gaze to where Plato had been, she realized she shouldn't have taken her eyes off him because he'd taken that moment to disappear.

CHAPTER SIXTEEN

"I know, I know. I'm late." Paris rushed into the Fantastical Armory, used to Papa Creola's usual greeting.

Father Time casually looked up. He held a rag in his hands and was polishing what appeared to be a large river rock. He was wearing a tie-dye T-shirt as usual. This one's hippie phrase said, "Wasn't it beautiful when you believed in everything?"

His long stringy brown hair was obstructing one eye. With the back of his hand, he pushed the strand away. "You're not late."

"I'm not?" Paris looked at one of the many grandfather clocks on the wall. "You told me to come over right after class and I—"

"Stopping to talk to King Rudolf Sweetwater wasn't the best use of your time," Papa Creola cut in. "However, that trashcan needed replacing, and now it will be. Well, after they peel Ramy Vance off it."

"You really do orchestrate everything, don't you?" Paris slid the tray of chocolate fudge, chocolate chip cookies onto the counter in front of Subner, who hadn't looked up from his book to acknowledge her.

"No, I can't take credit for everything," Papa Creola answered. "Mama Jamba and a select few share the blame there too. Then there are a few variables that always keep us on our toes."

Paris smirked at him, grateful that she wasn't late. "Well, I got here—"

"When you were supposed to," Papa Creola interrupted again. "You got the information from the lynx, and now you're ready for the next pieces of the puzzle, which I'm going to give you."

She laughed at this. "You're in on this Faraday business as well, huh?"

"As you know, it involves time travel and so, of course," Papa Creola answered. "I need you to fix this business, which is why I consented for Faraday to be your companion for the mission."

Paris crossed her arms and leaned back casually on the glass counter. "Wouldn't it be easier if you told me all this stuff instead of letting me fall in the rabbit hole?"

"That's what the Beaufonts always say," he muttered, continuing to polish the large stone. "No. Things happen because of the way they're set up. If I told you spoilers, you'd mess up everything with anticipation."

"Thanks for the vote of confidence," she remarked dryly.

"You sound like your mother with that sarcasm." Subner finally spoke, pulling the tray of cookies toward him without saying, "thank you."

"Speaking of which, I'm not here to see my parents am I?" Paris questioned Papa Creola. "I'm here for this puzzle piece then?"

"We're not to your parents yet." Papa Creola laid the polished rock onto the countertop in front of him.

That answer filled Paris with dread. What if she wasn't seeing them not only that day but for a while? Could it take another fifteen years for them to recover? That would make things super weird.

Papa Creola held out his hand, and another large river rock appeared in his palm. He went straight to work polishing it. "I need you to get the puzzle pieces of this Faraday situation back together and get things back in their time."

"You mean that since Faraday time-traveled, he has to go back?" Paris hid her instant remorse. Her job was to put Faraday back in his time. Of course, the talking squirrel was stuck, not only as a woodland creature but also in this timeline, which wasn't his real one. She didn't want to lose her friend, and yet because he was her friend, she had to.

"Yes, I need you to fix this time travel issue and more," he answered cryptically.

"Please don't explain," Paris jibed. "I definitely don't want to know what the 'more' part is."

"Good, I'm not telling you," Papa Creola said flatly, still polishing the stone.

"Sarcasm is the language of the uncouth," Subner advised through a mouthful of crumbs.

"You're welcome for the cookies," Paris said to him.

The greasy-haired hippie ran the back of his hand across his mouth. "I didn't say, 'thank you.'"

"That's my point." Paris still leaned on the counter and wondered if she'd get in trouble for killing Father Time's assistant.

"Did you bring any milk to go with the cookies?" Subner asked.

Paris chuckled, looking down at her crossed arms. "Does it look like I brought you a jug of milk?"

He shrugged while chomping into the next treat.

She shook her head and returned her attention to Papa Creola, who had conjured another river rock and was polishing it. "These puzzle pieces? You have them for me? Are they enigmatic bits of information that lead me on a wild goose chase?"

"They aren't ready yet," Papa Creola answered simply.

"Do you have an ETA? Being the guy in charge of time and all?" Paris asked.

He shook his head. "That's up to you."

She rolled her eyes. "Are you serious? Does this get any more confounding? How can it be up to me when I get these secret puzzle pieces for a mystery I didn't know I had to solve?"

"When you're ready, they will be." Papa Creola kept polishing the third rock.

"Is this like that philosophy that when the pupil is ready, the teacher will appear?" Paris joked.

"It's more like when you're ready to see your parents and not looking for tactics to stall, that the pieces will be available." Papa Creola glanced up at her. "I'm getting tired of polishing, so maybe we can progress."

Paris' mouth fell open. "Wait, I do get to see my parents. But you said—"

"He said, we're not to your parents yet," Subner cut in.

"So I do get to see them today?" Paris questioned, her heart suddenly beating fast in her chest.

"Do you want to?" Papa Creola asked, eyeing her.

"W-W-Well, of course," she answered.

"Your stuttering doesn't make you sound convincing," Subner said dryly.

What Plato had told her had made her feel better about seeing her parents, but it didn't take away all of the nervousness. Even if she knew they'd love her no matter what, she was still anxious about the whole thing.

As with any new situation, like attending Happily Ever After College or going on her first missions, there would be butterflies. That had to be expected. Paris reasoned that there would be something wrong with her if she weren't nervous about seeing her parents after everything they'd all been through. It was a big deal.

It was also the beginning of something wonderful she believed at her core when she allowed herself to fantasize. That was the thing. She had such high hopes for the life she'd have with her parents.

There. I admitted it. I have high hopes. Yes, I'll be disappointed if my relationship with my parents doesn't meet my expectations, but at least I'll know. There's nothing wrong with wanting the best.

Paris pushed off the counter, standing tall. She gave Papa Creola a sturdy look with conviction in her eyes. "I'm ready. I want to see my parents."

He sighed and placed the river rock with the other two on the countertop. "Good. The puzzle pieces are ready then. Go through the door at the back and descend the stairs. Your parents are waiting."

CHAPTER SEVENTEEN

Each step down the long staircase felt like part of a mediation. Paris wasn't rushing or taking her time as she descended to Papa Creola's "office" where her parents were recuperating.

The area was totally different than the last time that Paris had been down there. Instead of a set of cozy couches and armchairs, there was a large dining room table next to the roaring fire. Standing in front of the long table, set with elegant plates, stemware and a beautiful bouquet, were the two most loving faces Paris had ever seen.

She wasn't sure what she'd been worried about as her feet carried her quickly across the rug-covered floor and into the widespread arms of her parents. Her mother pulled her in tight, and her father wrapped his strong arms around them both. They stayed like that for a long time…the perfect amount of time.

When Paris peeled away, she discovered tears in her eyes. Her parents shared the same appearance, both warriors wiping them away as they straightened, checking her over.

"It's so good to see you, Paris." Her mother continued to push away the tears with the side of her palm. "You'll have to excuse us the last time you saw us. We were pretty comatose."

"Well, it's understandable." Paris smiled as her eyes ran over her parent's faces. "How do you feel?"

Her father slid his hands through his jet-black hair. He was undoubtedly attractive with his piercing blue eyes and chiseled jaw. "It's been quite the transition. I can't tell you how many times we tried to wake up."

"I'd manage to sit up and stir this once," Liv motioned at her husband. "He'd rouse, and I'd pass out."

"A moment later, I would too," Stefan admitted with a laugh.

"It went like that for days," Liv stated. "I'm proud to inform you that we've been awake for a solid six hours."

"That must be why Papa Creola finally allowed me to see you two." Paris now studied her mother's face. She was incredibly beautiful with serene bluish-green eyes and balanced features. None were overly pronounced, and they all complemented each other. Her long blonde hair fell past her shoulders and was slightly unkempt in that beach wave look.

"We asked that hippie to send you right away," Liv explained. "He said you had to kill someone first."

A laugh burst from Paris' mouth. "Yeah, apparently Papa wanted a new trashcan for Roya Lane."

Stefan shook his head. "Such strange priorities that man has."

"When you're timeless, you care about trash receptacles," Liv joked. She smiled so wide at Paris that her shoulders bunched up high. "It's so perfect seeing you. We can't tell you how incredibly surreal this is."

Stefan chuckled. "Can you believe we were nervous to see you? We thought you wouldn't like us, or we wouldn't know what to say or that it would be awkward."

"But it's not at all," Liv added. "It feels like no time has passed and we are a family once more…well, always."

"Familia Est Sempiternum," Paris' father said proudly.

"Familia Est Sempiternum," Paris echoed.

"Well, like no time has passed, and also you and I can share clothes," Liv teased, looking Paris over. She patted her husband's shoulder. "She's gorgeous."

"She looks like you," he said fondly, looking at his daughter.

It should have been odd that the couple in front of Paris, her parents, were physically only in their early thirties when she was twenty, but it wasn't. To her surprise, it was the most normal thing in the world. Paris reminded herself that she was a halfling with demon blood and her "normal" would never suit another—as it shouldn't. Paris' life should only ever fit her.

Liv clapped her hands together, looking over her shoulder. "Are you hungry? Papa prepared us some food to celebrate the reunion."

Paris tilted her head in surprise. "Father Time cooks? Then why did he make me bring Subner cookies?"

Both of her parents laughed. Liv added, "Oh, Papa can do takeout like nobody's business. I don't know how that man survived before Uber."

Stefan nodded. "The cookies were a goodwill present to try and make Subner feel better. The grouch will be sour that Liv is awake."

"That's what Plato said," Paris offered.

At the mention of the lynx, Liv looked like she might start crying again. "You talked to Plato? How is he?" She waved forward. "What am I saying? He's always been the same. Timeless and mysterious."

"He missed you painfully," Paris informed. "He says that the last fifteen have been his hardest ever, and that seems like it's saying a lot for a timeless being."

"Well, I can see why. Without me, there's no one to roll my eyes at his dry sense of humor."

"He also said that he did what you asked and ensured that someone always watched me." Paris detailed the whole Faraday situation.

"I knew he wouldn't let me down," Liv said when Paris finished talking. "I mean, I didn't know I was gone fifteen years, but once I did, I knew our family and friends would've taken care of you."

"Everyone took care of me in their way." Paris explained how each person took a various role to protect her until she was ready to face the Deathly Shadow.

Stefan closed his eyes for a moment, shaking his head briefly. "Wow, I had no idea how much everything would have had to change in our absence. However, now that I'm coming to, it all makes sense. You had to be protected. So you were raised on Roya Lane?"

Paris nodded. "Uncle John became a detective for the Fairy Law Enforcement Agency. FLEA for short."

"I'll have to check into that," Liv joked. "I'm not sure I like another magical organization policing on my lane."

Paris chuckled too. "Apparently, everything had to be restructured."

"I'd say." Stefan ran his hands through his hair again, looking overwhelmed. "The House of Fourteen has two new Warriors and all because Clark and Raina married to save our positions."

"Imagine everyone's faces when we waltz back in there." Liv hunched up her shoulder, relishing the idea.

"I think that's still going to be a while," Stefan added.

She nodded. "Still, the sooner, the better. There have been a lot of lives uprooted all because of that. John isn't with Alicia. She and Clark have a sham of a marriage. Your sister, well, she married a werewolf."

Stefan laughed. "I don't know. She probably likes Fane. Raina likes hairy men."

"Fane, the Warrior on the Ludwig side, is a werewolf?" Paris realized how much she had to learn as well as explain to her parents.

"Not only a werewolf, but the leader of the entire pack," Stefan explained. "He's part of the originals who are the only ones who can spread werewolfism."

Paris' mouth popped open. "Wow, that's really cool."

"My point remains." Liv turned to her husband. "We have to get back to normal. Then everyone else can…well, sort of. I think we need to get our friends a nice gift basket to thank them for all they did."

"They did it because of who you both are," Paris cut in. "I want to hear all of your stories, but Aunt Sophia, Uncle John, Uncle Clark,

Rudolf, and Rory have all told me about you two. You were beyond loved…you are beyond loved."

Liv looked on the verge of tears once more. She shook her head, recovering. "I'm sorry for any precious brain cells that the king of the fae has made you lose. I'm guessing he hasn't changed in the last fifteen years."

"He was giving a tour of Roya Lane earlier when I arrived," Paris offered.

"Oh?" Stefan asked.

"Yeah, he was telling anyone who would listen that Abby Lincoln signed the Gettysburg Address on a park bench on Roya Lane."

The three laughed easily.

"Yes, Ru hasn't and hopefully won't ever change," Liv said fondly. "He might have the IQ of a set of sticky notes, but he's also just as helpful. If you ever need something, he will drop everything and risk his life for you."

Paris nodded. "I've sensed that. You two have some amazing friends."

Her mother smiled at her father. "We do. I can't wait to get back up to that world of the living." She pointed at the ceiling where many stories up, Roya Lane buzzed with life.

Stefan nodded. "First, we have to recuperate fully. That's the deal we made with Papa Creola. Then we can assimilate back into the real world."

"And kick some ass," Liv said with a wide grin.

Returning the expression, Stefan said. "Absolutely. I'm guessing the demon population is sorely out of control with me gone."

"Well, you know the best way to get back to normal?" Liv turned for the table at their backs.

"How?" Paris and her father asked together.

Liv spread her arms wide, and a feast with tons of Mexican food options magically appeared on the table. She glanced over her shoulder at her family. "The way to recover is nachos, of course."

CHAPTER EIGHTEEN

Paris was extremely full. Not only her belly, which required that she unfasten the first button of her pants, but also her heart.

For hours, she and her parents dined on chicken taquitos, carne asada tacos, cheese quesadillas, roasted salsas, and of course, nachos piled high with all the trimmings. She wasn't sure why she'd ever been nervous but was relieved that they had been too. Among the three of them, the conversation flowed easier than the margaritas.

Apparently, Papa Creola had encouraged her parents to drink up, saying they had to refill their reserves and tequila was good for that. Not only that, but the alcohol would loosen them up and allow their bodies to assimilate to the time change.

Paris and her parents laughed until they had tears in their eyes again, but for different reasons. They exchanged stories, her parents from before she was born or when she was little. Paris told them about growing up with Uncle John and how he was always full of love and thoughtfulness.

The reunion didn't meet Paris' expectations. It far exceeded them. She would never have imagined in a million years that there would be two people that she loved so completely. As soon as she returned to Happily Ever After College, she automatically missed her mom and dad. However, Papa Creola had all but kicked her out, saying that they needed their rest and she did too.

The father of time thrust the large river rocks into her hands, saying they were part of the puzzle related to time travel. Then he ushered her up the stairs to make the trek to the top of the Fantastical Armory. Paris blew a kiss to her parents with a promise to return soon.

Presently, she stood in front of the fairy godmother mansion with so many good wholesome feelings billowing out of her. She glanced down at the pile of rocks in her hands, realizing that the fun was over and the next adventure was starting. These were pieces to the Faraday puzzle, and she had no idea how to put them together. Starting for the mansion cloaked in the darkness of the night, she hoped that the squirrel did.

The fairy godmother estate was quiet when Paris made her way up to her room. She was grateful for that since she didn't want to explain why her arms were full of polished river rocks. Her brain was also full of all the various things she and her parents had discussed.

When asked about what Plato said about her familiar also fulfilling a deal, Liv explained that it was much like the situation with Paris and Faraday. Liv's parents—Guinevere and Theodore Beaufont—had known Plato and asked him to watch after Liv if anything ever happened to them. Something did, so he did. However, when his service to Liv was up he had realized that the deal had helped him to meet his best friend.

Fondly, Paris' mom explained that Plato had never left her side since he showed up many years ago. Secretly, Paris hoped that Faraday had formed that kind of bond with her, but she couldn't shake the nagging thought that he was simply doing all this out of obligation.

She sighed, turning the corner on the second story to her room. It all didn't matter. If she did her job, Faraday would be changed back to whatever he was and returned to his timeline. That was probably for the best, but she had to admit, she'd miss the strange squirrel.

Paris fumbled with the door handle given her full arms but

managed to get it open finally. Faraday was sitting in his usual place in her half-open sock drawer. His eyes darted to the rocks and widened suddenly.

"What are those?" He scurried out of the drawer and onto the top of the dresser, where Paris relieved her burden.

She stood back and looked at the rocks, which were quite similar. "Puzzle pieces. Do you have any idea how to put them together?"

He leaned over to study, sniff, and scratch them. "No, but they aren't normal. There's something unique about them."

"I'd say." Paris plopped down on her bed. "They were given to me by Papa Creola."

"Oh?" His gaze slid to the side.

"Yeah, this is part of the puzzle that will put you back on your timeline." Something caught in her throat.

His tail flicked. "So you know that much."

"Yes, and I know that you can't tell me anything until I go into the Bewilder Forest and find the last two puzzle pieces. Plato told me that much."

Faraday sighed. "Oh, good. So you talked to the lynx."

"Yeah, about that…" Paris measured him up, studying the squirrel. "I was a deal, huh?"

"It's not like that," he replied.

"Plato came to you, stuck in squirrel form and in the wrong timeline, and told you to accompany me and help me until I recovered my parents, and in return, he'd help you with what you need? Is that correct?"

"Well, when you put it that way, it's kind of how it happened," he answered. "But there was more to it than that."

"Like what?" Paris challenged.

"Well, I wanted to come to Happily Ever After College and help you," Faraday replied. "It was a noble mission, and I got to learn about things of interest to me."

"Now that you've fulfilled your end of the bargain, Plato says that he's put everything in motion to hold up his end of the deal," Paris offered.

The squirrel glanced down at the wood grain of the dresser, apparently studying the pattern. "That's incredible. I didn't think it was possible, but if anyone could pull it off, it's him."

Paris motioned to the river rocks sitting next to Faraday. "Papa Creola gave those to me. They're other parts of this weird puzzle. Apparently, that's what we need to put you back on your timeline."

He glanced at the rocks and nodded, not looking particularly excited. "That computes."

"Does it?" Paris questioned. "How do some shiny rocks help you to time travel to whenever you're from?"

"It's complicated," he answered simply.

She nodded, having expected this answer. "So you can't tell me what time you're from, can you?"

He opened his mouth as if he was going to say something, then shook his head. "It appears I can't."

Paris threw herself back on the bed. "Yeah, Plato said you couldn't tell me everything until I retrieved the last two puzzle pieces. At least Papa Creola gave me these for the time travel business."

"So you're going to help me?" Faraday asked tentatively.

She bolted upright, surprised. "Of course."

"Even though I wasn't completely honest with you from the beginning?"

Paris thought about this for a moment. "Honestly, it doesn't sound like you could. You never lied to me, right?"

Immediately, he shook his head. "Everything I told you about my family and my desire for knowledge and being spelled was true."

"It sounds like your agreement forced you to leave out some details," she reasoned. "Albeit what seems like the pertinent, juicy details."

He nodded. "But I didn't lie to you."

"Well, and you risked your life to help me face the Deathly Shadow, which I couldn't have done without you."

"That's true," Faraday chirped, perking up.

"Still, I haven't forgotten that you got me in a fair amount of trouble with the Serenity Garden business and trespassing into the Bewilder Forest at night."

His cheerfulness receded once more as he hung his head. "Curiosity has always been my downfall."

Paris nodded. "I have a feeling that I'm going to learn how it's the culprit to you being a time-traveling, talking squirrel."

He simply returned the nod.

"Speaking of going into the Bewilder Forest at night, you know where I have to go to find the other two pieces of the puzzle?"

His large brown eyes widened. "That will be dangerous. I'll go with you."

"You better." She grinned and laid back on the bed once more. "I hope the puzzle pieces aren't river rocks. Otherwise, you might have to get used to that body and this timeline."

"I'm prepared to do that." His voice turned melancholy.

Feeling bad for him, Paris reassured him, "Don't worry. I won't stop until I help you. We'll get you back to whatever and wherever you came from."

"Thanks, Paris. You're a true friend."

She laughed. "Even if circumstance originally forced you to be that."

He flicked his tail. "I was asked to help you. I'm the one who decided to be your friend."

CHAPTER NINETEEN

"Doing this research without a computer is tough." Christine lounged on the straight-back tufted sofa in the front sitting room of the mansion. Casanova, the fluffy orange oversized cat, was sitting on her lap. Paris knew he was a tattle cat, but she didn't see that as much of a problem since they were working on a mission for the headmistress—although it was on the down-low.

Paris was pacing in front of the large window that overlooked the Enchanted Grounds. She pointed at Wilfred Biltmore—the AI magitech butler for Happily Ever After College—standing at attention beside the sofa. "He's a computer."

Christine sighed while petting the cat. "I can't type on him. Well, I could, but I don't think he'd like it."

"I would prefer that you did not," Wilfred said in his posh, English accent, his hands pressed behind his back at waist height.

"You have a preference," Paris sang, wagging her finger at the butler.

"I'm not sure what you're getting at, Miss Beaufont."

"Well, if you can prefer things, you can be amused by them," she stated while continuing to pace.

"Are you trying to get the AI to laugh?" Christine appeared entertained.

"It's a worthy cause," Paris said. "I have to figure out what material does it for him. So far, it's not knock-knock or blonde jokes."

Christine shook her head. "If he laughed at those, I'd be worried there was something wrong with his programming."

"I don't know," Paris retorted. "A dragon told me a few really funny knock-knock jokes recently."

Throwing her arms out dramatically, Christine sighed. "Oh my gosh. You hang out with Father Time and dragons and get to have cool fiestas with your long-lost parents. Why is it that the coolest thing about my parents is that my dad won at enchanted bingo at the Magic Disco recently on Roya Lane?"

"That's pretty cool," Paris marveled.

"Yeah, it would have been, but you know what the prize was? Birkenstocks! My dad won a pair of Birkenstock sandals. Do you know who needs to wear Birkenstock sandals? If you answered no one, ever, you are correct. But my dad is going to wear them and worse...." She covered Casanova's ears and whispered, "With socks. Birkenstocks with socks..."

Paris laughed and shook her head at her friend. "Anyway, I think Wilfred is the perfect computer because he's much more than that."

"By more, do you mean that I'm a multifaceted piece of magitech engineered to serve, inform, and also teach?" Wilfred asked.

Paris shook her head. "No. I mean that you have multiple functionalities that you don't know how to use unless guided. So, my point is that you have untapped potential."

"I don't know if that is accurate," Wilfred answered dryly.

Christine sighed and sat up on the couch. Casanova took the spot next to her. "Will, you were able to hack into news sources and plant bogus articles to pit McGregor Technologies and Rose Industries against each other."

He cleared his throat. "I wasn't aware that was something within my capabilities until Miss Beaufont informed me of such."

"So, untapped potential." Paris looked at Christine. "What do we have him do so we can research this social media scandal with FriendNet?"

"Well, it's believed that the social media source is causing breakup, lowering the love meter," Christine mused. "So, Will, can you run a search on couples who have recently unfriended each other on FriendNet?"

"Running report now," Wilfred stated, his eyes glazing over momentarily. "I have results of one hundred and twelve thousand couples who have severed ties on FriendNet—"

Christine gasped. "Wow, that's a lot—"

"In the last twenty-four hours," Wilfred added.

Paris whipped around to face Christine directly. "In the last twenty-four hours. That has to be a lot more than the average."

"Wilfred, can you tell us how many couples unfriended each other, let's say, last month?" Christine asked.

Again, the AI butler's eyes glassed over before he straightened once more. "In total last month, there were one hundred and sixty thousand couples who severed ties on FriendNet."

"Whoa!" Paris exclaimed. "So in twenty-four hours, there were roughly as many breakups as in a month. How many for this week in total?"

"There were approximately seven hundred thousand and thirty breakups on FriendNet in the last seven days," Wilfred answered.

Paris continued her pacing. "That's a significant increase."

"At that rate, no one will be together in a month," Christine stated.

"Well, I'm no mathematician, but there's roughly three billion of the world's population on FriendNet, so I don't think it will be that extreme," Paris explained. "However, your point remains. We could see the love meter go into the negative if this continues."

"The fact that you said you're not a mathematician and threw out the statistics on FriendNet is pretty entertaining," Christine teased.

"Touché," Paris replied. "Still, I think we've determined that the rise in breakups isn't a fluke. Something is the cause of it."

"That's what we have to figure out next." Christine pushed up to her feet.

"Got any ideas?" Paris asked.

Christine nodded victoriously. "Yeah, I'm going to go get on my FriendNet account and hit up all my ex-boyfriends. The best way to get information is to use your resources. They are all stupidly in relationships, or they were, so I'll find out if they're one of the statistics. Then we'll go from there. I suggest you do the same thing. Do some investigating, and we'll reconvene."

Paris nodded victoriously, grateful that she'd enlisted her friend on this mission. Christine was savvy and clever, and hopefully, together they could fix what was destroying relationships on social media. If they couldn't, love was at stake worldwide.

CHAPTER TWENTY

The Enchanted Grounds felt different at night. The temperature was always the same, but the glow from the fairy godmother mansion on the lawn created an eerie quality that wasn't present during the day.

The foreboding feeling on the Enchanted Grounds probably had a lot to do with the looming Bewilder Forest and the fact that Paris knew what was in there.

"Are you sure it has to be at night?" Hemingway asked at her side.

"It's what the lynx said." Paris turned to face the dark, haunted forest.

"Is it worth pointing out that you're taking instructions from a talking cat?" Hemingway joked.

"I'm not sure what the issue is there," Faraday said from the grass on the other side of Paris.

"Right." Hemingway drew out the word. "I'm obviously the weird one since I don't know any talking animals who send me on dangerous quests."

"That's very peculiar," Faraday teased.

"I can loan you one," Paris offered, nodding in Faraday's direction.

Hemingway had agreed to accompany her into the Bewilder

Forest since it had to be at night, and he was the only one who could control the ghost of his dead mother—of course, Paris hoped that he could. She listened to him the last time, but she was a deranged ghost who killed herself and haunted the forest at night.

"So let me get this straight," Hemingway began, looking out at the forest, the same as the other two. "You have to go into the Bewilder Forest at night to find a puzzle piece, but you don't know what you're looking for. That's so you can fix the talking squirrel, which I'll remind you, I warned you shouldn't be talking at all."

"The fact that I can talk isn't the issue," Faraday chimed in.

"I think it's more the fact that he's a squirrel," Paris added.

"Of course, that's the issue." Hemingway nodded but wasn't cynical about the whole thing. "The talking squirrel ironically can't tell you why he's an animal, how he got that way, what we're looking for, or anything of use to help fix him. Do I have all that correct?"

"You forgot that he time traveled, and Papa Creola requires that I put him back on his timeline," Paris explained.

"I didn't, actually," Hemingway replied. "I'm still digesting that part. You have the strangest friends."

"Coming from the guy whose mother haunts the Bewilder Forest, that doesn't hold much weight," Faraday imparted.

Hemingway held up his hands. "Hey, I'm not saying I don't have strangeness. I'm a magician disguised as a fairy, and my oldest friend is a magitech AI."

"What do you think would make Wilfred laugh?" Paris cocked her head to the side.

"Have you tried tickling him?"

"Do you think that would work?"

"No, but it would make me laugh to see you try."

"Fine, I'll keep working on ideas." Paris let out a breath, realizing that they were all stalling, each for different reasons. Hemingway didn't want to have another confrontation with his ghost mother. Faraday seemed reluctant about this whole thing since Paris explained what they had to do to fix him—which she didn't understand. She thought he'd be excited to be whatever he was before a squirrel. If she was honest with herself, Paris knew she'd lose her friend when he returned to his timeline. However, all three of them had to face their demons.

She forced a smile and looked between her two companions. "Well, shall we enter the haunted Bewilder Forest to find something that we don't know what it is?"

"Well, when you put it that way…" Hemingway swallowed and turned his attention back to the dark forest. "Let's get moving. Stay close to me."

Paris and Faraday nodded, starting for the forest. Hemingway hunched his shoulders and led the way.

CHAPTER TWENTY-ONE

As soon as the three entered the Bewilder Forest, darkness cloaked them. It took Paris' eyes a moment to adjust.

"Watch where you step. There are bewitched vines at night. They have just been popping up," Hemingway murmured over his shoulder.

Paris froze. "What are bewitched vines?"

"Think of them as regular vines, but they come alive and wrap around you."

"Then what?"

"They keep doing that."

"Until..."

"Until they cut off your circulation."

"What a fascinating plant," Faraday mused.

"Killer," Paris corrected. "You meant killer plant. Why do they do that?"

Hemingway shrugged. "That's their thing. They've been springing up more and more, which is another reason that the Bewilder Forest is off-limits at night. There are a few plants that have been making a sudden appearance lately."

"Like the deadly nightshade," Paris offered.

"Yeah, and I've been pulling it up when I find it in the forest, worried that the woodland creatures would eat it," Hemingway explained, carefully stepping along the path.

"Well, if the bunnies had the diet of my friend here, that wouldn't be a problem," Paris joked, indicating Faraday.

Hemingway paused to get his bearings. "Yeah, but most bunnies don't eat nuts."

"He's allergic to nuts," Paris remarked.

"You're kidding," Hemingway said.

"She's not," Faraday answered. "I prefer soup and sandwiches."

"You're a very strange animal, or whatever you are." Hemingway continued down the path.

"How are we supposed to avoid these strangling vines?" Paris couldn't see where she was going in the blackness of the Bewilder Forest.

"Keep going," Hemingway urged.

"Isn't it cute how he says, watch out for these killer plants, but we can't see anything in here, and his answer is to keep going?" Paris asked Faraday.

Paris could hardly make out the worried expression on the squirrel's face, but she sensed his trepidation.

"It's only a little farther." Hemingway moved swiftly now, his posture straightening with confidence.

"A little farther until wha—"

Paris was interrupted when the flowers with tiny bulbs illuminated across the forest, making her startle. Remembering that the twinkling flowers had turned on the last time she was in Bewilder Forest, she relaxed, grateful that they provided light for them. They were mesmerizing to look at, tiny twinkling bulbs like fireflies strewn for as far as she could see.

"Twinkling flowers are another plant that only comes out at night in the Bewilder Forest," Hemingway said proudly, looking out at the now bright woods.

"Yes, but they're harmless, right?" Paris questioned.

He nodded. "Yes, and if we stay on the path, we're most likely safe from the bewitched vines."

"Stay on the path." Faraday ground his teeth with obvious nervousness.

"I wonder why deadly nightshade has been sprouting up around the forest lately," Paris mused, moving at the same pace as Hemingway now.

"I have a theory on that." He searched the forest.

"Which is?" she inquired.

Hemingway shook his head. "It's only a theory. I need to keep working on it before sharing."

"Theories is Faraday's middle name," Paris joked.

"It isn't actually," the squirrel answered quite seriously.

"Thanks," Paris chirped, shaking her head at him. "So, the deadly nightshade. Do you think it has to do with the college remaining stuck in the Dark Ages?"

Hemingway glanced at her, a hesitant expression on his face. "Like I said, I'm still working it out. But strangely enough, I had some in the greenhouse go missing recently."

"Say what?" Paris nearly exclaimed. "That stuff is lethal. Did you report that?"

He shook his head. "The headmistress has enough to worry about with Agent Topaz poking around. I'm sure that Wilfred threw it out or something. He gets on cleaning sprees and goes a little nuts. One time he threw away a bunch of depours I had in a bucket, thinking they were loose rose petals meant for the trash."

"Depours?" Paris hadn't heard of them.

"Depending on the color of the depour, it can create different elements," he explained. "You know, fire, rain, snow…"

"Oh, they sound helpful." Faraday hopped along the path.

"They are and are especially nice when we want to have a winter wonderland at Happily Ever After College for Christmas," Hemingway stated. "However, the AI didn't know any better."

"It seems that's exactly what he should know," Paris countered.

"Well, he probably thought the deadly nightshade was a weed," Hemingway declared.

"Guys." Faraday's voice vibrated.

"Yeah?" Hemingway turned to look at the squirrel.

"If the twinkling flowers turn on when someone enters the Bewilder Forest—"

"Humans," Hemingway interrupted. "They turn on when humans enter the forest, which is why you didn't activate them the first time you came in here alone at night."

"My point is, doesn't that alert a certain someone to our presence?" Faraday asked.

"You mean the ghost who haunts the forest?" Paris looked around the illuminated woods.

The squirrel nodded.

"Yeah, but as long as you're with me, you're okay," Hemingway imparted.

Again the squirrel nodded roughly. "Good, good. Then we don't have to worry about that?" He lifted his paw, indicating the glowing figure soaring in their direction from across the Bewilder Forest.

CHAPTER TWENTY-TWO

Protectively, Hemingway stuck out his arm, holding Paris back. "She probably won't hurt you."

"Probably?" Paris questioned with doubt in her tone.

"This is untested territory," Hemingway explained. "She doesn't bother me, but..."

"You're her son." Paris filled in the blanks. She watched as the ghostly figure streaked through the trees in the distance, her strange howling rising in volume. Before, the ghost of Hemingway's mother seemed to beeline for them. However, she was taking a more zigzagging approach now that they'd halted.

"Maybe we'll go this way." Hemingway pointed at a fork in the path ahead that led away from the direction of his ghostly mother.

"Well, since we don't know where we're going or what we're looking for, any path could get us there," Paris offered.

Hemingway glanced down at Faraday. "Any chance you can give us a hint about what we're looking for?"

Faraday, as before in Paris' room, opened his mouth as if he was going to say something. After a moment, he shook his head.

"He's spelled and can't say," Paris offered.

Hemingway gave her an annoyed expression. "You have the weirdest friends. Like, why can't they simply tell you?"

"Because it's part of my journey to figure things out on my own," Paris answered. "Apparently, if I knew what to do, I'd screw it up with anticipation, according to Papa Creola."

"Well, since the only person who puts me on quests is Chef Ashton when he asks me to forage for truffles, I'll take your word for it." Hemingway pointed in the direction of the fork they were going to take.

Paris glanced over her shoulder at the ghost, who hadn't gotten any closer. Hopefully, she'd leave them alone. "So your mother…"

Her words trailed away, unsure how to say what she was thinking.

Hemingway glanced sideways at her and read her uncertain expression. "You wonder why I don't have her released, don't you?"

"Well, the fairy godmothers could do it, right?" Paris asked.

He nodded. "Of course. They've offered. No one has pressured me, and Headmistress Starr says it's my decision, but…"

"Then you'd have to let her go," Paris guessed.

Hemingway chewed on his lip. "I never knew my mother. Not when she was alive. Now, it's hard to know a ghost. Obviously, I never knew my father. I don't even know life outside this place." He motioned around, referring to the entirety of Happily Ever After College and its grounds. "So yes, it's hard to let her go. I know she's not alive, but she's also here."

"She's an imprint of who she was," Faraday imparted, scurrying beside them, having to move fast to keep up. "She's a frozen moment in history."

"That's true. It's like a picture, and we keep looking at it, thinking that it's reality, but it's not. It's a snapshot of a past reality." Hemingway shrugged, walking faster now as if spurred on by the words. "I know I have to let her go, but I haven't found the proper motivation to do so."

"Well, as you said," Paris began. "You don't know life outside of Happily Ever After College. Maybe that's the motivation. Maybe her being here is keeping you stuck here."

He halted, a sobering look in his eyes.

"I'm not saying you're stuck," Paris nearly stuttered. "I was saying—"

"It's true though," Hemingway cut in. "I am stuck. The idea of leaving this place is unfathomable. That's why no one can know that I'm a magician. They'd kick me out, and I'd have to find a life away from Happily Ever After College. I don't know what that would look like."

Paris nodded. "I get that. I'm not judging you. I've never been in your situation, so how should I know how I would deal with this."

He offered her a sensitive smile. "You should not judge. You should understand. Those are the words from the famous Hemingway, but they're relevant because that's what Paris Beaufont does. She tries to understand. Most don't..."

Paris blushed. She shrugged to cover the expression. "I try to understand. I mean, I had never lived or been anywhere before Roya Lane. Coming here was scary." She glanced down at the squirrel moving beside her. "Then I found a friend, and it's amazing how you can overcome fears when you have someone by your side."

"I was happy to be that for you," Faraday squeaked.

Hemingway flashed them a grin before taking off again. "You two are cute. I might miss you, Faraday, when you become whatever you are."

"I bet he was a short giant who made a wish to be shorter on a genie's lamp all so he could fit in a proper-sized bed," Paris joked. "Because genies are crafty and deceptive little creatures, he made you into a squirrel."

"Yes, that's what happened," Faraday remarked dryly.

"You know firsthand how genies are crafty with their wish fulfillment," Hemingway said to Paris.

She nodded. "Apparently, if you ask them for something, they give it to you but while blowing a raspberry of sorts."

"Well, maybe it wasn't a genie," Hemingway joined in the speculation. "I bet he was a gnome—"

"I'm allowed to tell you what I wasn't," Faraday interrupted. "I definitely wasn't a gnome."

"A man with an aversion to being cool?" Paris mused.

He shook his head.

"A fae with a fascination with his shadow?" Hemingway questioned.

"Nope," Faraday answered.

"How about a magician who—"

A loud howl cut through the air, interrupting Paris. All three turned and froze. The ghost was close. Really close. Also, she was speeding in their direction. Her mouth was open, making the horrible sound emanating through the Bewilder Forest. Her hollow black eyes were ominous, and her clawed hands outstretched like she was about to grab one of them.

Hemingway spun to face Paris, an urgent expression in his eyes. "Run! Run and don't look back! Don't stop until you're far away. I'll take care of her!"

Paris jerked her head down and gave Faraday a fevered look. He didn't need any more encouragement. The squirrel took off, sprinting down the path ahead. Paris launched after him, speeding far away from the angry ghost, leaving Hemingway to deal with her, and hoping that he could.

CHAPTER TWENTY-THREE

Paris' feet moved faster than ever before, spurred on by self-preservation. She didn't know if a ghost could do anything physically to harm her, but she didn't want to find out. She also knew that the worst traumas were often emotions.

Although Paris didn't like abandoning her friend, she also suspected that Hemingway would be fine facing his mother. She wasn't going to harm him, and he had to deal with the traumas his mother had left him with when she abandoned him. That was his ghost to deal with—both figuratively and literally.

Paris looked down and was shocked to find that Faraday wasn't right beside her. Sensing she'd put distance between her and the ghost, she slowed, turning to look over her shoulder. She was right, and Hemingway and the specter of his mother were far down the path, hardly noticeable even with the twinkling flowers. However, Faraday was nowhere in sight. She didn't understand how she'd lost him. He had taken off before her.

"Faraday," she whispered, squinting as she looked around the forest for a small creature. Something rustled in the distance. Honing her attention on it, she tried again. "Faraday?"

Something moved. Something large. Something that couldn't possibly be Faraday. A giant animal with hooves and antlers and a menacing glint in its dark eyes emerged from the shadow and the trees—and it charged straight for her.

CHAPTER TWENTY-FOUR

Paris didn't wait to find out if the giant stag charging in her direction would weave around her or take a detour or wasn't after her at all. She took off running. Something in the stag's eyes told her that it was trying to mow her down, and she trusted nothing at night in the Bewilder Forest.

She didn't know where Faraday took off to but hoped he was all right. Trying to avoid exchanging one danger for another, Paris ran in the opposite direction of Hemingway's ghostly mother. Behind her, she heard the stag's thundering hooves.

When she glanced over her shoulder, she didn't have to question if the beast was after her. It was charging straight for her. Paris didn't know if, once again, it was her demon blood that made the stag come after her. She also didn't much think it mattered why the animal was racing in her direction.

Another glance over her shoulder told her that she was about to lose the race. The giant deer had its head down, the large rack of sharp antlers pointed in her direction. Its hooves shook the ground under Paris' feet, which were moving so fast she thought they'd come out from under her. Several times she nearly tripped on the path, eating dirt. Then the chase would surely be over, and she didn't want to see what happened next.

Knowing that she needed a different strategy, Paris made an impromptu decision. She did the thing that Hemingway had told her not to. Paris veered off the path, jumping over ferns and bushes and into the thicket of the Bewilder Forest.

CHAPTER TWENTY-FIVE

Weaving through the dense vegetation, Paris tried to make it difficult to follow her. However, the stag had gone off the path with her and made quick progress through the Bewilder Forest. It was now undeniable that the angry creature was after her. Before, she could have reasoned they were both using the path to travel through the Bewilder Forest. Now that she was in the crowded woods, zig-zagging around the trees, it was clear the animal was following her. She couldn't fathom why.

Damn demon blood. She made a mental note to ask her dad about this later…if she lived that long.

Several times, Paris nearly tripped on thick roots or vines, which she didn't want to think about, assuming they were the killer type. She moved so fast, leaping and jumping, her feet hardly touching the forest floor, that she reasoned nothing could catch her…well, besides the beast that was huffing and racing in her direction.

Considering her options, Paris debated using her magic to fight the animal. However, that felt wrong. Maybe it was frightened. She didn't want to harm an innocent animal. Although Paris didn't want to die either, and if it was between "kill or be killed," the options were clear.

Still, Paris thought she could come up with a different strategy. Something that she could live with…if she lived. Glancing around as she sped through the Bewilder Forest, she considered climbing a tree using magic like the first time a hoofed animal had charged her. However, she didn't think she could do it while running, and her climbing skills without magic were pretty untested.

Deciding that her best option was to out-think the stag, Paris scanned the upcoming area of the forest, searching for an opportunity. If she could find a place to hide, maybe she could buy some time. The twinkling flowers made concealment difficult since their bright lights illuminated everything.

Ahead, Paris spied a low branch that looked quite sturdy. If she could grab it and swing her body on top of it, she could scale the thick tree and get to safety, at least for a brief moment before the angry stag charged the tree with its hooves.

It was the best plan Paris had so she sucked in a breath, swung her arms fast at her sides, and prepared to leap for the low branch. She was so focused on the tree ahead that she didn't see the thick roots on the ground. The tip of her boot snagged a particularly stubborn one that didn't give when she caught it, sending her face-first to the forest floor.

CHAPTER TWENTY-SIX

Before she fully connected with the forest ground, Paris whipped around, rolling onto her back. It was too late.

The stag raced straight for her. Paris didn't have a chance to jump to her feet before the beast halted straight over her. Its hooves were on either side of her. The stag lowered its antlers, staring straight down at her. Its hot breath knocked her in the face. The looming expression in its dark eyes sent a chill down Paris' spine.

She choked on a mouthful of dirt she'd nearly swallowed after the fall. The beast watched her as she held her breath and considered her options.

Paris, out of options, prepared to use a spell when the stag opened its mouth and said, "Who are you, and how did I get here?"

Of all the things that Paris expected, that wasn't one of them. The stag spoke…like Faraday. He had a refined voice and carefully enunciated each word. She pressed her hands against the ground and scooted back, stealing a few inches away from the stag.

"Y-Y-You can talk," she stammered.

"Who are you, and how did I get here?" the stag repeated.

Paris nodded and wiggled back a few more inches. "I'm Paris

Beaufont, and I'm not sure how you got here. Can you give me more information? I'll try and help."

The stag swung its head back and forth and huffed. Paris used this opportunity to push back and up, staring up at the large animal.

"I was in the woods in upstate New York," the stag said, his voice very distinguished. "Then yesterday, I woke up and I was here. Where is this place?"

Was this what Plato had arranged? Was the stag a piece of the puzzle? This was growing more confusing, offering more questions than answers.

"You're at Happily Ever After College." Paris tried to catch her breath between words, her heart racing.

"Is that connected to Copper Union?" the stag questioned.

Again, this wasn't how Paris saw interaction with the stag going when it had raced after her like a bull ready to mow her down. Really, she didn't expect to be talking to a stag, but she was still alive, so she wasn't complaining.

"It's a college where fairy godmothers are educated and trained," Paris explained. "This is the Bewilder Forest, and through there or there…I'm actually really turned around, there are the Enchanted Grounds."

The stag thought this over, strange wisdom in its eyes. "So we aren't in upstate New York then?"

Paris shook her head. "I'm not sure where the college is. I know that sounds weird, but it exists in a bubble of sorts due to its magic."

He nodded. "I know magic well and how it can do strange things."

"So you are…were…" Paris left the sentence unfinished, hoping the stag would fill in the words.

"A magician, yes," the stag stated.

"Can you tell me how you became a….well, you know…?"

The stag opened his mouth, but nothing came out. "Unfortunately, it appears that I can't."

"Okay." Paris drew out the word. It appeared she was going to have to play twenty questions like with Faraday. "Do you know a talking squirrel?"

The stag's eyes widened, surprise written on his face. "Faraday?" He looked all around. "Is he here? Where? This is very, very important."

Paris wanted to jump up and hug the stag, but that would have been awkward because she didn't know his name yet. Plus, he was a stag…who could talk.

"He's here." She looked around the forest. "Well, he's somewhere. I lost him when a ghost was chasing us. Then you came after me, and I'm really lost now."

"I'm sorry," the stag answered. "I haven't seen anyone since I awoke here. I was confused, and I have to admit a little unnerved. We should start over." The stag backed up and lowered his head as if he was bowing to her. "It's a pleasure to make your acquaintance, Miss Paris Beaufont. I am Edison."

CHAPTER TWENTY-SEVEN

*E*dison. The name seemed strange. However, Paris didn't think he could answer her burning questions. It appeared that someone had spelled the talking animals not to share their secrets. It was the story of her life at this point. However, she was unweaving this mystery, and hopefully, she'd found the next to last puzzle piece.

"Nice to meet you, Edison. So you awoke in here?"

He nodded. "Faraday is here. That's superb news. I'd all but given up trying to find him."

"You've been searching for him?"

"Yes, for a long time," Edison answered.

"Because you have to be reunited for you to turn back into a magician and return to your timeline, then?" Paris guessed, putting it all together.

"You know that I'm not from this time?" Edison sounded surprised and also relieved.

She nodded. "Yes, I've been sent to find you and another piece of the puzzle, which I think is also in the Bewilder Forest."

"Curie," Edison stated.

Paris let out a giant breath. She was finally making progress on this mystery. The stag could give her a tiny bit of information. Maybe the farther she progressed, the more he and Faraday could reveal. That seemed about like Plato's and Papa Creola's styles.

"Curie." She mused on the name. "I'm guessing that's another talking animal?" '

Edison nodded.

"You three have to be reunited. Then the stones send you back to your timelines and change you back." Paris observed the stag for a hint she was on the right track.

"I can't really say, for I simply don't know. Although I can affirm that putting us together would be progress."

Realizing she was still sitting on the forest floor, Paris pushed up to her feet and wiped her hands on her pants. "So you three turned yourself into animals, time traveled, got separated, and got stuck both in the future and also as animals?"

Edison huffed again, swinging his head back and forth. "If you can help me, I would be forever grateful. I'll reward you for your efforts handsomely."

Paris grinned but shook her head. "That's kind of you, but not necessary. Faraday is my friend, and I want him to be happy. However, it sounds like I still have to find Curie." She looked around the Bewilder Forest. "Hopefully, that won't take very long. Then I'll return with the stones, but I'm not sure what happens then."

"Curie will know," Edison said with confidence. "She knows the spell that can change us back, but we must be together for it to work."

Again Paris wanted to jump up and down with excitement. Things were finally coming together. "Father Time gave me the stones to send you back to your timeline. So I need to find Curie…somewhere in here."

"Very good," Edison said proudly.

"Oh, and I have to locate my squirrel too," Paris added.

"I'll be ready when you are then," Edison stated. "You can find me at the sharp bend in the stream here."

Paris didn't know where that was, but she knew someone who

knew the Bewilder Forest well, and he would help. She had to find Hemingway on the long list of people she was tracking down.

"Great," Paris said with a relieved smile. "I look forward to seeing you again, Edison."

Again the stag bowed to her. "You as well, Miss Paris Beaufont. Thank you greatly for your help."

CHAPTER TWENTY-EIGHT

Paris was doubtful that she'd have luck finding Curie or anyone else in the Bewilder Forest since she was completely and utterly lost. In her attempts to get away from the racing stag, who was a friend and not a foe, she'd gotten so far off the path that she didn't know which way to go to get back to it.

The forest was as its name indicated and totally bewildering. Paris turned several times, doubting the direction she'd chosen. Through the twinkling lights, she didn't see anything that marked the territory, like the fairy godmothers' mansion through the trees.

Careful to watch where she stepped, Paris worked to avoid any bewitched vines or anything else that could harm her. When an owl hooted overhead in the trees, a chill ran down her back. She suddenly wished that Edison hadn't left her side since she didn't know what other creatures or ghosts could be hiding in the Bewilder Forest.

To keep her from thinking about what dangers could be lurking in the trees, ready to swoop down and gobble her up, Paris thought about what she'd learned. Edison, Faraday, and Curie had apparently done some experimental spell. That's what she was assuming based on the little that the stag could share. They would have had to transform to animals to time travel, as Mae Ling had hinted. Then as talking animals, they'd become stuck in that form, seemingly lost their ability to do magic, and gotten locked in the future.

It was a relief to know that the three had to be reunited to do the magic. To further help, Curie knew the spell that would change them back. Then they could return to their timeline and go back to their real lives.

It simultaneously made Paris relieved and remorseful to know she was so close to putting the puzzle pieces together and fixing this mess with Faraday. She'd miss her squirrel sleeping in her sock drawer and offering his advice on her missions. Of course, she'd find herself in fewer sticky situations without the curious squirrel getting her into trouble. However, she would miss that too.

Paris' feet ached, and she was exhausted when she finally stumbled upon the path that snaked through the Bewilder Forest. She was so relieved to have made that progress that she immediately perked up.

Picking the direction she thought would most likely take her to the Enchanted Grounds, Paris hurried down the path with a renewed sense of energy from her victory. When she spied the forest thinning, a sign she was coming out of the woods, light was growing on the horizon. It was morning, and the sun was rising.

Slowly the twinkle flowers dimmed as Paris strode down the path. By the time she made it to the edge of the Bewilder Forest, the lights were all out, and the sun was shining as morning dawned over Happily Ever After College.

Paris had thankfully made it out of the forest alive. However, she hadn't slept at all and now had hardly any time before classes would start.

Trudging across the Enchanted Grounds for the fairy godmother mansion, Paris laughed, thinking that Faraday had better promise to do all her homework that day. Otherwise, she was going to threaten to make him into her next assignment for Magical Cooking.

CHAPTER TWENTY-NINE

"That's, like, the tenth time you've yawned," Christine said from the couch in the sitting room of the fairy godmother mansion, where she was lounging. "I guess I'm boring you."

"Zero things are boring about you, Miss Drama Queen." Paris shook her head. "I'm tired from spending the night talking to a stag and getting lost in the Bewilder Forest."

Paris hadn't told her friend about Hemingway's mother haunting the Bewilder Forest. She trusted Christine, but that wasn't her secret to tell, and she'd promised Hemingway. However, Paris had told her about Faraday and the mission to recover him and the others. Her friend thought it was cool that she was breaking the rules and going into the Bewilder Forest at night—but that was also on par for Paris Beaufont's behavior.

Christine sighed. "Again, why is it that you get a cool talking sidekick squirrel and all I have is this guy who only sleeps?" She pointed at Casanova, who was snoozing on her lap. The fat orange cat had taken to Christine, always finding her lap when they worked on the FriendNet case. Christine had said it was because they were both gingers and she understood him like no one else.

Paris didn't know if it was that, but she noted that the tattle cat made an appearance during their meetings. Still, he worked for the headmistress mostly, sharing things that went on at the college with her. Willow had assigned Paris the FriendNet case, so she rationalized it was fine. Maybe the cat did like Christine because when she wasn't wearing the blue gown, her hair was the same orangey-red as the cat.

"I won't have a talking sidekick for long," Paris remarked, working to keep the remorse out of her voice.

Christine petted the fluffy cat. "Knowing you and your awesome life, you'll probably upgrade and get a unicorn or centaur or something."

Wilfred cleared his throat, standing beside the couch. "According to several sources, centaurs do not socialize well and prefer to live outside of magical societies, on their own."

"Yeah, but our odd defiant halfling will probably be the first to tame the wild centaur. Then she'll have a cool sidekick and a ride," Christine joked.

"You realize that you're incredibly ridiculous, right?" Paris asked her.

"Oh, want to know how ridiculous I am? Ask my ex-boyfriends," Christine related.

"Yeah, what have you found out with your investigative research of FriendNet? I updated my account and tried to investigate, but none of my exes wanted to talk to me. Is anyone else shocked?" Paris hoped to stay focused on the mission at hand. It would also help keep her awake and not thinking about Faraday, who she hadn't seen since returning from the Bewilder Forest. She hoped that he was okay and had made it out okay—Hemingway too, although she suspected he could handle himself just fine.

"Well, I learned that I dated a whole slew of narcissists, most of whom have advanced degrees in manipulation and gaslighting," Christine said dryly.

"Oh, that sucks," Paris offered sensitively. "I'm sorry."

Christine shrugged. "Honestly, I think that reflects worse on me than them. I did choose those psycho-pants."

"Well, did you learn anything related to the FriendNet mission?" Paris asked.

"Yeah, there were some interesting correlations I found when doing my social media away from the college." Christine glanced at Wilfred. "Seriously, I don't know why we can't get a special router that gives the fairy godmothers access to the internet. This is the twenty-first century."

"Saint Valentine has been trying to change the regulations on that but has met a lot of resistance from the board," Wilfred offered.

Christine sighed dramatically. "It should be the headmistress' decision."

"Although I agree," Wilfred began. "It is the board who has the final say on curriculum, rules, and regulations at Happily Ever After College. Even Saint Valentine can't overrule a majority vote."

"Sounds like we need a new board," Paris remarked.

"Well, at least you have messaging on your phone." Christine pointed at Paris' mobile sitting on the side table.

"Yeah, we seriously live in a removed bubble here, don't we? So, this correlational evidence that you found regarding FriendNet. What was it?"

"According to Jerk Wad Number One," Christine began, "he wasn't surprised to hear from me, although probably a bit put off. He says that for some reason, FriendNet has been suggesting friend matches with many of his ex-girlfriends."

"That's interesting," Paris muttered while thinking.

"Psychotic Number Two," Christine continued, "his feed on FriendNet had only been either ex-girlfriends or girls he was interested in. So he broke up with his current hussy because—drum roll, please—he wanted to upgrade. However, that didn't work out because he got dumped for someone the new hussy thought was better."

"Wow, it's like the platform is luring people into old or new relationships," Paris mused.

"Then there was Inflated Ego Number Three," Christine went on, "who said he was fighting with his train wreck girlfriend all the time. When I dived into it, he was always in a bad mood lately because his feed on FriendNet displayed all things he can't stand, meaning people doing better than him. He was like, 'did you know that so and so won the lottery and my old high school buddy owns a jet, and my rival is marrying a supermodel?'" Christine had broken into a deeper voice to impersonate her ex-boyfriend, making Paris laugh.

"It's starting to sound like someone or an organization or something is intentionally doing things to make people unhappy in their relationships and break up," Paris offered.

"Then here's my last piece of anecdotal evidence, which I think might mean we're dealing with something much bigger than Big Brother," Christine said in a conspiratorial voice. "According to Personality Disorder Number Four, every time he'd pick his girlfriend up from work, as soon as she got in the car, our song would start playing."

"Your song?" Paris asked. "Like, the one that you and he listened to romantically when you were together?"

She nodded. "*With or Without You* by U2. Which, looking back, said a lot about our relationship."

"Yeah, that song isn't as romantic as one might think," Paris agreed.

"No, it's perfect for codependent lovers who also like to play the hot and cold game," Christine stated. "Which pretty much defined our relationship."

Paris twirled a strand of her hair around her finger. "I don't understand. What's the significance of the song coming on when the girlfriend got into the car?"

"Well, Train Wreck was one of my old best friends until she stole my boyfriend." Christine nodded. "Yes, I get how my poor decisions are all starting to come out and hit the fan now. Anyway, Train Wreck knew that was our song together. Strangely, even though Personality Disorder Number Four said he didn't have *With or Without You* on any of his current playlists, it would always switch over when his girlfriend got in the car. He would try and explain that it was a fluke, but it happened so many times that she finally got fed up with him, keyed his car, and hit on his best friend, who turned her down."

Christine sat back proudly. "I mean, who says we can't get our happy endings? I feel like everyone got what they deserved."

Paris laughed and glanced at Wilfred. "Can you confirm any of this correlational data by looking into the back doors of FriendNet?"

"I've already been doing that during this discussion," Wilfred answered. "According to my research, a year ago, the person who Miss Welsh describes as Personality Disorder Number Four, posted on FriendNet that the U2 song, *With or Without You*, was his anthem to her. Furthermore, I found evidence that FriendNet powers the music app that Personality Disorder Number Four uses."

Paris' mouth popped open. "So it's entirely possible that the beast that is FriendNet has the information and capability to create drama for couples."

"Moreover, Miss Beaufont and Miss Welsh," Wilfred continued. "Using discreet and illicit means—"

"Meaning you hacked," Christine interrupted.

The magitech AI butler nodded. "Yes, and I discovered that there is an exponentially high number of words exchanging in chat messages, posts, and related apps owned and operated by FriendNet. Everything from negative restaurant reviews to services is on the rise."

"That's right," Paris said with sudden realization. "FriendNet runs that review site, Yap."

"There's also strange activity on that app in particular," Wilfred explained. "Many of the most recent reviews mention how poor service or food ruined a date."

"I contend that if two people have chemistry, they'll make the most of a bad restaurant," Paris argued.

"Yeah, but it does seem as though someone is messing with multiple factors that would affect relationships." Christine absentmindedly petted Casanova.

"Many of the reviews mentioned that they were given gift certificates to restaurants based on contests they entered on FriendNet," Wilfred informed them. "However, even having a free meal didn't undo the bad experience."

"How can FriendNet or whoever is behind this make service and food bad?" Paris questioned.

"Good question," Wilfred stated. "I looked into this, and there are several factors that seem to be of interest. Some of the gift certificates were part of dating apps connected to the social media platform. There's also a high proportion of people who were given and used gift certificates for cuisines that they later mentioned weren't their favorites. In other incidents, people randomly ran into exes, rivals, or enemies who contributed to them not having a good dining experience."

"Whoa," Christine said, her eyes wide. "Someone is pulling a lot of puppet strings and causing a ton of heartache for people."

Paris nodded. "The questions are, who is it? Why? How do we stop them?"

Christine suddenly looked overwhelmed. "I don't know, but they seem very powerful, using a lot of information and resources to create chaos and break people up. This isn't a coincidence."

"Yeah, the love meter proves that," Paris stated. "We need to proceed with caution. I think what we need is another reconnaissance mission."

A smile lit up Christine's face. "Are you thinking we disguise ourselves again and sneak into FriendNet?"

Paris matched her grin. "The best way to find out what's going on is at the very source."

Christine rubbed her hands together eagerly. "Oh, I want my disguise to be good. Something repulsive and annoying."

"You want to be a hippie?" Paris questioned.

Christine nodded. "Yeah, that will work. My name can be Rainbow or Clover or something ridiculous."

"Great, and maybe I can be—"

"My support dog!" Christine exclaimed.

"Wait, I can't do that type of transformation work yet."

"You haven't tried yet," Christine argued. "You're brilliant at it. Your sidekick knows how to do transformation work, obviously, so he can help. Or Mae Ling can."

Paris chewed on her lip. "I don't know…"

"Even with magic, it's going to be hard to do covert investigating at a powerful place like FriendNet," Christine countered. "But let's say I show up under the guise of a consultant, and my support cat or llama or parakeet gets away. They won't question that animal when they find it pecking at the keys of the CEO's computer or whoever we need to investigate to find answers."

"I think I might have some leads on who you should inspect," Wilfred stated. "My research shows that many of these new trends on FriendNet are linked to a specific programmer, although I need more time to look into this."

"You're brilliant, Will," Christine said excitedly, turning her attention back to Paris. "What do you say? Will you be my support chimp?"

"No," Paris answered at once. "But how about I bring along my support squirrel, and he can do the investigating while we cause a diversion? Faraday is much better at hacking and all than me."

"Fine, but maybe one day you'll be my purse dog." Christine pouted slightly.

"I can't believe that's a dream of yours." Paris was about to say something else when she was interrupted. Through the glass-paneled doors of the sitting room, she watched as a group of strangers strode through the entrance of the mansion, marching down the hall. They weren't fairy godmothers, but their starched black suits and serious expressions told her right away who they were—agents for FGA.

CHAPTER THIRTY

Although Paris knew she and Christine needed to devote their time and attention to the FriendNet case, they also couldn't ignore the sudden appearance of a bunch of agents from FGA.

"What do you think they're all doing here?" Paris whispered to Chef Ash over lunch from across the dining room table.

He glanced toward where all the guys in matching black suits were filing through the buffet line, about to take a seat for lunch. "I'm not sure, but I don't like it at all."

"Maybe Agent Topaz got lonely since we all have personalities, and he wanted his boring friends with zero senses of humor to join him," Christine teased.

Hemingway slid his plate onto the table next to Paris. He also focused on the preponderance of agents across the room.

"Hey, there you are," Paris murmured when he sat.

He nodded, his gaze still on the agents. "How did it go last night?"

"I met a stag," she said so only he could hear her.

His eyes widened, and he bent close to her. "There aren't any stags or anything close to that in the Bewilder Forest."

"There is now," Paris whispered back. "His name is Edison, and he's like Faraday."

"In that, they both have names of scientists?" Hemingway questioned.

"They both can talk," Paris answered.

He shook his head. "You have the strangest friends."

"I count you among them." She grinned. "How did everything go for you last night?"

Hemingway glanced down at his sandwich, ambivalence written on his face. "About like usual."

"I'm not sure what's usual about your situation."

He shrugged. "We will have to talk about it later...like, much later. For now, it seems we have other fish to fry." His eyes drifted up to the agents on the other side of the room. "Any word on why they're here?" Hemingway asked the group.

"Not a clue," Chef Ash answered.

"I heard one of them mention that Saint Valentine would be arriving soon," Penny said in a meek voice, looking around self-consciously.

"Does he visit Happily Ever After College often?" Paris asked.

"Never," Chef Ash answered.

Becky Montgomery leaned over from a few seats down. "Mother says that the FGA agents are here because Agent Topaz has found too many questionable practices here at Happily Ever After College."

"Like, that we're educating aristocrats who care more about their selfish gains and reputations than about creating love for all?" Paris jibed.

Becky narrowed her eyes. "As in we're educating magicians and considering allowing technology into the college and changing curricula which have served us for ages."

"I don't know," Christine said, a mock look of uncertainty on her face. "I think all that sounds like a good evolution for the college. I'd contend the problem is educating snobs and allowing them to spread their arrogant attitude in an establishment meant to spread love."

"I know what you're insinuating," Becky fired back.

"Oh, I hope so, or you might need to think about dropping out of Happily Ever After College because you're not bright enough," Christine teased. "I hear Tooth Fairy College is looking for students, and all they have to be able to do is tie their shoes and stomach watching bad reality television. Do you think you can handle that?"

Becky gawked at her. "As if! I'd never be caught dead at that college."

"Yeah," Christine reasoned. "I didn't think you could get in either."

"Make your insults now," Becky threatened. "You wait. The FGA agents are going to do their assessments. Then Saint Valentine will come here and make changes."

"I happen to know that Saint Valentine is very open to evolving the college as well as FGA practices," Chef Ash stated.

"Well, then maybe he's part of the problem," Becky retorted. "Maybe once the agents make their assessment and give their recommendations to the board, it will be to do some serious trimming, starting with those at the very top."

Paris didn't know enough about the structure and politics of FGA and Matters of the Heart, Saint Valentine's office, but she knew enough about corruption to conclude there was a power game operating. She didn't know which side was right, but she heavily suspected that those who didn't want change served only their purposes. It should have been about love, but it appeared that over time, FGA had lost its mission. She only hoped that she could be a part of the change that created love instead of inhibited it with rules and outdated practices.

CHAPTER THIRTY-ONE

Paris would have spent her afternoon working on the FriendNet case, attending classes, or spying on the FGA agents. However, when Father Time messaged you and granted you an opportunity to see your long-lost parents, you didn't delay.

After hurrying down the tons of stairs to the basement of the Fantastical Armory, Paris was nearly breathless when she got to the bottom. To her surprise, the basement wasn't dark or full of furniture or a roaring fire like before. Instead, it looked a lot like the apartment where Uncle Clark and Aunt Alicia lived.

The walls and floors were all white, but the furniture had some color, although still the modern vibe. The ceilings were high, with elegant chandeliers, and many windows let in cheery sunlight. Outside the windows where there shouldn't have been a view was a balcony and scenes of West Hollywood where Uncle Clark's apartment was.

Paris paused, spying her parents standing arm in arm and looking out the bank of windows, her mother's head on her father's shoulder. Sensing her standing there, they turned, but not with the reflexes that she felt they possessed but rather dulled ones as they got reacclimated to this time dimension.

Liv's face brightened at the sight of her, and she rushed over at once, hugging her tightly. When she released Paris, her father was next to hold his daughter in tightly.

He peeled back, and her mother must have sensed the confused expression on her face. "This is how our old…well, our home looked. Papa made this for us to help us reenter the real world." She held out her hand, indicating the large open floor space and oversized furniture.

"It looks like Uncle Clark's place…but with color," Paris admitted.

Liv grimaced. "Yes, that's our old place. It appears that my dear brother has redecorated in his boring way as only he can."

"This is what your old place…our old home looked like?" Paris felt a sudden pang of nostalgia.

"Well, there's a lot of history to it. This was my place from back in the day. When I left the House of Fourteen, after my parents were killed, I got the job working for John at the electronic repair shop. He rented me a one-bedroom studio above the shop for practically nothing. Then, once I went back to the House of Fourteen and got my magic reinstated, Clark and I started to renovate the studio apartment using magic."

"I have a lot of history to catch up on it seems." Paris felt overwhelmed as she looked around.

Stefan nodded. "Your mother has had quite the wild ride when it comes to life."

Liv scoffed at him. "You're one to talk, demon hunter."

"About that." Paris looked intently at her father. "I forgot to tell you that much about the showdown with the Deathly Shadow."

"I don't think it's as much forgot as haven't had a chance yet," a familiar voice said at Paris' back.

In front of her, Liv gasped. A smile broke across Stefan's face. Paris whipped around, spurred by the excitement exuding from her parents.

There, standing in the middle of the bright white marble floor and contrasting boldly, was the magical and mysterious lynx—Plato.

CHAPTER THIRTY-TWO

Liv rushed around Paris but stopped short of the black and white cat. She stared down, vibrating with excitement, but it seemed like she didn't know how to proceed.

"Plato." Liv smiled at her familiar.

"You want to hug me, don't you?" he asked dryly.

Liv jerked her head to the side, her nose in the air. "Of course not. I mean, I was only gone a day."

"Yet, you still missed me," Plato said.

She scoffed. "I didn't."

A Cheshire grin spread on the cat's face. "Well, I missed you."

"Starting when?" Liv joked, crossing her arms over her chest. "When I'd been gone ten or so years?"

"Starting the day you left, and it appeared you might not come back for an uncertain amount of time." Affection seeped into his tone.

Liv gave him a fond and gentle look. "I missed you too. It never takes long."

Stefan stepped forward, his hands on his hips. "In fifteen years, it appears you haven't aged a single day."

"I'm more mature on the inside," Plato stated smugly.

"Oh, like you're going to stop cheating at board games finally," Liv joked.

"I said mature, not stupid," Plato retorted and glanced at Paris with a twinkle in his eyes.

"Hey Plato," she said in greeting.

"I hope you don't mind me crashing your get-together," Plato said to her.

She grinned. "Not at all. I guess you finally got clearance from Papa Creola."

"Strange that he relented when he did," the lynx said coyly.

Liv laughed. "Papa said that his food has quite literally been disappearing right in front of him all day."

Stefan nodded. "Yeah, his sandwich vanished from his grasp while he was putting it in his mouth. He grumbled about starving to death although I think that's impossible."

"He gets really grumpy," Liv imparted. "Well, grumpier than usual. So, Plato, you wouldn't know anything about the food bandit on the loose, would you?"

"I can't say that I do," he replied.

"Is that a piece of pastrami on your whisker?" Liv pointed at the cat's face.

He lifted his paw and wiped it away. "Probably. It had too much lettuce on it for my liking, but beggars can't be choosers."

"More like stealers can't be choosers," Liv teased. "I'm glad you wore Papa down. It makes me feel normal to see you again."

Stefan nodded. "Hopefully this means we'll see others soon too."

"None of them have really changed," Plato offered dryly.

"It's been fifteen years," Liv argued. "Clark and Raina are married to Alicia and Fane. Rory is a best-selling author. Sophia has saved the world a dozen times over, most likely. John is a pretend fairy and a detective. Rudolf…well, he's probably still brain dead."

Plato gave her a wise look. "For the most part in life, circumstances change. Rarely do people."

"Oh, nothing has changed about your cynical nature," Liv sang. She turned, grabbed Paris' arm, and tugged her toward the couch. "Now, you were going to tell us about the showdown with the Deathly Shadow, which I'm still amazed that you fought and won against."

"Not that we're surprised that you were able to," Stefan added. "It's that it was a force that eluded us for so long and defeated a lot of powerful people. You were very brave to face that monster."

"Well, I didn't have a choice once I learned the truth," Paris remarked, suddenly feeling nervous. "But that's what I wanted to tell you. I was only successful because I had help."

Liv glanced at Plato who was casually licking his paw. He glanced up at her. "I didn't help, although I was there—in the distance."

Paris shook her head. "I didn't see you."

"That's how he does things," Liv offered. "You don't know he's there until later he points out that you were picking your nose. Go ahead and assume that the great lynx is always watching."

"Unless the finals of *Eurovision* is on. Then I'm watching that," Plato teased.

"Note to self, not to get myself in trouble during that broadcast and need your help," Liv retorted.

The lynx ran his paw over the side of his face, continuing to bathe himself casually. "You have hardly ever needed my help."

"Except that one time," Liv replied playfully.

Plato shook his head at her. "I told you that hot air balloons were unpredictable modes of travel."

Paris giggled, suddenly feeling giddy, being around her parents and the ancient and mysterious lynx.

Stefan glanced at his daughter. "They're like this nonstop. It's cute."

"We're adorable," Liv said dryly. "Like a newborn kitten."

Plato shivered with disgust. "Why did you have to pick the least adorable creature in the world?"

Liv laughed. "Because I know how much you detest the little animals, like you once weren't one."

"I wasn't," Plato said plainly.

Stefan smiled thoughtfully at Paris. "So you had help defeating the Deathly Shadow. I'm glad for that, but I'm sure that your success was because of your strength and courage."

"I did have help," Paris admitted. "Faraday—"

"The talking squirrel," Liv interrupted.

Paris nodded. "Yes, who Plato is helping me to turn back into whatever he was and put him back on his timeline."

"That doesn't sound like Plato," Liv joked, glancing at the lynx. "Maybe you have changed in the last fifteen years. Have you softened up?"

He shook his head, eyeing his paw. "Not in the least. By 'help,' your daughter means that I put two puzzle pieces in a haunted woods and told her to find them."

"Let me guess," Liv said dryly. "You didn't tell her what the pieces were, did you?"

Plato looked up, a sneaky grin in his eyes. "What do you think?"

Liv nodded. "There's the Plato I know and love."

"They're two talking animals," Paris explained.

"See, I knew you'd figure it out," Plato admitted. "Why spoil the surprise?"

Paris couldn't help but laugh. "Well, because then I wouldn't have run from a confused stag thinking he was trying to stampede me, thereby getting lost in that haunted forest in the middle of the night."

"Well, where would the fun in avoiding that be?" Plato retorted. "I've simply given you the opportunity for an experience. Think about what a great story that makes to tell at dinner parties."

"Strangely enough, I don't get a lot of invites to dinner parties," Paris remarked.

Plato lowered his chin, giving her a pointed expression. "Maybe that's because you don't have any good stories to share."

Liv shook her head. "Do you see what I mean? Being helpful is what he tries to be, but it always turns into something less so."

"I'm glad you survived the stag and all," Stefan offered.

Paris nodded. "Yes, and despite his mysterious efforts, I was able to find the clues that Plato left for me. Well, I found one of them. I still have another animal to locate."

"Look in the trees," Plato said discreetly.

"Because it's a bird?"

"Because I lost a pocket watch there and thought you could locate it while you're hunting around."

She nodded, already at home with this banter, and returned her gaze to her parents. "As I was saying, Faraday helped, fixing the magitech that I used to open the vortex that brought you back."

"Sounds like a smart squirrel," Stefan offered.

"Probably not a squirrel," Paris retorted, looking at Plato, but he offered up no extra information.

Liv waved at the lynx. "He won't tell you something extra unless you're nearly dead and bleeding, and even then, you have to be on his good side."

"Most no one ever is," the lynx stated dryly.

Paris nodded. "Anyway, then Uncle John's locket, well, I think it originally belonged to Aunt Sophia."

"The one with the Rumi quote that said, 'You have to keep breaking your heart until it opens?'" Liv asked.

"That's the one," Paris affirmed.

"That belonged to my mother," she stated.

"Yeah, that one." Paris had a moment of remorse. "Sorry, it's broken now. Anyway, Uncle John's chimera was locked inside that."

"What?" Liv asked. "Pickles was in the locket?"

Paris nodded. "He burst out in chimera form and helped me to gather up the bits of the Deathly Shadow that had splintered or something. I'm not sure. I didn't know how I'd collect him, then all of a sudden, the chimera took over and helped. It was amazing, although I'm not sure where Pickles is now. He quickly disappeared."

Stefan smiled. "It sounds like it. What a wonderful set of tools and friends that came to the rescue to ensure you were successful."

Paris smiled at her father. "The most unexpected came from you."

He tilted his head, obvious confusion in his eyes. "It did? What was it?"

"Your demon blood," she answered. "It was what overpowered the Deathly Shadow and also nearly killed me."

CHAPTER THIRTY-THREE

This news visibly shook Liv. "You still have demon blood? But the genie…"

"The genie made her half-fairy to combat the demon blood," Plato explained.

"My wish was that my daughter wasn't a demon," Liv argued, shaking her head.

The lynx's white-tipped tail flickered as he stretched to a standing position. "She's not thanks to the fairy part of her, which counteracts the demon part that she inherited from Stefan."

"She still has the blood of a demon." Her father looked down at the floor with shock written on his face.

"Naturally," Plato answered. "You still have demon blood. It's that you also had the antidote so it didn't change you."

"Well, technically it did change me," Stefan admitted.

Liv balled up her fist and held it in the air, shaking it slightly. "That damn genie. They can't fulfill a simple wish, can they? He was supposed to make it so Paris wasn't a demon."

"She's not," Plato repeated, the voice of reason in the room. "It's that she has an aspect of the demon still. You can have something without being it."

Liv shook her head. "Can we stop splicing semantics?"

"Again, where would the fun be in that?" Plato asked playfully.

Liv leveled her gaze at the lynx. "Tell me what you know on this subject and don't hold back, or I'm opening up that vortex we came through and tossing you into another dimension."

"Meow." Plato drew out the word and swiped his paw through the air, his claws retracting.

Liv glanced at her daughter. "Can you get that device to open the vortex again?"

Paris laughed, enjoying the repartee between the two.

"Technically," Plato began, "Paris is half-fairy and let's say about forty-nine percent magician."

"With one percentage of her being demon," Stefan guessed, worry in his eyes.

"Yeah, but if I had one percent cheetah in me, you wouldn't find me identifying as that," Plato explained. He shivered with disgust. "I mean, even if I were fifty percent, you wouldn't find me saying I'm a cheetah."

"Can we not make this about your prejudices?" Liv questioned.

Stefan focused on Paris. "So you said that the demon part of you helped you in the fight but also nearly killed you. What happened?"

"Well, I didn't know how I'd overpower the Deathly Shadow," Paris answered. "Papa Creola wouldn't tell me. He kept saying I had to do it to contain him."

Liv nodded. "That's his way. His favorite thing to do is to send me on missions with zero instructions. I think he needs a hobby since that's how he derives entertainment."

Paris laughed. "Yeah, he told me that if he explains how to do something, I'll overthink it and screw it up."

Liv pointed at the cat. "Yeah, that's probably why this one doesn't provide much information."

"No, it's because I derive entertainment from watching your confusion," Plato retorted.

"Seems about right," Liv muttered.

Stefan sighed, staring at Paris. "You see how it's tough to stay on a subject with these two around?" He indicated his wife and Plato. "Anyway, the demon part of you helped you overpower the Deathly Shadow? I can see that happening. It makes the most sense because a demon's worst enemy is another demon."

"That's what makes your father such a successful demon hunter," Liv explained.

"Well, and my nunchuck skills." Stefan winked.

Paris chuckled. "So your demon blood, what does it do to you?"

"The antidote made it so that I didn't turn into a red-faced gross demon," Stefan explained. "Thankfully, I got many of the best aspects of the demon without being a stinky soul-sucking beast."

"He has their strength, agility, speed, and longevity," Liv cut in.

"Plus I'm able to sense them, which makes it easy to track them down," Stefan stated.

"There's a drawback, isn't there?" Paris sensed a caveat coming.

Her father nodded. "As with all things, there are tradeoffs. My demon blood compels me to stamp out evil."

Paris blinked in surprise. "That doesn't sound like a bad thing."

"It is if he will kill himself to accomplish that goal," Plato imparted.

Stefan nodded. "I'm addicted to ridding the world of evil. If I'm not careful, it will exhaust me. Own me. Push me to my very limits."

Paris' mouth popped open. "Wow. I guess anything taken to an extreme is dangerous."

"We've figured out how to manage it over the years," Liv explained. "Stefan is the best demon hunter, and that's the perfect job for him as a Warrior for the House of Fourteen. However, he's not so good at other cases because he loses his objectivity when evil is part of the equation."

Stefan nodded. "Demons are easy because regardless, we have to rid this world of them. However, I'm not the right warrior to deal with werewolves, vampires, or certain monsters."

"Because they need to be dealt with rather than killed?" Paris guessed.

"That's right." Stefan looked fondly at Liv. "Your mother is the perfect Warrior for that because she's excellent at finding strategic solutions to dealing with villains, which isn't always to kill them."

Liv smiled at her husband before returning her attention to Paris. "You said that the demon part of you almost killed you. How?"

"When I tapped into it, well, it became overwhelming," Paris sheepishly explained, feeling shameful at the confession. "I felt this intoxicating power, and like a drug, it took over my objectivity. I wanted to cause pain to the Deathly Shadow."

"That's when he was able to take advantage because you slipped up, having gotten distracted by the rush," Stefan guessed.

Paris nodded. "It all happened so fast."

"That's exactly what happens to me when I'm around strong sources of evil," he admitted, a heavy expression on his face. "No one has ever understood that feeling the way that I think you probably can. The rush takes over, and it's impossible to think, and it feels like you're losing your mind to the hunt to root out evil."

Liv pressed her hand into Stefan's shoulder consolingly before looking at her daughter. "You didn't let the demon aspect of you take over completely?"

"Well, I almost did," Paris admitted. "I worry that it will happen again. I mean, even if I'm only one percent, that's enough that it angers horses when I'm around them."

Stefan laughed abruptly. "Yeah, horses hate me. Take me to a rodeo, and it quickly turns to chaos. I also don't do well in churches. My skin starts to crawl."

"It's weird that you got all the best aspects of the demon and hunt evil but have an aversion to churches," Paris remarked.

"He is technically a demon who was cured," Plato imparted. "That's why sources sensitive to demonism will either cause him problems or be repelled. Stefan registers as a demon, as you will too. The differences are that he had the antidote and you have your fairy blood that combats it."

Stefan nodded and gave Paris a caring look. "I can help you learn how to control this part of you. I'm guessing that it will push you to want to fight evil, much like me."

"Oh, it does," Plato said. "That's why she's been taking the law into her hands for the last ten years, putting bullies in their place."

Liv threw her hands into the air victoriously. "That's my girl."

Paris lowered her chin, blushing. "Yeah, but I've also given Uncle John quite a few headaches. Poor guy has had to bail me out of trouble too many times."

"He has?" Stefan didn't appear put off by this news.

"She has a rap sheet to rival both of yours," Plato supplied.

To Paris' relief, both of her parents grinned.

"Yeah, that rap sheet is why I'm at Happily Ever After College," Paris admitted. "It was our agreement to keep me out of jail after the last incident."

"Well, and also, I'd made arrangements." Plato glanced to the side with a mischievous expression in his green eyes.

Liv nodded appreciatively at the cat. "I couldn't have thought of a safer place for Paris to protect her from the Deathly Shadow."

"And a half-fairy, half-magician is probably going to make the best fairy godmother in history," Stefan stated.

"No probably about it," Liv said proudly.

Stefan smiled at Paris. "You'll have objectivity when it comes to love while also seeing things the way a fairy does with rose-colored glasses."

"I want to hope so," Paris said, chewing on her lip nervously. "However, I worry about this demon part of me. What if I can't control it when in high-octane situations? What if it overwhelms me and takes over?"

"That's not going to happen because your father will teach you how to control it," Liv stated. "Like him, you'll leverage all the advantages of your demon blood while not suffering the consequences of the disadvantages."

"I bet you're fast," Stefan said proudly.

Paris shrugged. "I haven't had a chance to test it or know how to compare myself to others."

Plato chuckled at this, gaining everyone's attention. "Yeah, because a tiny little fairy should be able to best a giant in a fight. You thought that was normal?"

Liv's mouth fell open, her eyes wide. "You beat up a giant? Nice!"

Heat rushed to Paris' face, making her face feel on fire. "I always thought my advantage was being smaller and having the clearance to move faster."

"Oh, it definitely is," Stefan stated. "Like your mother and Sophia. It sounds like you're also faster and stronger because of the demon blood."

"I guess so." Paris continued to chew on her lip, the nervousness not having faded away.

"Don't worry about the negative aspects of being a demon," Stefan continued. "I sense evil acutely, and I don't sense anything evil about you. You're all the best parts of a magician, fairy, and demon with none of the shortcomings."

Finally feeling more relaxed from those words, Paris let out a weighty breath, hoping that her father was right.

CHAPTER THIRTY-FOUR

Relief flooded Paris' chest when she entered her room that night to find Faraday sitting in her sock drawer. His head popped up, and he seemed to share the feeling.

"What happened to you last night?" Paris looked the squirrel over.

"I got lost in the Bewilder Forest," he answered, also searching her. "What about you?"

"I met a talking stag," she answered.

His large eyes widened. "Edison. So Plato did find him…"

Paris nodded, explaining what the stag had told her.

"It sounds like you've put together a lot of it," Faraday said when she concluded, jumping over to the bed.

"Well, there's the whole how you all got turned into talking animals that I need to have filled in. Still, it sounds like what's preventing you from telling me everything is wearing off. We need to find Curie. By chance, can you tell me what animal she is?"

Faraday opened his mouth to reply, but nothing came out. After a moment, he shook his head. "I'm sorry, but I can't. I would if I could."

Paris slumped on the bed beside him. "That's fine. I think it's part of the unraveling that gets me to the solution."

He nodded. "Yeah, it's like a complex equation. It's not enough to know the answer. You have to work out how to get it. Otherwise, reversing the operations to check your work never works."

Paris laughed. "I'm going to miss your strange examples that are totally un-squirrel-like."

Faraday slid his gaze to the side, hiding the expression in his eyes. "Yeah, really? I didn't think you'd care when I left. I've mostly gotten you in trouble although my job was to watch out for you."

"I think you did watch out for me," Paris argued. "You always seemed to know what was happening to me before I faced the Deathly Shadow."

"Well, I tried…"

"Also, if it weren't for you, I never would have survived the Deathly Shadow," she stated. "You fixed the device just in time."

He turned his head up, smiling at her. "I'm glad I could help."

"Yeah, so, of course, I'll miss you, although it will be nice not to have a bunch of torn-up socks," she teased.

"I'll replace them," he offered.

Paris shook her head. "That's okay. I'll be happy to return you, Edison, and Curie to your real lives. I'm sure you're excited."

Again the squirrel averted his eyes. "Excited isn't the word I'd use."

"Well, you are a master of picking the right word," Paris stated. "Hey, were you an author in your previous life? Is that why you're always spouting off definitions?"

He opened his mouth, but again, nothing came out. Finally, he shook his head. "It appears I can't tell you who I was."

She shrugged. "That's okay. We only need one last piece of the puzzle. Then you and I can have a cup of coffee, and you can tell me everything before I send you back."

"I don't know this," Faraday began, "but I'd suppose that we have to travel back in animal form."

"That makes sense," Paris related. "Because animals can time travel more easily."

"We'll have to consult with Curie, but I think she'll know the process," Faraday said.

Paris nodded. "That's what Edison said. So I guess we won't have coffee but rather an overdue heart-to-heart where you tell me your story before I send you home."

He nodded. "I look forward to sharing with you."

Paris stretched to her feet, noticing the sun retreating over the horizon through her open window. "Well, since it's almost night, you want to go have another adventure in the Bewilder Forest? I think Hemingway will be down to help."

"Yes." Faraday sprang for the open window, intent on taking his usual path to the Enchanted Grounds. "I'll meet you beside the woods."

"Okay, and this time, don't get lost," Paris warned, heading for the door. She hoped they'd find Curie that night and also she slightly wished that they didn't, buying her a little more time with Faraday.

CHAPTER THIRTY-FIVE

"I think I know what we're looking for," Hemingway said as they set off for the Bewilder Forest.

"A talking animal," Paris offered sarcastically.

"Well, I haven't met one of those." Hemingway pointed at the squirrel scurrying beside them. "None besides him."

"I can introduce you to a talking stag or a lynx or dragon," Paris bragged.

"Do you ever start to question your sanity?" Hemingway teased.

She nodded. "Every. Single. Day. More and more with each passing day."

"You should," he offered. "I don't know if I believe half the stuff you tell me regularly."

"Well, if I were telling tall tales, they definitely wouldn't paint me as a halfling with demon blood whose best friend was a talking squirrel," Paris related.

Faraday halted in the grass and looked up at her. "I'm your best friend?"

Paris paused and regarded the squirrel, suddenly feeling self-conscious. "Yeah, I guess so. I mean, you do sleep in my sock drawer."

"Which isn't weird at all," Hemingway teased. "Especially if you were once a man, which is what I'm supposing."

"I wasn't that type." Faraday crossed his tiny arms over his chest.

"It's not weird at all," Paris argued.

Hemingway chuckled. "Yeah, a girl and her squirrel."

"Well, some of us don't have angry horses who charge first and ask questions later," Paris joked.

"I don't think they ask questions at all," Hemingway retorted.

Paris laughed and continued to walk. "Well, my demon blood does more than turn horses into my foes. According to my father, who I inherited the demon blood from—"

"You do get how statements like that make Christine envy you?" Hemingway interrupted.

Paris shot him a mock look of offense. "Christine is ridiculous and knows it. Anyway, according to my dad, I have increased speed, strength, longevity, and an irresistible craving to hunt down evil due to my demon blood."

Hemingway stifled a fake yawn. "Have you considered taking up a hobby to make yourself sound more interesting?"

An abrupt laugh fell out of her mouth. "Maybe I'll take up arranging complex mysteries for others to solve. That's Papa Creola's and Plato's hobbies, apparently."

"Again, you're not interesting at all and know the dullest people," Hemingway pestered. "Maybe you should get on FriendNet."

"Yeah, no thanks. I avoid drama at all cost," Paris replied.

"Good call," Hemingway said as the three entered the Bewilder Forest.

"Do you think that we'll have another confrontation with…" Paris trailed away, not knowing what to call the ghost of his mother.

He shook his head. "I put up some wards earlier. They won't last long, but they should keep her corralled to a small section of the Bewilder Forest. Hopefully, your talking animal won't be in that area."

"Yes, the wolf is definitely in this part of the woods." Paris glanced sideways at Faraday, looking for a reaction.

He shook his head.

She shook her head at Hemingway. "It's not a wolf we're looking for."

"Good thing," he said with exaggerated relief. "As I said, I think I found evidence of what we're looking for."

"Oh?" Paris was curious.

"Yeah, I found droppings that I haven't seen before."

"Velociraptor?"

"Surprisingly, I don't know what those dinosaur's droppings look like."

"Well, it's never too late to learn," Faraday chimed from the ground where he was hopping along beside them.

"Actually, I think it is," Hemingway replied. "No, I think it's—"

The loud hooting of an owl cut through the air, interrupting him.

All three halted and looked up as the twinkling flowers turned on, illuminating the Bewilder Forest. Paris tensed, watching as the bird of prey swooped down from the canopy of trees and soared in their direction.

CHAPTER THIRTY-SIX

Protectively, Paris jumped in front of Faraday, knowing the owl diving in their direction was looking to feast upon the small woodland creature. However, he was fast and ducked under some ground cover—hurrying away unseen.

Having lost its opportunity for a snack, the bird of prey swooped back up toward the tree branches, flapping its expansive wings.

"Owl," Hemingway said simply.

"Thanks," Paris muttered dryly. "Even if I grew up in the center of London on Roya Lane, I still can identify my birds."

He shook his head. "No, the animal who is new to the Bewilder Forest is an owl."

Paris' eyes widened. "Oh...I mean OH! The owl is Curie!" She craned her head to search the dark canopy of tree branches and leaves overhead for the large brown owl. There was some rustling in various spots, but it was hard to make out anything. Yanking her chin down, she stared around the forest floor. "Wait, but why did Faraday run? Didn't he know that his friend or whoever she is, turned into an owl? Or doesn't she know that her key to freedom is a talking squirrel?"

Hemingway shrugged. "This is all brand-new territory for me. I know you're shocked, but this is my first 'reunite magicians-turned-animals and stuck in the future' case."

Paris knelt, searching the ground cover for Faraday. "Really? What have you been doing with your life? Have you considered getting a hobby?"

"Maybe I should." Hemingway studied the trees for the owl. "I only garden, fish, take care of the stables, tend to the grounds, forage the woods, and teach."

She yawned this time. "Sorry, I dozed off there for a bit. What did you say?"

Hemingway shook his head at her and pulled something from his pocket. Straightening, not having caught sight of Faraday, Paris looked at him. "Are you hungry? Is that a snack?" She watched as he pulled a piece of beef jerky from some wrapping.

"Yeah, I decided I'd take a break and gnaw on some jerky," he retorted. "What else is there to do than protect your squirrel from the owl we're supposed to befriend? No, I thought what better way to lure a hungry bird of prey down from the canopy." He waved the beef jerky in the air.

Paris nodded. "That could work. Or we could try my approach."

"What's your approach?" He looked at her curiously.

She cupped her hands to the sides of her mouth and angled her head toward the canopy overhead. "Hey, Curie! My name is Paris. Edison and Faraday sent me to recover you. I can reunite the three of you, which is what you need to get back to normal."

She lowered her hands and waited, listening to rustling in the trees. Remembering something, Paris cupped her hands to her mouth again. "Oh, and Father Time gave me the way to send you back to your timeline."

Immediately, the branches *swished* overhead, and a large dark owl dove in their direction.

CHAPTER THIRTY-SEVEN

Instinctively, Paris covered her head, worried that the clawed bird would attack her like she thought Edison was going to. To her surprise, Hemingway also covered her, grabbing her and putting her swiftly behind him, blocking her with his body.

However, both were relieved when the large brown owl landed on a low branch, blinking at them as she settled her wings into place.

"You know my name," the owl said in a female's sophisticated voice and hooted softly.

Hemingway pulled his arms away from Paris, allowing her to come around beside him to face the bird staring at them.

Paris needed to take a moment to catch her breath so she took in the appearance of the large owl. She was beautiful with her dark feathers and wise eyes. She revolved her head around, taking in her surroundings from her new perch on the low branch.

"You're Curie?" Paris asked.

"You know my name," the owl repeated. Her eyes opened and closed in long blinks as she spoke.

"I also know the names of your friends," Paris said.

"I wouldn't call them friends," the owl replied. "More like associates."

"Wow, a talking owl." Hemingway shook his head next to Paris. "Now I've seen it all."

"No, for that, you have to see the talking stag," Paris remarked.

"That's Faraday's shape?" Curie asked. "He's a stag?"

"He's a squirrel," Paris answered.

"Oh…" Remorse edged into Curie's tone.

Paris nodded and looked around at the ground cover again. "I think you nearly ate him."

"You can't fault a woman for being hungry," Curie replied.

"Edison is the stag," Paris continued. "How is it that you don't know what shapes your associates took?"

"Everything that got us to where we are was very fuzzy for a long time," Curie answered. "I don't understand it now. We shifted. Time traveled. Performed the spells, and then I lost a lot of my memory. It got more complicated recently when I awoke in this strange place." She revolved her head. "Where am I, and how did I get here?"

"The Bewilder Forest at Happily Ever After College," Hemingway replied before Paris could. "It's where we educate fairy godmothers."

"Fascinating." Curie hooted again.

"It sounds as though someone transported you here for this reunion, much like Edison," Paris imparted. "Faraday made a deal so that you all could come together and return to your real lives."

Curie glared at Paris for a long moment, a very calculating expression before she said, "That was very selfless of Faraday."

"Thanks!" the squirrel chirped, popping out of the ground cover, his little head the only visible part of his body.

The owl rotated her head smoothly, taking in the squirrel and blinking at him. "Faraday, is that you?"

He nodded. "Curie, it's…well, right now I see you. That's what I'm doing."

"Usually, most say, 'It's good to see you,'" Hemingway whispered in Paris' ear.

The owl spun to face him at once. "We aren't friends."

"You've mentioned that in so many words," Paris remarked.

"Associates," Faraday echoed.

Paris watched as the squirrel jumped out of the ground cover, arriving beside her. "Are you okay?"

He nodded. "Sorry, my protective instinct took over."

"As it should have," Curie announced. "I was going to eat you."

"Then you would have regretted it because I think you all three have to be reunited to go back to your lives," Paris stated.

Curie nodded. "That's correct."

"Edison said that you'd have the spell for returning to your original forms," Paris continued.

"Yes, but we can't do it until we return to our timelines," Curie said.

Paris glanced at Faraday. "As you suspected then."

"We can't go to our timelines without magic," Curie stated. "Which means we can't go to our timelines. That's been the problem all along."

"Well, and that we were separated and needed to be together for the spells to work." Faraday sounded surprised. He put his paw to his mouth. "I can say more than before."

Paris nodded. "Yeah, as I recover the puzzle pieces, you all can share more. The more I learn, the more I can learn."

"That's pretty cool," Hemingway offered in awe.

"So you three have to be reunited for the spell to work to transform you?" Paris asked the owl.

"For us to start the transforming spell," she explained. "As I said, it has to be completed when we time travel to our original timelines, which are all different. Also, like I said, we can't do magic, so we can't do the transforming spells."

"Well, maybe I can help with that," Paris offered. "I'm a magician. Well, and a fairy…and more."

Hemingway held up his hand. "I can help too."

The owl didn't look impressed. "Although that's nice of you two, all the magic transforming us won't help if we can't move to our timeline. That's where the final transformation can take place, and the last time I checked, simple magicians can't do that type of work."

"Simple magicians can't," Paris offered. "But Father Time can. He gave me three stones that he said would put you on your timelines. If I give them to you, do you know what to do with them?"

The owl bobbed her head suddenly. "Time rocks. Yes! That's exactly what we need. You got those from Father Time? That's perfect."

Paris beamed, looking between Faraday and Curie. "Then we have everything we need. We only have to meet Edison at the sharpest bend in the river." She turned to Hemingway. "You know where that is?"

He nodded. "Yeah, I can take you there now, if you'd like."

"Not now," Curie interrupted. "We can only do the spells on a full moon due to the gravitational pull on the Earth, which is needed for the transformation to work."

Hemingway sucked in a breath before looking at Paris. "The full moon is in three nights."

She smiled. "Then we have a date. We'll all meet then."

CHAPTER THIRTY-EIGHT

Thankfully, Paris was able to finally sleep, having returned to Happily Ever After College at a reasonable hour that night. She awoke still groggy and slept in a little, thinking that her extracurricular activity warranted an excuse.

She was surprised to find Faraday still snoozing in her sock drawer when she awoke. Thinking that he was exhausted from the excitement of being able to return to his old life, she got ready and tip-toed out of her room, careful not to wake him.

Having missed breakfast, Paris grabbed a protein bar from the kitchen and hurried to ballroom dancing. She didn't regret missing Art of Love the way she would have if the headmistress had been teaching it. She assumed that Agent Topaz was grateful not to have to deal with her contentious remarks.

With her stomach rumbling from missing too many meals, Paris slipped into ballroom dancing class. Wilfred was at the front, explaining how to do the rumba.

Using the opportunity to stay at the back of the group, Paris unwrapped her protein bar carefully, trying to sneak bites. Many of the students caught the noises and gave her punishing looks over their shoulders.

"Sorry, I missed breakfast," Paris whispered when given a particularly scathing look from some hippie student.

"Rumba is the dance of love," Wilfred said from the main part of the floor while rhythmically gyrating his hips.

"I thought that was the tango," Poppy said.

"No, that's something else," Chef Ash corrected.

"What is the tango then?" Lilly Pad asked.

"It's the dance that you must have two for," the chef builder answered.

"But don't you need two to dance?" another student questioned.

"Not necessarily," Wilfred cut in, stepping forward. "Dancing is about mastering the steps on your own so that you complement your partner. The next part is pairing those steps together to create something beautiful."

Paris held up her hand. "Yeah, quick question."

"Yes, Miss Paris Beaufont." Wilfred pointed at her as she crammed a bite of the protein bar into her mouth.

"How is this relevant to creating love?" she asked through the food.

The magitech AI butler sighed, starting to get annoyed by her "act."

"The rumba is a romantic dance that can both encourage love and also be part of a discipline," Wilfred explained. "I think you'll find that when you master the grace that goes along with ballroom dancing, you'll understand a lot more about the heart than you thought."

"Not only that, but no man wants someone who can't dance," Becky commented, rolling her eyes over her shoulder.

"That's definitely not true," Hemingway countered.

"I think one of the main points is that grace is attractive." Wilfred tried to regain control of his classroom. "When we possess it, only then can we teach it."

"So I teach Cinderella to rumba, and hopefully she lands a man who can buy her a Roomba vacuum to clean her floors, right?" Paris teased. "That's the dream, is it?"

"The dream is to find love that fulfills its purposes," Wilfred said, always the picture of patience. He clapped his gloved hands. "Now please break into pairs and practice today's dance, the rumba."

The students moved off, picking partners.

Hemingway made a beeline for Paris, to her relief, because everyone was getting picked up—everyone but Becky, who most were over at this point. If Paris had to dance with that witch, she would sweep her legs out from under her and run.

However, before Hemingway made his way over to Paris, Wilfred intersected, holding up his hand to block them. "Miss Paris Beaufont will be dancing solo in this class."

"I've been dancing solo," Paris argued.

"Yeah, you keep saying she has to master dancing alone and know the moves on her own before she can dance with someone else," Hemingway added.

The butler nodded. "That's correct. In the last class, I was Miss Beaufont's partner."

"And I was excellent and knew all the moves." Paris had tried to do better although the whole thing seemed silly.

"Yes, but your problem now is that you refuse to let others lead," Wilfred stated.

"So, shouldn't I practice with a partner to get better at that?" Paris asked. "I mean, maybe I'm leading because I'm not used to having someone else."

"Although that's an evident point," Wilfred began, "I think it means you haven't figured out how to dance alone enough to dance with another. Love is about loving yourself as much as it's about loving another. We have to get good at being solo before we can have a partner."

Paris lowered her chin and regarded the butler with hooded eyes. "You know, for someone who is supposed to have no emotions, I think you got more than you let on."

"My programming is intuitive." Wilfred bowed and disappeared back onto the dance floor of students.

Hemingway gave her an apologetic smile and also bowed. "I hope to dance with you soon, Miss Beaufont."

She nodded regretfully at him, watching as he disappeared onto the dance floor too, also wondering when she'd be ready for a partner. Paris felt as if she'd danced solo her whole life, but maybe she'd only learned to "dance."

CHAPTER THIRTY-NINE

"The full moon has long had a significant impact on the human psyche," Professor Joyce Beacon began as she walked onto the stage in the auditorium of the observatory.

Paris rolled her eyes. *Here we go again with this unfounded baloney.* Although she tried to keep an open mind, the astrology class at Happily Ever After College had tested her patience more than a few times. She wanted to believe that there was something the star charts and phases of the planets could tell them about love, but so far it was all founded in superstition and misleading correlations.

"The werewolf turns on a full moon—signaling the aggression it causes," Professor Beacon continued, her long gray dreads swaying as she paced in front of the class.

"Some packs of werewolves turn every single night despite the phases of the moon," Paris interrupted, all eyes in the auditorium turning to look at her.

Because of a conversation she had with her parents about the werewolf her Aunt Raina Ludwig married, she knew a little more about werewolves. Fane Popa-Ludwig was from Lupei and the leader of the original pack of werewolves in Romania. A unique property of that pack, according to Paris' mother, was that the werewolves turned every single night regardless of the moon's phase.

"Where have you learned such a false notion?" someone asked from the back of the room.

Everyone turned to see an agent for FGA standing at the back of the room. Rumors said that his name was Agent Ruby. He wore a jet black suit like his counterparts but also had a bowler hat covering his hair.

"From a Warrior for the House of Fourteen," Paris stated, not allowed to say it was her mother or that she was back yet. Only a few knew that until Liv and Stefan were ready to reenter the world and take back their positions as Warriors.

The man laughed coldly. "Because your parents used to be Warriors for the House of Fourteen, you think that makes you an expert on such things, do you, Miss Beaufont?"

Paris narrowed her eyes at the man. She wanted to blurt out that her parents *were* still Warriors for the House of Fourteen, but she couldn't. That was fine. She knew how to combat this guy, who looked more stern and rigid than Agent Topaz.

"My uncle happens to be a Warrior presently for the House of Fourteen and also a werewolf, who turns every single night." Paris made the statement with confidence, allowed to say that much—although Liv had shared something else about the Lupei pack that she wasn't allowed to share with anyone…ever.

Agent Ruby sighed dramatically as if this news was of great disappointment to him. "That doesn't surprise me. Magicians are notorious for making illogical choices when it comes to appointing people into powerful positions."

What the hell was this guy's problem? Paris reflexively wanted to punch him in the face. She worked to quell her demon blood, which was suddenly boiling. Losing her temper would only make her look worse in this situation.

"The House of Fourteen is the governing body for all magical organizations," Paris argued. "I would be careful about insulting their decisions."

Agent Ruby lifted his chin, revealing a wicked grin. "We operate independently of any governing body per the authority of Saint Valentine."

"Who was appointed by Mother Nature," Paris cut in.

"Who was appointed by the board," he argued, his smile disappearing.

"I guess I'll have to call Mama Jamba and tell her that her authority can't trump a board of fairies," Paris said with satisfaction, seeing the rise she was getting from the agent.

"You don't know Mother Nature," he spat bitterly.

Casually, Paris brushed her hair off her shoulder. "We had dinner last week."

Professor Joyce Beacon cleared her throat, working to regain the class' attention. "Well, an uncle who is a Warrior and a werewolf and dinners with Mother Nature. That's quite impressive, Paris."

Unhurried, Paris turned back to face the front of the auditorium.

"I didn't know about this pack of werewolves who can turn every night," the professor continued, striding the length of the stage again. "A full moon affects the tides, the seasons, circadian rhythms, REM cycles of sleep, emotions, and hormones. It is well-documented that a full moon increases aggression resulting in higher incidents of violence."

"I'm going to have to stop you right there," Paris interrupted. She knew she would create trouble for herself. However, she simply couldn't help it. Mae Ling encouraged her to speak out about things she didn't agree with at the College, and Paris' recent research on the full moon seemed appropriately timed.

When Curie had said that the spell to transform herself, Faraday, and Edison had to be on a full moon due to its gravitational pull, Paris had done some research. She'd found some powerful things related to magic on a full moon, as Curie had stated. There was also a lot of often-popularized wrong information.

Professor Beacon halted, staring down at Paris. All eyes in the auditorium were on her once again.

"Although it's true that the moon affects sleep and the tides," Paris began, "there is no evidence to support the notion that it increases aggression or influences hormones or emotions."

"Is this more false information that you learned from magicians at the House of Fourteen?" Agent Ruby strode down the center aisle of the auditorium and stopped right in front of Paris.

"A book in the library here at Happily Ever After College," Paris retorted, copying his smugness.

This answer threw Agent Ruby off his game. "Was it a fiction book?"

"Yes, and I read Harry Potter to learn how to do my spell work," Paris replied sarcastically.

Some students behind her gasped at her boldness. A few snickered. She guessed some of them were Christine and Penny, who would appreciate her reply.

"I'm not sure what type of behavior you were used to getting away with at the school for delinquents that you came from," Agent Ruby scolded, his eyes narrowed on Paris, "but here at Happily Ever After College, we expect a high level of decorum."

Paris nodded. "Yes, and the ability to digest whatever wrong information is shoved down our throat from FGA. Is that right?"

The fury on his face deepened. "I would make the excuse that it's because you're half-magician that you behave so poorly, if it hadn't recently come to my attention that you're not only a halfling, you also have the blood of a demon."

Paris froze. Everyone around her fell silent. She felt as if everyone in the room peeled back away from her in total fear.

CHAPTER FORTY

"Where did you learn that?" Paris tried to breathe past the sudden tightness in her chest. Only Hemingway and Penny, at the school, knew that she had the blood of a demon. Why would either one of them share that information with FGA, who were already scrutinizing her and looking for a reason to kick her out of Happily Ever After College? Suddenly she felt betrayed in a way she'd never expected.

A triumphant smile spread on Agent Ruby's face. "So you don't deny it then?"

"Who told you that?" Heat built in Paris' face, spurring her anger, making her think it would overpower her.

The agent folded his arms over his chest. "My source isn't relevant since you've now confirmed that it's true. I'm certain that this will be of great interest to the board."

"I'm not sure that this conversation should be the business of the entire class," Professor Beacon cut in, stepping down off the stage beside Agent Ruby.

Paris was relieved to see she wasn't keeping her distance from her, although she'd sensed many of the students around her pull back—fearful of her.

"I think if we have a demon in our midst, that all should be notified of it," Agent Ruby argued. "I'm sure many of the families of our students will find this to be very disconcerting."

"I'm not dangerous," Paris remarked, sitting up straighter, trying to feign confidence.

Agent Ruby ran his narrowed gaze over her. "You refuse to wear the school uniform, argue with your professors, and make a mockery of our curriculum. I fail to see how you can argue that you're not a hazard to this college and all who attend."

Paris stood, facing him directly. "I also helped the love meter to recover, matching up Amelia Rose and Grayson McGregor. I bring value to Happily Ever After College."

He sighed, shaking his head—unfortunately undeterred. "I do believe that the love meter is at a record low. Apparently, your efforts weren't as successful as you thought. This is a perfect reason that the board is looking into the matter of students working on fairy godmother cases. That should be the job of our graduates and not those who will invariably flunk out or be expelled."

Momentarily speechless, Paris felt her breath seize up. This jerk was threatening her in front of the whole class. If she weren't the talk of Happily Ever After College before, she would be the newest hot topic. Not to mention that everyone would treat her as if she had the plague. Right then, she felt like she did.

"The love meter is down because FriendNet is breaking up relationships," Paris insisted, not wanting this agent to best her.

His eyes turned into sharp slits. "How do you know about that?"

"My source isn't relevant." Paris copied his exact wording from earlier.

There was something all wrong about the expression on Agent Ruby's face. He suddenly appeared flustered, whereas before his confidence and arrogance had been building. "I think now that we've confirmed you have the blood of a demon that the board will have to reconsider your enrollment here at Happily Ever After College. A magician doesn't belong here, but a demon, well, they shouldn't belong in this world."

"Agent Ruby," Professor Beacon barked, shock written on her face. "I really must insist that you—"

"Thank you, Professor, but I think Agent Ruby is only proving who the real monster is," Paris interrupted, her penetrating gaze on the man before her.

A few students gasped.

"Burn," Christine said from somewhere at Paris' back.

Agent Ruby's face turned an awful shade of red—matching his name. Paris wasn't going to allow him to best her like this. All she had to do was turn the tables.

"My demon blood doesn't make me dangerous," she said, her confidence bolstered by her friend's reaction. "Quite the opposite. It compels me to stamp out evil. I can sense it with incredible accuracy. It draws me to it and is invariably repelled by me, which means those who have a problem with me are usually the problem."

The insinuation that Paris had spouted caused many around the classroom to break into whispers. Agent Ruby's eyes darted around, taking in the many students who were suddenly talking in excited voices before his scrutinizing gaze landed on Paris.

"You are very confused if you think that fairy godmothers are supposed to fight evil, Miss Beaufont," he said through clenched teeth. "Their job is to promote love. It sounds like you belong elsewhere, and I'm sure that many others will vehemently agree."

Before Paris could respond, Agent Ruby did what any coward would when someone had outmatched them and retreated for the exit.

CHAPTER FORTY-ONE

"I promise that it wasn't me," Penny said, nearly in tears when Paris confronted her after the class let out. Professor Beacon didn't try to resume the lesson after the disruption. Instead, she encouraged everyone to try and relax after the explosive argument, sending the students to dinner early.

To Paris' surprise, many of the students didn't treat her differently as they filed out of the observatory and strode toward the mansion. Some offered consoling smiles. Others seemed extra fascinated by her, not hiding their stares.

"You didn't tell anyone that I have demon blood?" Paris questioned, striding beside her two friends.

"Hey, why didn't you share that information with me?" Christine sounded offended. "I can be trusted."

Paris rolled her eyes. "As if I needed another reason for you to think I'm a cool zoo animal."

"You totally are." Christine heaved a dramatic sigh. "I mean, does your life ever stop getting any cooler? What you said to Agent Ruby makes sense. Your demon blood makes you fight evil."

"Yeah, it's why no one is afraid of you," Penny added, indicating all the students still staring at Paris as they neared the mansion.

"Well, it's true," Paris said. "I inherited the blood from my father, and he says if anything, the demon blood makes us so we can't stop until we've extinguished evil. We're compelled almost to our detriment."

Christine threw her hands up. "Seriously, I only inherited my father's big feet and red hair. This isn't fair."

Paris and Penny laughed.

"I promise," Penny said when the laughter had subsided. "I would never share anything you told me about you with anyone, especially that demon eater, Agent Ruby."

"Nice one." Christine held out her hand for a high five. "He's totally a demon eater, and I hope he chokes on Paris."

Penny, looking unsure of the gesture at first, clumsily threw her palm up to meet Christine. "It's true though. That guy is wrong on so many levels."

Paris nodded. "Yeah, I don't get a good feeling about him. He's somehow worse than the other agents."

"Trust that," Penny encouraged with a serious expression.

"I will," Paris stated. "I believe you if you say you didn't tell anyone about my demon blood. However, that means that if it wasn't you, it was only one other person."

Christine grunted with frustration. "Seriously, why am I not in the circle of trust? I'm loud but a total vault when it comes to secrets."

Paris laughed again. "You are trusted. I haven't had much opportunity to share this. I only told Penny because she gave me advice. This other person figured it out."

"The tattle tale," Christine offered.

"Yeah," Paris admitted, anger starting to brew in her again at the idea that Hemingway shared her personal information. "I'll catch up with you two at dinner. I need to take care of something first."

Christine glanced at Penny. "She's going to go take someone out. Listen for the screams."

Paris shook her head, cutting away from her friends, heading for the greenhouse where she'd caught sight of Hemingway. She hoped that she didn't have to take him out, but if he'd told her secrets after everything, she was definitely going to give him a black eye…maybe two.

CHAPTER FORTY-TWO

"Right or left?" Paris asked Hemingway when she entered the greenhouse. Thankfully he was the only one in there.

He looked up from a particularly hairy-looking plant. Seeing her, he smiled wide before confusion covered his face. "Right or left what?"

"Do you want me to punch you in the right or left eye?" She held up a fist and brandished it in his direction.

He cocked his head to the side. "I'd prefer neither. Why would you punch me?"

"Because only two people here knew that I had my father's demon blood," Paris explained. "Now the whole college knows. Actually, all of FGA will know soon, and it looks like it might get me kicked out of Happily Ever After College."

His eyes widened with horror. "Paris, I didn't tell anyone. I promise. I never would do that. I'm so sorry, but Headmistress Starr will never let them kick you out of the college."

She didn't know if she could believe him. She wanted to. He appeared earnest, worry springing to his features, but what if he'd let it slip and was lying?

Paris shot him a challenging expression. "If she can't prevent you from being tossed out for being a magician, do you think she'll be able to stop the FGA board if they don't want a demon at the college?"

"You're not a demon," he replied, a sensitive expression on his face.

"I have demon blood," Paris argued. "I spook horses. I also despise evil, but most won't understand that. It's not like I can point at my father and say, 'Well, he has demon blood and saves the world. I'm good too.' You might remember that no one knows my father is back or that he has demon blood. I'm on my own, and it's FGA's perception that counts."

"I know how you must feel—"

"Do you?" Paris interrupted. "I don't think you do. Your secret is still safe because I didn't tell it."

"Paris, I didn't tell anyone about your demon blood. You have to believe me. I'd never do anything to betray your trust."

He was pleading. Paris wanted to believe him, but someone shared this information, and it wasn't Penny. If it wasn't Hemingway, she didn't know who else it could have been.

"Remember when I quoted the famous Hemingway?" he asked.

She shrugged. "Which time?"

"When I told you, 'The best way to find out if you can trust somebody is to trust them.'"

"Yeah, so you're telling me that I can't?" she asked.

He shook his head. "When you lie to deceive someone, they can't ever trust you again. I'd never do that to you. I would never risk losing your trust because without that, we have nothing. You may not see it, but I want a lot more from you than your trust."

Paris tensed, feeling suddenly nervous rather than angry. She bit her lip and lowered her gaze. Finally, when she forced herself to look back at Hemingway, she felt a new tension between them. "So you didn't tell anyone about my demon blood?"

He shook his head and stepped forward.

"Then how do the FGA agents know?" Paris questioned.

"I don't know," Hemingway said thoughtfully. "But I'll do whatever I can to help you figure it out."

Paris knitted her fingers together, so many worries streaming through her mind. "Honestly, I have so many other problems to deal with." She threw her arm in the direction of the mansion. "I have to go to dinner, and I'm pretty sure that the rumors of my demon blood will have spread throughout the college. Everyone will soon think I'm some evil that will hurt them. I don't know if Headmistress Starr knew I had demon blood. She might be the first to kick me out, thinking that I'll infect the college."

Hemingway shook his head. "She's not like that."

"She's already in so much trouble," Paris argued. "The board will be upset. Donors will be breathing down her neck. I don't know if I can fight this."

Taking another step forward, Hemingway gave her a steady look. "Then we will fight it together. Because you're right, it's perception. Those stupid, uptight agents think they know everything, but they're so stuck in old ways of thinking that they can't see reason. I mean, they're feeling-feeling fairies, but they're also afraid of change. That's what you represent. You've been able to do the one thing I've wanted to do for a long time."

Paris blinked at him. The look on her face said, "What?"

"Be myself," Hemingway said. "You are unapologetically Paris Beaufont, and that's a beautiful thing."

She blushed and pushed an errant strand of hair behind her ear.

"So you know what you have to do now?" he asked.

Paris shrugged, not at all knowing what to do at that point.

"You have to go to dinner with your head held high," he stated. "They all will be talking. Let them. You're the best of all worlds, and they aren't worried about what evil you're capable of. They're terrified of how you're going to revolutionize the fairy godmothers in all the best ways, spreading love everywhere, because let's be honest, that's exactly what you're doing."

CHAPTER FORTY-THREE

If Paris had any doubts about whether the rumors of her demon blood had spread around Happily Ever After College, her curiosity settled the moment she and Hemingway entered the mansion's dining hall. Everyone halted their conversations and looked directly at her. There were a solid few seconds where most stared. A few backed up as if afraid she was about to breathe fire on them.

Paris reminded herself that to most uneducated types, demons were only evil. There was no gray for them. They wouldn't know about a cure or a wish from a genie who made it so that she wasn't a demon. That's why Paris decided to address the matter straight on instead of skirting it. If the FGA board kicked her out of Happily Ever After College, at least she'd know that she made an effort.

Paris held up her hands, making some scream like she was about to curse them. A few fairies jumped back, covering their faces.

Paris shook her head at them. "Look, by now you all know that I have demon blood in addition to being half-magician and half-fairy. However, I'm not a threat to you or anyone else. A genie made me what I am at my parent's request. Therefore, although I have demon blood, I only possess the best parts of it. I can sense evil. I have the hunger to fight it. I have the skills of the monster to win. Someone recently told me a demon's worst enemy is a demon, and that's me in so many ways. I intend to become the best fairy godmother because I want anything that blocks love, such as evil, erased. You all might try and create love, but because of my demon blood, I can't physically stop until I've rid the world of bad. Until I've made a path for love. So talk about me. Stare at me if you must. But don't fear me. I'm not like you. I'm a different type of fairy godmother, but I'll make a good one."

The room fell silent as Paris concluded. All eyes were on her, and she didn't know what else to add now that she'd said her piece.

"A great one," Headmistress Starr said from across the dining hall, smiling proudly at Paris. "And a well-said speech that hopefully puts all the rumors to rest. We do have other matters to attend to."

At that, everyone in the room broke out of their trances and went back to getting food, eating, or conversing.

Paris let out a breath of relief and charged for the buffet line, hungry now that she'd given herself a chance to tap into her feelings.

She and Hemingway took their usual places at the dining room table, earning sneaky grins from Chef Ash, Christine, and Penny.

"Yeah, yeah." Paris rolled her eyes at her friends. "I get that I made a scene, but what else was I supposed to do?"

"I thought it was grand," Christine gushed.

"Me too," Penny admitted.

"Oh, I agree," Chef Ash stated. "I think it's awesome that with everyone's attention on Saint Valentine in attendance, Paris was able to steal his thunder."

Paris nearly dropped her fork on the way to her mouth. "What? Saint Valentine is here? Where?"

Chef Ash nodded toward the head of the table to the left. "Down there. He's the one intently watching you."

CHAPTER FORTY-FOUR

Of all the times that Paris picked to make a huge display, of course, it had to be when the leader of the fairy godmothers visited the college.

She slid down in her seat, not daring to look toward the end of the table at Saint Valentine. Paris needed a moment to regain her composure first. She was pretty sure that announcing that she had demon blood in front of the college wasn't going to go over very well with him. It would play straight into Agent Ruby's hand. She'd taken the speculation out of the whole rumor, admitting to everyone who she was.

Paris remained convinced that it was a matter of time before the FGA board met, voted, and kicked her out of the college. Headmistress Starr, as supportive and open-minded as she was, wouldn't be able to save her. Paris had dug her own grave at this point.

Christine waved down the table. "Hey there!"

"Oh, don't do that," Hemingway scolded, also sliding down in his chair.

"Why not?" Christine asked. "He's gawking at me. Oh, and he brought a bunch of his cool agents from Matters of the Heart. That one is cute."

Penny giggled. "Saint Valentine is staring at Paris."

"You don't know that," Christine joked. "He could be staring at me because my parents are both accountants who cheat at card games on the weekends and…" She leaned forward, her voice suddenly conspiratorial. "I heard that my mom got bitten by a scorpion and had—"

"Scorpions don't bite," Hemingway corrected.

Paris shot him a pursed expression. "Really? That's your takeaway from what Miss Ridiculous said?"

He nodded. "Sorry, I also wanted to say that accounting is a noble profession."

"Yeah, right," Christine challenged and pointed at Paris. "We're all at a dinner party, and this one tells people that her parents were Warriors for the House of Fourteen. Then I get to follow with, 'my parents did the taxes for farmers in Kansas.' Guess who is getting her drink refilled with follow-up questions? Then guess who is getting sent to the kitchen for more little smokies."

"Why does everyone think I go to dinner parties?" Paris stared at her plate of food, suddenly not hungry at all.

"That would be one of my questions too," Becky Montgomery cut in from a few chairs down. "I mean, you're not dinner party material."

"I'd invite you, Becky, if I were having a slumber party," Christine chimed. "I mean, we have to have someone who puts everyone to sleep."

The group all laughed, excluding Becky, of course.

She glared at Paris. "You know, you might think you can convince others that your demon blood doesn't make you dangerous, especially to fairies who those demonic monsters aren't interested in. However, some of us will never trust you. Mother says that if it's your fairy half that subdues your demon blood, that doesn't mean it's totally under control. You could turn on any of us fairies at any point."

"You know what—"

Paris cut off Christine, who was probably coming to her rescue, holding up a hand—a sudden realization occurring to her. "It was Penny who said that bit about how demons didn't go after fairies because they are so loving and emotional, not Hemingway."

She looked at him, and he nodded in reply. "I told you it wasn't me who told."

Penny's mouth fell open, and tears instantly filled her eyes. "Paris, it wasn't me who told. I promise."

"I know," Paris replied. "Because the school found out about my demon blood, but if Becky here has been talking to dear old mother about it, then it sounds like she's known for a good bit. What, were you spying on us?"

Becky leaned forward with a petulant glint in her eyes. "Maybe you shouldn't talk so loudly."

Paris shot her a murderous glare, feeling the heat rise in her face again like before with Agent Ruby. "I would guess that it was Mrs. Montgomery who took it upon herself to pass along this information to FGA, hoping to get me expelled."

Smugly, Becky shrugged. "If the truth gets you kicked out of Happily Ever After College, is that my fault?"

"If your snobbery gets you put in a headlock, is that my fault?" Christine asked, mock curiosity on her face.

Becky tightened her mouth, looking between Paris and Christine, trying to craft a retort. "Face it. No matter how you spin it, no one wants a halfling with demon blood here at the college. You might as well pack your bags because you don't have long."

"I don't know," a melodic voice said from directly beside them.

Everyone's heads whipped up to see a very handsome man in a dark suit standing behind them. He had salt and pepper slicked-back hair and a cunning expression in his blue eyes. In the lapel of his jacket was a lush red rose, and on his face was a slight smile. Paris knew immediately that this had to be Saint Valentine.

"I, for one, think that a halfling with the advantages of a demon could make a great addition to the fairy godmothers." He looked at all of them briefly before settling his gaze on Paris. "Maybe instead of packing your bags, you'll join me in the conservatory for a chat?"

CHAPTER FORTY-FIVE

If all eyes hadn't been on Paris before, they were definitely watching her every move when Saint Valentine led her out of the dining hall. She had hardly taken a sip of air after the elegant man asked her for a private conversation. Paris had caught the look of total horror on Becky Montgomery's face as well as the shock in her friends' eyes.

The conservatory was empty and mostly dark since the sun had set at Happily Ever After College. Saint Valentine held out his hand, and a silver cane appeared at once. He flicked it slightly, and many of the Tiffany lamps around the room flickered to life, spilling warm light over the space.

Saint Valentine turned to her and waved the cane in a presenting fashion at the sofa in the middle of the room. "Shall we take a seat or would you prefer to stand? I would like you to be comfortable for this conversation."

The leader of FGA and Matters of the Heart had quite publicly said that he thought Paris could make a good addition to the fairy godmothers, easing some of her worries. He'd told her not to pack her bags, so maybe he wasn't put off by her demon blood like the conservatives such as the Montgomerys and Agent Ruby.

Paris drew a breath and forced herself to sit, watching as Saint Valentine gracefully copied her—sitting on the other side of the sofa.

"That was quite the speech you made at dinner," he said in a smooth voice. The man didn't seem old nor young, but he was the epitome of sophistication. Paris instantly liked him, whereas Agent Topaz and Agent Ruby had made her skin crawl.

She lowered her chin. "I'm sorry for that. I didn't realize you'd joined us for dinner. I'd just been outed in astrology and felt that I should cut off the rumors before people started making me out to be some devil worshipper who ate kittens for breakfast."

Paris pressed her eyes closed, realizing that she'd said way too much and way too casually. *Why couldn't I simply have apologized?* She felt mortified.

However, to her surprise, a soft chuckle fell out of Saint Valentine's mouth. She opened her eyes to find an amused expression dancing around in his bright blue eyes. "I've heard of your sense of humor, but witnessing it is much more delightful."

"You have?"

He nodded and rested both of his hands on his ornately engraved silver cane pinned on the floor. "Yes, I've heard a lot of interesting things about the halfling born to extraordinary Warriors, the niece to a dragonrider, and a formidable force of her own on Roya Lane. I dare say, the criminals are getting away with a lot with you here at Happily Ever After College."

She laughed. "Yeah, but now you know I have demon blood."

He waved off her worry. "That doesn't seem like a problem to me. Your explanation makes perfect sense."

"It does?" Paris needed him to tell her more—make her feel better about this all after the afternoon she'd had. In a few short hours, Paris had her secrets revealed to the college, had a public argument with an FGA agent, thought that Hemingway or Penny had deceived her, and learned that a powerful family was trying to destroy her. Needless to say, she needed a morale booster.

"A very thin veil divides love and evil," Saint Valentine explained. "It is love that makes people do the greatest acts of goodness and also drives them to the craziest ones of desperation. I can wholeheartedly believe that your demon blood fuels you in ways that will make you passionate about creating good. I dare say it is usually those who have experienced trauma who want to heal the world. It is those who have lost everything that want to ensure no one goes without. All too often, it is those who have not had their loved ones in their lives, who want no one ever to feel lonely, like they once felt."

Goosebumps rose on Paris' skin. It was as if Saint Valentine was looking into her soul. Even more chilling, he appeared to like what he saw as he smiled serenely at her.

"That makes sense." Paris hoped he'd keep talking, enchanted by his voice and words.

"Also, there is a choice involved when people have a drop of demon blood in them or whatever the equivalent could be in other examples," he continued. "When you found out that you had demon blood in you, what did you think?"

"I was afraid that it would corrupt me," she answered at once. "I worried recently and consulted with an expert." Paris trusted Saint Valentine without knowing why, but she didn't think she should tell him that her parents were back. That was their job, not hers.

He nodded. "You see, you want to be good. Your demon blood can make you evil or fight evil. It's always been your choice, and it seems clear what you've chosen."

"I won't ever let it turn me the other way around," Paris stated with confidence.

"No, and you wouldn't be here if that was a possibility," he agreed.

"I appreciate your encouraging words on this, but there are a lot of other people who don't want me here," Paris admitted, needing to be honest and forthright.

He tilted his head back and forth. "Unfortunately, I can't quell all the skeptics. Honestly, there's a lot of division at FGA."

"Because some don't want things to evolve for FGA and here at the college?"

"Yes," he affirmed with a kind smile. "The world has changed, and yet, we haven't at FGA. I've been fighting to adapt old practices and met with much contention." Saint Valentine's light expression fell away. "I don't know. Maybe I'm wrong to want things to change."

"But they should," Paris countered with conviction. "I mean, I'm sorry. I shouldn't speak out of turn."

He grinned at her. "I think you should."

Paris swallowed, mustering courage. "Well, I want to be a fairy godmother. I really do, but I feel like we're using an old manual, and it needs updating for the modern age. We focus on creating matches for the elite and famous, but I want to create love for all. Also, dating has changed, but we haven't. I think there are so many things we could do differently, but of course, I'm only a young mixed-up halfling who gets herself in trouble more than she fixes things."

He chuckled again, a nice sound. "I think sometimes we have to create a bit of trouble to fix things. Sometimes things have to be broken so we throw them out and start over with something new."

"So you think I'm right?" Paris asked.

Saint Valentine thought for a moment. "I think that I need to keep an open mind. Change can't happen overnight. That would be unwise, both out of respect for tradition and because many are stuck and need time to adapt. Also, strategy should be a part of the equation. Not all of the fairy godmother's practices are bad because they're old. For me, I think that a new generation of fairy godmothers who don't fit the old cookie-cutter shape would be good. A nice mix of old and new. Of tradition and modern thinking. In that way, we can complement each other's best attributes."

Paris smiled. "I like that idea."

Saint Valentine nodded. "Me too, but we'll see how it happens. I have the board to convince, and they aren't the most open-minded." He winked at her. "Some aren't as flexible in their old age as me."

Paris laughed easily, grateful that this man was Saint Valentine. There were a lot of things that she believed needed to happen to bring the fairy godmothers into the twenty-first century, but she thought that there were only opportunities ahead, especially with a man like this in charge.

"I wanted to take this opportunity to introduce myself," he continued. "I realize now that I never formally did that." Extending an elegant hand to her, Saint Valentine steadied his cane with his other one. "I'm Saint Valentine, and it is a delight to meet you, Paris Beaufont."

Paris blushed as she took his hand, allowing him to bring it to his lips and kiss it politely. "A pleasure to meet you, sir."

Releasing her hand, Saint Valentine looked at her intently. "I know that you're receiving a lot of attention and not the kind that most would want. I also wanted to take this opportunity to tell you that Matters of the Heart fully supports Headmistress Starr and her decision to educate you. I've also heard of your work on the recent missions. Your approaches, while unconventional, are very intriguing."

Picking up his cane and pointing at her with it, Saint Valentine's eyes twinkled. "I'm going to keep an eye on you, our halfling godmother. I think you'll go on to do great things, and my job will be to ensure that you have all the resources to grow and spread your wings so you can achieve greatness."

Paris suddenly felt so much better than before. She was grateful her secrets had come out and that she'd had this opportunity to show herself to Saint Valentine. Also, to hear his encouraging words. She now knew that everything would be okay—as long as the man before her remained in power at FGA, that was.

Their fond moment was immediately interrupted by running footsteps. Both of them tensed and turned to the hallway. A moment later, Wilfred burst into the conservatory, his eyes urgent.

"Saint Valentine," the magitech AI butler began in a rush.

Saint Valentine and Paris bolted upright off the couch.

"Yes, Wilfred? What is it?" Saint Valentine read the urgency exuding from the butler.

"It's one of your agents from Matter of the Heart," Wilfred said, his voice not as steady as usual. "He is dead. It appears to be from poison."

CHAPTER FORTY-SIX

All of the students were being ushered out of the dining hall by the staff. However, because Paris rushed in beside Saint Valentine, she was able to get into the crime scene.

She'd never seen a dead body. It was surreal and startling and strange all at the same time. The reason for the strangeness was that the agent from Matters of the Heart was face-down in soup and appeared to have drowned in the shallow bowl.

Saint Valentine halted, looking with wide eyes at the dead agent at the abandoned dining room table. Gathered around were other agents from FGA, Headmistress Starr, Chef Ash, and Hemingway.

"How do you know it was poison?" Saint Valentine keenly studied the crime scene while keeping a safe distance.

Chef Ash pointed at the soup. "That's not what I served. I don't know what's in it, but I know that's not the right color of the vegetable puree." He indicated other bowls of abandoned soup in various places. "Compare it with those others."

The other bowls were an orangish hue, whereas the one the agent had his face in was slightly purplish.

"Who would have done such a thing?" Saint Valentine looked at the headmistress for answers.

Willow looked utterly beside herself, her traumatized eyes pinned on the dead body. "I really don't know. Nothing like this has ever happened."

"You mean, nothing like this ever happened before certain students were allowed into the school," Agent Ruby said smoothly, his gaze unmistakably on Paris. All eyes darted to her.

Before she could defend herself, Saint Valentine stepped forward. "Paris was with me when this happened."

"She could have poisoned the soup before she left with you," Agent Topaz offered.

"Yeah, because not all eyes were on me the entire time I've been at dinner," Paris retorted sarcastically. "I kind of was the center of attention, unfortunately, even with Saint Valentine in attendance."

"Who was sitting right there," Chef Ash said in a startled voice as the realization suddenly dawned on him. He pointed at the seat where the dead agent still perched.

Willow gasped. Paris drew in a breath. Saint Valentine narrowed his blue eyes and nodded.

"You're right," he affirmed. "Agent Opal must have accidentally taken my seat when I left, thinking it was his."

"Which means that the poisoner intended the soup for you," Hemingway added, pure shock written on his face.

Agent Ruby shook his head and clicked his tongue. "How disturbing. This is unprecedented."

"It is," Willow agreed, visibly still shaking. "I don't know what protocol is for this type of thing."

"I do," Paris cut in.

Agent Topaz nodded. "Why am I not surprised?"

She glanced at him. "My uncle is a detective for the Fairy Law Enforcement Agency."

"Adopted uncle, I'm guessing," Agent Ruby said flatly.

No one knew or could know that Uncle John wasn't a fairy. It would blow his cover, which was also keeping Alicia's story under wraps until Liv could take back her position as a Warrior for the

House of Fourteen. Therefore, Paris simply had to ignore this statement.

"I don't think it's relevant how they are related." Hemingway turned to Paris. "Can you call your uncle to investigate?"

"I've already done that," Wilfred said from the entryway. "It made the most logical sense and was what I assumed the headmistress would order once the shock wore off."

"Good." Willow sighed. "We will need to open up a guest portal for Detective Nicholson."

"I've already taken care of that," Wilfred stated.

"Well, it appears that as usual, you have everything under control, Willow," Saint Valentine said, the picture of poise even standing next to a dead body. "I trust you will relay all details directly to my office once the investigation is underway."

She nodded while knitting her hands together.

"I also assume that Detective Nicholson will take care of the body and all." Saint Valentine still looked intently at Willow.

She nodded again.

"Then I think it best that I take my leave," Saint Valentine stated. "I'm not sure why someone would want me dead, but I trust that extreme measures will be in place from here on out."

"Sir, I think that under the circumstances, we might consider closing the school," Agent Ruby stated. "There's a killer in our midst."

Saint Valentine shook his head. "There's a coward for sure. Poison is the coward's murder weapon."

"We can't shut down the school," Willow argued. "The students shouldn't be negatively affected by this."

"What if it's one of them who did this?" Agent Topaz countered.

"Strangely enough, this only happened once agents infiltrated the school," Paris boldly challenged.

"Strangely enough," Agent Ruby echoed smugly, "this happened when someone with demon blood entered our college."

"Yes, and it was you who announced this information to the entire class," Paris remarked and stood straighter. She knew someone was setting her up. It had to be, but she needed more information. "Brilliant timing, right before something scandalous happened."

"I don't know what you're insinuating, Miss Beaufont," Agent Ruby said in a cutting tone.

"I think it's quite clear," Paris replied. "What motive did you have for sharing my secret with the school? A secret that was shared with you by the Montgomery family, who aren't quiet about wanting me out of Happily Ever After College."

"The Montgomery family wants what's best for the college," Agent Ruby stated. "And there is zero way an agent is behind this treachery. Murder simply isn't in our being. Fairies create love. It is magicians who are notorious for creating wars."

"Magicians create order. We create change based on evolving ideas," Paris argued. "From my observations, there are a lot at FGA who are resistant to such things, especially if they lose control."

Agent Ruby sighed impatiently. "Again, Miss Beaufont, fairies simply aren't capable of murder."

"That's false," a familiar voice said from the entryway.

Paris turned to find one of her favorite people striding over. Uncle John looked so out of place based on where she was used to seeing him, but he was the most welcome sight. His long brown trench coat billowed out behind him as he made his way over to the group.

His kind eyes skirted to Paris, a slight look of comfort in them before he focused on Saint Valentine. "I'm Detective Nicholson, and I'm sorry for your loss. I'm sure this is very disturbing for you."

Saint Valentine nodded, although still the pillar of strength.

Uncle John ran his hands through his white hair as he looked at the dead body at the table. "Although I know fairies prefer to focus on love and positive emotions, I'm sorry to inform you that outside of Happily Ever After College and FGA, quite a few criminals belong to our magical race. Actually, because fairies tend to be governed by their emotions, they have a tendency toward desperate acts."

"That's simply unfathomable," Agent Ruby refuted. "If that were the case, we'd know about it at FGA."

"How would you with your head stuck in the sand and your obsession with only focusing on matchmaking for the famous and elite?" Paris challenged.

All eyes swiveled to her. Agent Ruby winced as if she'd whipped him with her remark.

Before he said anything, Saint Valentine held up a hand, pausing the two's argument. "It's true that acts of violence would go unnoticed by the Matters of the Heart office or anything I govern. I suspect that FLEA has a much better grasp of such instances."

"I can take over from here." Uncle John pulled a vial from his jacket pocket.

"I'm not sure how comfortable I feel with the detective on this case having a connection to one of the suspects," Agent Ruby said bitterly.

"Paris isn't a suspect," Willow argued. "Saint Valentine stated that she was with him in the other room when Agent Opal was poisoned. There's simply no evidence to support such a notion."

Uncle John nodded, using a dropper to fill the vial with the supposedly poisoned soup. "All are assumed innocent until proven guilty. I will need to question everyone present when the murder happened privately."

He turned his attention to Saint Valentine. "Since you and Paris appear to have been the only ones not here, I will need one of you to take this vial for testing. Timing is crucial, and the longer there's a delay, the less viable the results."

Saint Valentine nodded and leaned on his cane. "I am fine with Paris taking the vial—"

"Sir, I must object," Agent Ruby interrupted. "There is simply too much speculation around the halfling."

"Again, agent, Paris isn't a suspect," Saint Valentine stated. "She is a change agent. She is an obstacle to those who prefer the status quo at FGA. But she is definitely not a murderer. Since my life as leader of FGA is in danger, I'm going back to Matters of the Heart at once." He gave Paris a sturdy expression. "I trust you can deliver the vial so that the investigation can proceed."

"Yes," Uncle John stated. "Paris knows the shop on Roya Lane and can get it there quickly. Only the potions master at the Rose Apothecary can tell us the composition of that poison and hopefully how and who made it."

Agent Ruby's gaze flickered to Agent Topaz and Saint Valentine. "Well, if that's the decision, I say we get going. The sooner this investigation is conducted, the sooner we can get answers. I, for one, am not at all comfortable knowing there's a murderer in our midst."

CHAPTER FORTY-SEVEN

It had been many years since Paris had been in the Rose Apothecary. She had little reason to enter the shop located next to Heals Pills, which she now knew was owned by her Aunt Sophia and King Rudolf Sweetwater. However, since time was of the essence, Paris kept her head down as she passed Heals Pills, hoping not to be diverted by the fae's antics or delayed by Ramy Vance accidentally killing himself.

The smell of sulfur and oranges was strong in the air when Paris entered the Rose Apothecary. It was such a strange combination that Paris didn't know whether to plug her nose or take in the odor out of curiosity.

The potion shop was mostly bare-bones with an open floor and the products lining shelves along the walls. On the far side of the store, two women looked up—one Paris recognized and one that she almost didn't. It had been a long time since she'd seen Bep, the potions master at the Rose Apothecary. This wasn't Paris' first time to run evidence from a detective case to Bep, although it had been a while.

The woman tilted her head, her short brown curls flopping to the side. She seemed to recognize Paris but not place her.

"Do you owe me money?" Bep asked her as Paris strode over to the counter where she sat.

"No, but she owes *me* money," Lee, the assassin baker, said from beside Bep and crossed her arms.

Paris scoffed at the co-owner of the Crying Cat Bakery. "No, I don't. What are you talking about?"

"Remember I did that one thing for you," Lee said critically.

"You let me use your shop to portal out of Roya Lane," Paris stated. "Is that what you mean?"

"No, remember I took care of that little problem for you," Lee explained. "Now that guy who yelled at your herd of alpacas is sleeping with the fishes."

"First of all, I hope you didn't kill someone for that," Paris began. "Second, I don't have any alpacas."

"Why don't you have alpacas?" Bep asked as if that was suddenly a burning question for her. "They are devilishly helpful animals. So many parts of them are useful in magical spells, from their saliva to their hair."

"How do you get alpaca saliva…you know what, never mind." Paris waved off the potions maker, returning her focus to Lee, too curious not to pursue this conversation. "We're only tabling this alpaca topic for a moment. First off, I'm here on official detective business for FLEA."

Lee's hands went for something in her back pocket. "We can make this hard or difficult, but I won't go down without a fight."

Paris shook her head. "No, I'm not here to investigate you. Hold your horses for a moment, and I'll get to you later."

"I don't have horses because they make the worst getaway vehicle," Lee mumbled, kicking at the floor. "I'm saving up for a stand up elliptical bike."

Even though Paris knew that the vial of poisoned soup needed immediate evaluation, she couldn't help herself. Blinking at Lee, she said, "Why would you use that giant contraption as a getaway vehicle? That has to be way worse than a horse. Why not get a bike?"

Lee shrugged. "I don't like spandex. And I don't want to ride anything. It feels unnatural. Instead, with a stand up elliptical bike, I feel like it's riding me."

"Again, I'm putting a pin in that conversation. First, Detective Nicholson needs Bep's expertise." She pulled the vial from her pocket and handed it to Bep. "He asked that you run tests on that for composition and anything else that you can determine about who made it."

Lee's eyes widened, and a grin spread on her face. "Oh, there's been a muuurrrrrder. Since we know it wasn't me *this* time, can I play detective too? I have a brand new magnifying glass."

"Thanks, Sherlock, but I think we're good." Paris shook her head. "I don't think it's wise to indirectly admit that you didn't do *this* murder, meaning you aren't innocent of others."

Lee rolled her eyes. "You're just like your aunt. Sophia was always like, 'Stop telling me about your murder weapons,' or, 'I really shouldn't know about your assassin activities.'" Lee shook her head. "It's like she didn't want to know anything about my life. I mean, I knew that she rode around on a winged Pegasus—"

"Dragon," Paris interrupted.

"Same thing," Lee said at once. "I know that she fights against stupidity."

"She upholds justice," Paris corrected.

"Again, same thing," Lee muttered.

Returning her attention to Bep, Paris watched as the potions expert swirled the vial contents around. "Do you think you can help? Unc—I mean, Detective Nicholson said that the poison was time-sensitive, and the sooner you examined it, the better."

Bep raised an eyebrow at her. "Why should I help someone who doesn't have a single alpaca?"

Paris sighed. She'd missed the loons on Roya Lane. These were the types of people who made for good stories at dinner parties. "Maybe this once you'll overlook the fact that I don't have an alpaca."

"Are you planning on getting one?" Bep held up the vial as though whether she examined it or not hung in the balance based on Paris' answer.

"I have a talking squirrel. Does that count?" Paris asked.

"Who doesn't." Lee scoffed.

Bep looked Paris over. "Where is this talking squirrel?"

She shrugged. "I don't know, trying to classify genomes or inventing something."

Bep shook her head. "I've changed my mind. You shouldn't have an alpaca. They like docile owners and not ones who will make them memorize the periodic charts."

"I don't make him… Actually… You know what, never mind." Paris decided to give up reasoning with these two. She figured she should pop some LSD and take the trip with them. However, Saint Valentine and Happily Ever After College needed her help. "Can you please help me with the poison? We need to know what's in it and who made it."

Bep pulled the cap off the vial and sniffed. "Besides carrots? There are definitely carrots in this."

Lee nodded. "That would probably send me to my grave too. Don't you dare put carrots in my drink."

"That's soup," Paris corrected. "Yes, we hoped you could tell us the poison and maybe who and how they made it. Anything that will help us to narrow down who did this."

Bep sniffed it again. "It was made by a fairy."

Paris' heart beat fast. That immediately absolved her of the crime, even if Saint Valentine and Willow weren't defending her innocence. "Not by someone who was a magician?" she asked hopefully, having to get the confirmation from the potion's expert.

Bep gave Paris an incredulous look as if this was the most ridiculous notion ever. "Does this look like something made with an acute eye for detail and precision? With a thorough working knowledge of how various ingredients interact?"

Paris tilted her head. "Nooooo," she answered with uncertainty.

"Of course not," Bep stated. "This is sloppy work."

"A fairy obviously made it." Lee glanced at the vial.

"How can you tell?" Paris asked.

"Well, it's an act of love," Lee stated. "That's apparent by how they made it."

"It is?" Paris questioned. "But they used it to try and murder Saint Valentine."

"Exactly," Lee reasoned. "Most murders are fueled by love. I mean, all of mine are. I love for all dumb people to be dead."

Paris stuck her finger in her ear and wiggled it around as if loosening wax or maybe more accurately trying to plug her ears. "Maybe less talk about the killing people thing you do."

Lee sighed. "It's always about the Beaufonts. Neeeeever about me."

"Also, if a magician made this," Bep continued, "the poison would have been slowly folded into the batch, making it blend in with color and odor. A fairy though, they don't think of spellwork as work, but rather as art. They approach most things that way as though they're making a Pollock-style painting. It's all haphazard paint flicking."

Paris nodded, thinking of all the ballroom dancing and cooking classes she'd been taking. "Yeah, they are more about crafting pretty things than making practical things."

"Exactly," Bep stated. "This will take a more thorough examination, but two things are immediately obvious to me about this potion."

"A fairy made it," Paris guessed.

Bep nodded. "The poison, which isn't blended well, is deadly nightshade."

CHAPTER FORTY-EIGHT

"Keep the coffee coming," Uncle John said to Wilfred as he poured him a cup of dark roast Columbian.

The mortal disguised as a fairy glanced up at Paris when she breezed into the sitting room of the fairy godmothers' mansion with a preliminary written report from Bep at the Rose Apothecary. Knowing that she needed written evidence for Saint Valentine and Willow, Paris had Bep write it out. However, the full report with details that could point to who made the poison would take more time.

"Hey Pare," Uncle John greeted as Wilfred held out a cup of coffee to Paris, offering to pour her one.

She shook her head at the butler. "I'm good, but thanks. Would you mind taking Casanova out of here? I have to talk to my uncle." Sensing the confusion on the magitech butler's face, Paris added. "He's allergic to cats." Paris pointed at her uncle.

Realizing that she had her reasons, Uncle John kept his lip buttoned and scribbled notes with his head down.

"Of course, Miss Beaufont." Wilfred laid down the cup and saucer on the coffee tray and shooed the fat orange cat off the sofa and out of the room. He pulled the glass doors shut behind him.

Paris slumped onto the sofa, suddenly feeling as exhausted as her Uncle John looked. "You've been at it all night, haven't you?"

He nodded. "There were quite a few people to interview. Over two dozen people in that dining room when the murder happened."

Paris threw her head back, suddenly having a surreal moment thinking that a murder happened inside Happily Ever After College. She didn't want to believe that she'd brought it on because she'd showed up with her magician half and demon blood. When she thought about it, Paris knew the truth. This was something that had been building for a while, and her presence had sparked it because the college was evolving. Some wanted that, and some didn't—so much so that they'd kill to stop progress.

"Why did you tell Wilfred I was allergic to cats?" Uncle John asked. "You know that I've never condoned you lying."

She nodded, slightly shameful. "I know. It's that Wilfred can't keep a secret if pressed and I don't like to put my friends in bad situations."

"Because you're a good friend," he offered.

Paris shrugged. "Anyway, Casanova is a tattle cat, and it's best if he doesn't overhear this conversation."

"Because you learned who did it?" Uncle John's eyes widened.

"Not quite," Paris replied. "But close. Anyway, because I wanted to ask about Pickles, and I didn't think you wanted anyone knowing that you had a chimera or are a Mortal Seven."

He understood at once and sipped his still-hot coffee. "Yes, I do appreciate that. I need to keep my identity under wraps until Liv and Stefan are ready. The timing has to be perfect. Alicia and Fane can't step down as Warriors for the House of Fourteen until they are ready to take their places. Therefore, I have to stay in place because if any of us abandons our roles, it makes the whole house of cards fall apart."

"We talked about this before, but will you go back to how things were when my mom and dad return?" Paris asked. "Before you said you wouldn't because without them, it would be too painful, but when they are back in their apartment above the electronic repair store, then will you?"

Uncle John considered this for a moment. "I think there's a lot to be decided. I haven't had the opportunity to see Liv yet."

"Yeah, hopefully soon," Paris added.

He nodded his head. "Yeah, hopefully soon. I do like my job as a detective for FLEA, although the hours are lousy. I guess we will see. We're all waiting for Liv and Stefan to come back. Then we can go back if that's what we want. It will be weird, especially at first."

"Fane and Alicia?" Paris questioned. "Will they willingly step down as Warriors for the House of Fourteen? They've had those positions for fifteen years."

"Both Fane and Alicia only ever took those positions out of obligation," Uncle John stated.

"Maybe they've grown into them now," Paris argued. "Because my parents have come back doesn't mean they'll want to part with them."

"I'm not sure. I can tell you that neither Alicia nor Fane would be alive or healthy or have had any further opportunities in their lives if it wasn't for your mother. She saved both of them. So I think when she and Stefan return, they'll be happy to step down. I know a little about Alicia, and I'm sure she'll look forward to returning to her passion for creating magitech. As for the rest of her life, well, she might keep it. I don't know. A lot changes in fifteen years."

"She still loves you." Paris sensed his hidden meaning.

He looked at her suddenly. "Did she say something to you about me?"

"Not any more than before," Paris admitted. "How can she not? I mean, I know she married Uncle Clark to take the position at the House of Fourteen, but that's like you making so many sacrifices. You all are amazing and did that to protect my parents and me. Soon you all can return to your old lives or new lives or whatever."

Uncle John reached out and patted her thoughtfully. "We will see, Pare. A lot of time has passed. I have no expectations because how can I?"

"Well, you're right that we're not there yet, but hopefully soon." Paris suddenly thought that maybe she did need a cup of coffee. "I wanted to ask you about Pickles. I haven't had a chance, but this seems perfect."

Uncle John chuckled and knocked back his coffee. "So he helped, did he? I'm glad for that."

"Yes, he saved my life. He was your protector as a Mortal Seven, and you had him locked in my locket?" Paris remembered the locket opening during her battle with the Deathly Shadow and being surprised by the chimera's sudden appearance.

"Pickles saves the day once again," Uncle John sang, shaking his head with gleeful laughter. "That's my boy."

"You gave him up for me," Paris argued. "I bet you missed him."

"I did," Uncle John admitted. "Remember that I couldn't be recognized as a Mortal Seven. It made the most sense that we put him in the locket to protect you if you ever needed it. That was our insurance, in a way, if anything ever happened and we couldn't save you. Your Aunt Sophia thinks of everything."

Paris nodded. "You did miss him. He's free now. Has he returned yet?"

Remorse covered Uncle John's face before he replaced it with a neutral expression. "Oh, he knows that things are like before. I'm a detective for FLEA. No one can see me as a Mortal Seven. Then everything will blow up in our faces before your parents can safely take their roles. That's the key. We all play the part a little longer, and when Liv and Stefan return, we can drop the act and do as we like."

"Soon," Paris said with confidence.

"Soon," Uncle John reiterated, not sounding as confident.

Paris pulled Bep's report from her leather jacket. "So, there's more information to come, but this will hopefully help with the investigation."

Uncle John gave her a heavy look as his eyes darted to the report she handed him and her eyes. "This has all been a lot for the college and Saint Valentine's office, and I'm sure you too."

"You heard that the school and soon the world has learned I have demon blood?" Paris asked.

He nodded gravely. "Willow told me. I'm sorry. I'm sure that wasn't something you wanted others to know. Then this mess happened." Uncle John tapped his notebook of interviews with the report. "I feel like there's something I'm missing in all this. I mean, the students don't have a motive to take down Saint Valentine. Many of the instructors do because he's in charge of so much of the college. It's FGA who is forcing his hand here. The leader of FGA had a lot of influence, but not totally. It's a very complicated mess of interworking relationships."

Paris nodded. "I suspect that the person who wanted to take Saint Valentine out wants total power. Right now, it's fluctuating between the board, the agents, and his office of Matters of the Heart."

"So it's someone who has partial power and maybe wants to take him out?"

"Well, it doesn't make any sense for someone at the college to do it," Paris pointed out. "Most feel supported by Saint Valentine. In my conversation with him right before the incident, he told me he wanted change, but not too fast. He wanted to do what was best. This isn't a person making sweeping changes."

"According to many, he is still open to new ideas, and that's met with hesitation from some."

"So someone has a reason to want him out," Paris muttered while thinking to herself.

Uncle John indicated his notebook with the folded report. "I have a lot of suspects. There are more than a few with a motive. The agents are here supervising at the board's request, meaning that it's against Saint Valentine's."

Paris nodded. "He's supposed to make recommendations about our curriculum based on the agents' review, but the board will make the final decisions."

"Very complicated organization the FGA has," Uncle John observed. "Then there are the old families with deep pockets who make up the board."

"Like the Montgomerys," Paris muttered. "They're the ones who outed me out for having demon blood. I'm certain they were trying to get me kicked out."

"Willow said you're safe."

"For now," Paris added.

"Then there are a few faculty and students who seem to think that FGA could run differently, but it's not clear if they think that's a management issue or a holistic one," Uncle John continued. "What's not clear is who had access to the soup right before Saint Valentine would eat it. No one saw anyone around his seat beforehand besides the agent who unfortunately died."

"Well, the preliminary report won't give you too many insights," Paris cautioned, "but it will give you a way to narrow things down. Bep will have more information in a day or two."

Uncle John opened the report and scanned it. His eyes sprang wide with relief as he read. "It says that a pure fairy most likely made the potion."

"That's not me," Paris confirmed.

"Good news," he cheered. "That will get many off your back after the reveal of your demon blood."

"Yeah, talk about timing," Paris groused. "The school finds out I'm a demon, and *bam*, there's the first murder at Happily Ever After College. It still seems like someone was gunning for me."

"If they are, I'll find them, Pare."

She nodded appreciatively.

He continued to read before lowering the report. "Deadly nightshade."

"It's been going missing lately," Paris offered. "Hemingway told me about it recently. Actually, it only recently started growing here at the college."

"How recent?"

"Like, in the last few weeks."

"So before the agents showed up," he speculated.

Paris nodded.

Uncle John's face went slack. "Do you think that a student or faculty member planted it to harvest for this exact reason?"

Paris gave him a pointed look. "Only one person will know."

CHAPTER FORTY-NINE

Hemingway glanced up when Paris and her Uncle John entered the greenhouse. He smiled at the sight of Paris and then, to her surprise, even wider after recognizing Uncle John behind her.

The sun was starting to rise over Happily Ever After College. Thankfully the fairy godmothers had set Uncle John up with a place for the night so that he didn't have to keep traveling back and forth. Portal magic might be fast and seemingly effortless, but it could be taxing on one's body—especially a mortal's.

Hemingway held up a small trowel and pointed it in Uncle John's direction. "That tip you gave me on fly fishing is going to come in handy."

Uncle John chuckled easily. "I'm telling you, it will have them jumping straight into your net."

Confused, Paris looked between the two. "Did you all talk fishing the entire time you interrogated him?" she asked Uncle John.

He shook his head. "I didn't interrogate. I questioned. There was no reason to question Hemingway Noble here. It was pretty obvious that he didn't have anything to hide and wasn't the murderer. After a while, you get a sense for these kinds of things, and Hemingway doesn't fit the bill."

Hemingway leaned forward and winked. "Also, I figured out straight away that Detective Nicholson wasn't a fairy."

Paris was about to spring into excuses, but Uncle John laughed. "Yeah, it takes an imposter to know one."

Totally confused, Paris looked between the two. "Wait, you two figured out that you both aren't who you say you are? Like, together?"

They both nodded.

"Oh, yeah," Uncle John stated. "I took one look at Hemingway and knew. What's funny is that he had the same moment."

"We're both connected to you, so we figured out that we were safe with each other's secrets." Hemingway heaved a giant sigh. "You know, before you Paris, no one knew my secret besides Headmistress Starr and Mae Ling. It feels good to be myself. To not be hiding something."

Still confused, Paris looked between the two. "So for you two, the glamour doesn't work? You both can see that you two aren't fairies?"

"Well, it's more like we recognized that we were disguising," Uncle John stated. "I've been doing it for so long that it felt like I was looking in the mirror."

Hemingway nodded. "During my private talks with Detective Nicholson, he explained why he pretended to be a fairy, and I can't think of a more noble reason."

"Says the man with the surname 'Noble,'" Uncle John said with a belly laugh. He pointed at Hemingway. "I like this guy so much that I gave him my best fly fishing tips."

Paris huffed. "You don't even tell me your fly fishing tips."

"I also don't take you fly fishing," he muttered and cupped his hand to his mouth, whispering loudly to Hemingway. "She talks…a lot."

Paris shook her head. "That's fine. I'm leaving you at home when I go…well, I have no idea where I'd go without you. You're so damn well-behaved."

Uncle John nodded good-naturedly. "I'm glad to hear it. I've always tried not to embarrass you, Pare."

She caught Hemingway smiling fondly at her and Uncle John. "What is it?"

Realizing that she'd caught him, Hemingway glanced down and

dug in the container he'd been working on when they entered. "Oh, nothing."

"What is it?" she pursued.

Hemingway didn't look up, just continued to dig around in the pot. "Nothing. You seem like such a loner but seeing you with your uncle, well, it makes you seem…"

"Human," Paris supplied.

To her surprise, Uncle John chuckled. "I know you two are friends, so I'll tell you, Hemingway, that when Paris came along, we all lost it."

Paris tensed, thinking he was about to tell how her existence brought great evil to the world, hungry for her. Instead, he smiled wide.

"I'd seen extraordinary magic and humanity clinging onto its very existence," Uncle John continued. "I'd thought I'd seen it all." He gave Paris one of the most sentimental looks she'd witnessed on his face. "It wasn't until we all laid eyes on Guinevere Paris Beaufont that we saw the magic of a real human. Soft like a fairy. Strong like a magician. And full of fire. I can't think of any better mixture." He nodded at Hemingway. "So, yeah, she's pretty human. The way Mother Nature intended them to be, a perfect mix of many races."

"Well, thanks." Paris blushed as her hands went behind her back. "Here I was, worried that my uncle coming to the college would be awkward."

Uncle John laughed and waved her off. "I'm here on business. You're helping. You too, Hemingway." He indicated the guy shaking dirt off his hands. "We hoped you could tell us more about this deadly nightshade that's gone missing."

"Oh?" Hemingway suddenly looked confused. "Do you think that deadly nightshade was involved in Agent Opal's murder?"

"We know," Paris answered. "The killer was fairy."

"Which is another reason I know it wasn't you." Uncle John winked.

"This fairy used deadly nightshade," Paris continued. "Since you said it went missing from the greenhouse, I hoped you could tell us about the timeframe."

"Yeah, when did it start going missing?" Uncle John added.

"Oh, recently," Hemingway answered at once. "In the last week, for sure."

"You said that it's increasingly been popping up in the Bewilder Forest lately," Paris began. "Do you think it's possible that someone started planting it to harvest it? Maybe for the exact purpose of taking out Saint Valentine?"

She was thinking of Becky Montgomery or one of the other more conservative students who kept a low profile but silently didn't like how things ran at Happily Ever After College.

However, to her surprise, Hemingway adamantly shook his head. "No one planted the deadly nightshade."

"How do you know?" Paris asked.

"Because the seeds are rare," Hemingway answered. "I had the same question, so I looked into it. The plant doesn't reproduce from seeds. Not usually."

"How does it sprout?" Uncle John asked.

"It's magical," Hemingway explained. "So magic brings it around or spreads other plants."

"Oh, so someone used magic to make the deadly nightshade." Paris ran through the options of who it could be.

"Yes, that's what I've decided." Hemingway dropped his gaze.

"They'd have to be someone powerful," Paris mused and chewed on her lip, trying to think.

Hemingway nodded. "Correct."

"Plus skillful," Paris continued.

Another nod. "That's right." Hemingway looked nervous.

"And I guess, someone who wants to cause harm," Uncle John supplied.

Hemingway held up a finger covered in dirt and paused him. "That's where you're wrong."

Paris and Uncle John both shot him confused looks.

"So this person grew a deadly plant but without the intent of using it for evil?" Paris questioned.

Hemingway nodded. "Yeah, I believe that the person who caused the deadly nightshade to grow in the Bewilder Forest is you, Paris."

CHAPTER FIFTY

It felt like Hemingway had knocked the air out of Paris without touching her. Her mouth hung open as she tried to will a breath into her lungs.

"Pare?" Uncle John finally broke the silence. "That doesn't seem right."

"I think it is, though." Hemingway wiped his hands on a cloth, cleaning off the dirt. "It's your demon blood." He gave her a consoling look, sensing her trepidation about the sensitive subject still.

"I'm not evil," she argued.

He nodded. "I know. I was confused at first when the deadly nightshade started popping up. In twenty years, I'd never seen it here in the Bewilder Forest. Then you showed up, and it did too. However, I know enough about plants and the earth to understand that it responds to those around it. At Happily Ever After College, we get certain plants that only grow around fairies, like honeysuckle and hibiscus flowers.

"Sweet flowers," Uncle John observed.

"Exactly," Hemingway affirmed. "However, when I showed up, Mae Ling pointed out all the succulents that started sprouting around the forest."

"Hardy plants that can withstand drought and harsh conditions." Uncle John grinned. "Like a magician."

"That's what got me thinking," Hemingway continued. "Certain plants are cued based on the magical race around them. Since you've shown up here, Paris, we've had hummingbird hawk-moths, a whole host of intelligent plants used in unique elixirs, and deadly nightshade."

"Because of my demon blood," Paris guessed.

"Yes, but it's not a bad thing," Hemingway pointed out. "Remember that deadly nightshade, when used correctly, is a wonderful sedative that is crucial in operations and medical treatments. It's all about the way you use it."

"Just like it's all about how you use your blood, Pare," Uncle John offered. "Like you use your demon blood to propel you for good."

Paris sighed, not having expected this. "So I made the deadly nightshade grow in the Bewilder Forest."

"Yes, but it was someone evil who took it to create a poison and try to kill Saint Valentine," Hemingway asserted.

"That's not on you, Pare," Uncle John emphasized, already sensing she was worried that she'd had a hand in this.

Paris nodded, deciding at once that she'd fix this the only way she could. "Yeah, so we have to figure out what fairy knew how to use deadly nightshade and stole it."

"Then we will find out who our killer is," Uncle John said victoriously, smiling proudly at his niece.

CHAPTER FIFTY-ONE

Headmistress Willow Starr kept looking over her shoulder toward the fairy godmother mansion. "You need to get out of here now. Mae Ling can't hold the FGA agents off for much longer."

The fairy godmother ushered Paris, Christine, and Faraday farther toward the Bewilder Forest. Thankfully, a large oak trunk blocked them from view from the mansion. Still, the agents had been patrolling all over the Enchanted Grounds, snooping, and there was no telling when one would poke his nose into their business.

"So you're okay with us going forward with this plan?" Paris needed to ensure she wasn't going to cause more problems for the headmistress after everything.

Headmistress Starr wavered. "I don't see what choice we have. The love meter is low. Saint Valentine doesn't feel that he can trust those around him at FGA. You two have found enough evidence to suggest someone is corrupting love and sabotaging relationships. At this point, our best bet is to gain more information. The FGA board wants us to do less than ever before. Plus, the divide between Matters of the Heart has never been so great. We have to do something. In light of the attempts on Saint Valentine's life, I have to do something major, and this is my best bet. I can't go. I have to play headmistress, but I can make an excuse for why you two are gone for the day."

"I have an awful headache," Paris supplied.

"I'm on holiday with my parents in the Canary Islands," Christine added. "They'd never holiday there because it's way too much fun and tropical, and we might have a good time."

"That's your excuse?" Paris teased.

Christine nodded. "Yeah, if I'm living vicariously through my fake self. Deal with it."

Headmistress Starr smiled pleasantly at the two. "Be careful. Don't take chances. I can't imagine what you'll face to investigate FriendNet for us."

"It's going to be awful," Paris admitted. "We're disguising ourselves as hippies." She twirled her hand, and Christine's blue gown disappeared, replaced with a long flowy linen shirt and bohemian pants.

"Oh, wow, this breathes." Christine squatted slightly. Her hair was up in a loose bun with flowers around it.

Paris made herself look similar, turning her shoulder-length hair into dreads and putting a fake tattoo on her forearm with the word "Perfectionist" crossed out. Above that it said, "Be Yourself." On the other arm were several bangles.

"You two look..." the headmistress paused. "Well, like individuals."

Paris sighed. "Yeah, right. Hippies conform to individuality in the most ironic of ways."

"You're a conundrum," Christine stated.

Paris nodded and gave the headmistress a consoling look. "We'll be fine. I know this isn't your usual protocol, but we have to figure out what's going on there. Someone is orchestrating all these problems with relationships."

"You think you can figure it out?" Willow asked.

Paris shook her head. "No, not at all." She pointed at Faraday on the grass beside them. "He understands programming and whatnot much better than us. I think if we distract the FriendNet folks, he can determine what's happening behind the scenes."

Not at all looking confident about putting this in two newbies' hands and a talking squirrel's paws, Headmistress Starr managed a forced nod. "Okay, well, still be careful. I'm counting on you. Saint Valentine, who is under a lot more scrutiny than usual, is counting on you. Still, that's not a reason to take any unnecessary risks."

Paris leaned down and plucked up the squirrel, snuggling him close. "Sounds like our kind of mission. Ready to be my support squirrel?"

He mock-grimaced at her. "I don't like the title, but sure." Then, as the portal to FriendNet materialized, Faraday added, "You're going to owe me for calling me a support squirrel."

She nodded as they stepped through to another place. "Yeah, how about I risk everything to return you to your old life?"

"That might do." Faraday snuggled in close as the portal absorbed them as if he was afraid it might swallow him whole otherwise.

CHAPTER FIFTY-TWO

"Oh. Gods. I'm in hell," Paris muttered when they entered the top floor of FriendNet.

"Yep, there is a land worse than the world of hippies," Christine declared, her arms opened wide. "The urban warehouse of hipsters."

Paris shook her head, hooking her temporary "Consultant" badge onto her flowing pants. Their magic had easily gotten them by the guards and the receptionist, who didn't appear to care that they were there. She had stated that appointments weren't static and had no idea if the head programmers were meeting with a consulting firm.

Paris made a note to take out all hipsters, right after all hippies.

"Oh, wow, your support squirrel really suits you," a guy with a long handlebar mustache said, striding over to Paris and Christine. He appeared to be wearing his younger brother's pants since they came up to his mid-calf. "I once had a snake as my support animal, but he ate my support mouse so I had to get rid of them both."

Paris wanted to clock Handlebar Mustache right then but thought that might blow their cover, so she refrained. "I'm sure they are both happy together now." She forced a smile.

"Let's hope so," the guy said. "So you're the consultants?" He stooped, eyeing her badge. "Oh, Starflake. What a great name."

Christine held out her hand, not having a badge. "My name is Rosewater." She had been so happy with the name she chose and couldn't wait to share it.

He wrung her hand. "Nice to meet you."

"Or meet me again," Christine stated. "We probably collided in a past life." She was enjoying the opportunity to be a dirty hippie.

"Right." Handlebar Mustache drew out the word. "So what do you want to see first? We have our creative space." He threw his arm wide at an area with a pool table and bean bag chairs. "Then we have our other creative space." He indicated an area with darts and records. "And we have the less creative space." The last area he motioned to was a set of offices with floor-to-ceiling windows.

Faraday tugged at Paris' linen top, which made her feel like she was a girl on a beach instead of trying to fix love for the human race. "How about I check out your tunes?" she asked Handlebar Mustache.

"I'd love to challenge one of you in some pool," Christine stated.

Handlebar Mustache chuckled. "No one wins or loses here. We are always winning if we're having a good time."

Again Paris had a moment where she fantasized about putting this guy in a headlock. Instead, she nodded. "That's what my friend meant. She wanted to have a good time at pool with you."

Handlebar Mustache grinned under too much facial hair. "I like you two, consultants. You know how to have fun and see how we operate. The last consultant only wanted to talk to Dash."

"Last consultant?" Paris asked as Handlebar Mustache walked away.

"Oh, yeah, this bloke in a total black suit that looked like it belonged to my dad," the guy stated. "He couldn't have been the least bit comfortable."

Paris and Christine both exchanged looks. Faraday tensed on her shoulder.

"Wow, he sounds like he was out of a Dick Tracy film," Christine joked.

The guy nodded. "Yeah, and he was wearing this hat like in the old films and had this serious look about him. Oh, and a ballpoint pen as if he would take notes at any moment or something. It was totally not of this world. I think there was a ruby heart-shaped gem on the top of his ballpoint pen. Like, is that legal by diamond rights?"

"Right?" Christine asked. "We should have gnomes check into this."

"Sounds magical," Paris said, giving Christine a pointed look. He also sounded like an agent, but he could have been some guy.

"Did Dick Tracy have a name?" Christine asked casually.

The guy shook his head. "If he did, I didn't catch it. We prefer not to go by names here. It weighs us down."

"Yeah, why be able to identify each other and avoid confusion when conversing," Paris pretended to agree.

"My point exactly," the guy stated. "Why not direct questions and statements to everyone? We're all friends here."

No, we're not. Paris wondered if she should punch the guy in the kidneys or the face when she finished here. She decided she'd sweep his little legs out from under him and let the concrete do the work.

"So this Dash," Christine said, twirling an errant piece of hair that had come loose from her messy bun. "Is he at yoga or something?"

Handlebar Mustache shook his head. "He's at the poker tournament in the breakroom. I'll get him and you two some craft beer if you'd like. How does that sound?"

"It sounds okay," Christine answered, the perfect picture of cool.

Totally buying the act, the guy trotted off, leaving the three alone in the middle of FriendNet Corporation.

CHAPTER FIFTY-THREE

"I'm going to kill these people," Paris whispered to her friends.

"Not if I kill them first," Christine replied. "Like, I've known people who were the worst, but these guys make them seem like rich panhandlers, who are the second-worst after these guys.

"Your example didn't have to be so literal," Paris muttered.

"Sorry," Christine muttered. "The lack of air conditioning and lack of paint on the exposed walls is getting to me."

"Did that consultant sound a lot like an agent for FGA?" Paris ignored the awesome and yet distracting humor of her friend.

"That definitely sounded like an agent," Faraday squeaked inconspicuously on Paris' shoulder so only she and Christine could hear him.

"I-I-I don't know," she stammered, looking around at the open space. "I think we need more evidence."

"Like shots from security cameras and whatnot?" Faraday asked.

"Well, I thought of asking the inner girl circle here for sketches of the most uptight guys to stroll in here in the last ninety days," Christine stated. "But I get now why you brought the squirrel. That guy is smart."

"I know." Paris winked at him. "So you think you can hack in and find the security system thing-a-ma-jig or whatever you call it?"

"Do you mean the security system?" Faraday asked.

Paris shrugged. "I guess if that's what you call it."

"That's what everyone calls it," he remarked.

"You can look through to see if one of the FGA agents has been here?" she asked.

"I can try," he answered. "Isn't my first job to determine if there's coding that's making it so couples are pitted against each other on FriendNet, resulting in breakups?"

Christine sighed dramatically. "While you're pretty much doing nothing, I have to maintain a conversation with a hipster about things that aren't cool and music that's irrelevant and doesn't sound good. And I might have to eat something like hummus to fool them into thinking I'm a hipster. Have you had hummus, Faraday? No one likes it. Ever…"

Paris had to stifle her laughter. "It's true. Hummus is for those who are trying to persuade themselves into believing that cheese isn't the nectar of the gods."

"Cheese isn't the nectar of the gods," Faraday corrected. "I believe that's—"

"Oh, would you go already and do your squirrel business?" Christine waved him off Paris' shoulder, where he ran down to the floor and scurried through the open space to the offices on the other side of the area

Paris laughed. "It's funny how you pretended that the squirrel wasn't our only way to figure all this out."

Christine forced a bored smile as Handlebar Mustache and another guy with a beard strode in their direction. From cracked lips, she said, "I gave our ride a way to call up our limo."

CHAPTER FIFTY-FOUR

"So play it cool," Christine urged as Handlebar Mustache and a guy with a big beard who was probably twenty-something ambled their way. "By cool, I mean, act like you don't care, and you also care a lot."

Paris gave her friend an annoyed expression.

Christine held up her hands. "What? It's hard being a hipster. I'm sure they're exhausted all the time. No wonder they drink so much coffee."

"Hi!" Paris squeaked as the head programmer walked over with the guy with a mustache. "We were hoping to chill with you two and understand your processes over some froyo if you're down with it."

The guy's faces went through a series of expressions but thankfully settled on passable by the end.

"I was going to grab us some craft beers after I introduced you to Dash," Handlebar Mustache said. He pointed at Paris and Christine. "This is Starflake and Rosewater."

"Cool to meet you. I think some frozen yogurt would be good for my gut health," the guy with the beard said. He shouldn't have one that large until he was a hundred years old, but hipsters excelled in growing facial hair. He turned to his friend. "Would you take our new friend to grab some for us from the organic, dairy-free, vegan, gluten-free shop down the way?"

"Wow, that place sounds so quaint," Paris remarked, sounding dreamy and hating every moment of it.

"It is." Dash looked at Christine. "Do you want to go with my friend to get us yogurt? He can fill you in on our ways during the errand if you like." He indicated Handlebar Mustache, who apparently couldn't have a name because that would make him known and real, and a hipster couldn't have that. Paris decided that after reinstating love, she was killing anyone who used a record player. She should warn them now to throw them out.

"Do I?" Christine gushed, batting her eyes at Handlebar Mustache. "I've already made a friendship bracelet, but let's wait until we've been friends for, like, five years. Then I'll give it to you."

Handlebar Mustache held out his arm to Christine, offering to lead her off, and smiled. "I feel like you might be my multi-soul mate. You get me like only a few dozen in this world might."

Christine nodded and strode off with the sad excuse for a human being, doing her best to keep their cover while Faraday did the real work.

CHAPTER FIFTY-FIVE

Holding out his arm at the open space, Dash glanced at Paris. "Well, what do you want to see? We've innovated things here at FriendNet, but we're always looking for ways to make things more synergistic."

Paris looked around where various people worked on tiny laptops or typewriters on the floor or were seated in the bean bag chairs. She swept her eyes over to the corner office where she'd seen Faraday run off to. Thankfully, he wasn't easily visible typing at a computer, although glass walls enclosed most of the offices. The chair in front of the desk obscured him from view unless she craned her head to the side.

Angling her body to the side, encouraging Dash to put his back to the offices, she pretended to study the area. "Well, my firm specializes in creating workspaces that support maximum inspiration," Paris said in an airy voice earning a smile from Dash.

"Now you're talking my language," Dash stated. "We're always trying to revolutionize our work environment. Like, check this out."

He picked up a small black remote that was lying on the shelf next to a record player. "We were sitting around in here one day. I was like,

I need some fresh air. Someone else was all, 'I wish we didn't have walls confining us.' Then I had this brilliant idea."

Dash clicked a button, and all of the floor-to-ceiling windows retracted, lowering and disappearing. The exterior barriers to the building had pretty much all disappeared, save for support beams along the walls and corners. A sharp breeze shot straight into the warehouse office space.

Paris covered her exposed arms, missing her leather jacket. "Whoa, aren't we on the twenty-sixth floor?"

Dash nodded proudly. "Yeah, pretty cool, huh? It's my outdoor-slash-indoor office."

Paris neared the closest windowed areas, which were completely open now. She peered over the edge where the window, a barrier, and wall of sorts, had been seconds prior. There was no guard rail. She looked down to the alleyway below, getting a daunting feeling as the crisp San Francisco winds swept into the office, not stopped by a window or a wall any longer.

Pulling back, Paris worked to keep the repulsed expression off her face. "Is that safe? Anyone could fall out."

"We've all embraced that could be our fate," Dash stated. "Isn't it worth it to have a conducive workspace? I mean, how are we supposed to do our best work with walls caging our creativity."

"Yeah, I feel you," Paris muttered, wondering if she'd get kicked out of Happily Ever After College for killing a bunch of hipsters. She reasoned that they were blocking love with their annoying ways.

"Do you want a tour of the floor?" Dash asked. "We can start with the most stifling areas, our offices." He indicated the area where Faraday was hopefully hacking into FriendNet—gaining covert information. "Then we can work our way to the more creative places and reward ourselves with a treat."

"I don't want to see the offices yet," Paris said in a rush, turning to face the record player. "How about some tunes? That's the best way to introduce me to a space."

"I agree." Dash picked up a record on the top of the stack. "Let's see. Have you heard Blind Pilot? They have a nice mellow sound."

Trying to be cool, Paris nodded. "Yeah, I love them."

He sighed and *chunked* the album onto another stack. "Oh, well, then I'll find something else. This is a new space to you, and you need new music." His eyes lit up. "Oh, in my office, I've got a brand new album that isn't yet released. It's by an experimental band that doesn't use instruments. Mostly, it's ambient noises like lights flickering to life or dishes being put away. Let me go grab that."

"No!" Paris exclaimed too loudly, making many in the open area look up at her. She forced a smile. "I mean, no, that's not my jam. I prefer the banjo."

"Banjo?" Dash asked.

"Only the banjo," Paris stated with conviction.

"You know what you like, and that's impressive." Dash smiled at her.

A cold wind swept through the open office, kicking up loose papers and making Paris' hair fly in her face.

Dash closed his eyes, enjoying the gust of wind that was disrupting the area. The winds on the twenty-sixth floor could be intense in San Francisco most days, and this one was no exception.

Stealing a glance at the office, Paris noticed Faraday getting blown around as he tried to type furiously on the computer. The wind was doing a number on the squirrel since the open wall was directly at his back. Plus, the draft from the opposite end of the large workspace where she and Dash stood was causing suction.

"Isn't this so good for our working spirit?" Dash opened his eyes and looked at Paris.

She jerked her head back, pulling her eyes away from where Faraday was working.

Dash glanced in the direction of the office, skeptical curiosity on his face. Paris desperately hoped he didn't see the look of worry on her face.

"Can I get one of those craft beers?" Paris asked in a rush. "I'm super parched, and I do my best work when I have a libation."

Dash nodded slowly, careful speculation on her. "Yeah, I'll be right back. Make yourself at home."

She plastered a serene, hippie smile on her face and nodded, waving and watching as he retreated for what she guessed was the breakroom on the far side of the open room.

CHAPTER FIFTY-SIX

Trying not to appear as if she was rushing, Paris dawdled along the space, pretending she enjoyed the brisk wind tearing through the open window walls. When she caught sight of Faraday clinging to the keyboard of the computer, his tail whipping in the torrential wind, she hurried, not caring if anyone saw her. She'd say that her support squirrel was exploring and had gotten lost. That had been the plan all along. However, she didn't think that he'd get lost by blowing out the open wall behind Dash's desk.

Nearly running, Paris rushed to the glass-enclosed office. Faraday jerked his head up when she entered the office—his eyes frantic.

"I found evidence of a program that uses algorithms at FriendNet to instigate tensions in relationships," Faraday said urgently, holding onto the mouse for dear life.

Paris looked around for a way to close the wall, but there wasn't one of those little black remotes, and Dash had pocketed the other one. Rushing behind the desk, Paris put herself between the squirrel and the open wall.

"It's incredible," Faraday related, scrolling through what looked like a foreign language to Paris. "There's a giant database full of each FriendNet member's dislikes, exes, allergies, phobias, aversions."

"He's using the data the social media source has on people to make them upset, fight, and break up," Paris said, confirming what she and Christine had speculated. "Can you shut it down? There's like one hundred thousand breakups a day because of this dude."

"I'm working on it but need another minute." Faraday swiveled around from the blistering wind.

"A minute to undo a program set up by this hipster. That's impressive for anyone, especially a squirrel." She worked to put her body more as a shield for the talking squirrel.

"Thanks," Faraday chirped, bouncing around on the keyboard, pecking at it with his paws.

Her eyes flickered to a graduate's diploma certificate on the wall from MIT. "And you're undoing the work of a software engineer from the illustrious Massachusetts Institute of Technology." Paris' eyes narrowed on the name of the degree, and she grimaced. "Oh, hipsters are the worst. Dash is short for raz8.dash."

"Yeah, I thought that was his user name at first, but it's his legal name," Faraday explained, his tail like a flag in the wind.

"Can you tell where the program originated?" Paris asked. "Maybe Dash isn't involved—but finding out where it originated is important. Can you link it to an agent at FGA?"

"I haven't had a chance to check the security cameras," Faraday muttered, the wheels of his brain spinning as he typed out what looked like code to Paris. "I'll try and look into that later, but this program originated from this computer. As far as I can tell, it's isolated."

"Meaning that the chief programmer is behind this. That's what we thought," Paris mumbled, her eyes scanning the admin area outside the office for signs of the hipster.

"Well, shutting this down will pause the problem," Faraday stated. "But he'll figure it out and turn it back on."

Paris tapped the desk impatiently. "That's fine. Just find me some evidence, and I'll snap a picture on my phone. It's all that Willow needs to turn over to Saint Valentine. Then his authority will shut FriendNet down."

CHAPTER FIFTY-SEVEN

FriendNet was hooked into everything. Not only that, but Dash had apps that gave him access to everything from traffic lights to convenience store security cameras. Using a picture he grabbed from the security footage taken in the lobby of FriendNet earlier, Dash uploaded it to his facial recognition app on his phone.

He sensed something was different about Starflake and Rosewater. However, that curiosity had quickly morphed into suspicion when Starflake started acting nervous. *And banjo, really.* He shook his head. Banjos were popular in the West Coast folk music scene. Anyone who had a true appreciation of music wasn't listening to the overly popularized folk stuff.

What made Dash wary of Starflake was that she felt similar to the fairy who had assigned him the breakup project—Agent Ruby. The magical creature from FGA had said that there would be someone who tried to stop their efforts. *Maybe it was a young hippie fairy.* Dash waited for the facial recognition results to populate.

A moment later they did, and his eyes narrowed. The results read:

97% facial match to a Paris Beaufont.

He scrolled through the information listed that was the private property of FriendNet. Although Paris wasn't very active on FriendNet, she had updated her profile recently. She'd been trying to get in touch with some of her exes, but they didn't appear to want anything to do with her.

Dash scrolled through various photos of Paris from the public cameras. She'd been all over recently. The images told a story that most would never have access to. Although much was unclear, one thing was evident to Dash—Paris Beaufont was no consultant.

CHAPTER FIFTY-EIGHT

Agent Ruby picked up the phone after the first ring, wanting an update from the chief programmer from FriendNet. Dash had delivered, doing an excellent job of breaking up couples. The love meter had never been so low.

The FGA board was furious with Saint Valentine, believing his mismanagement led to these problems. No one had connected the plummeting levels of love to FriendNet. Well, no one but Paris Beaufont from what Agent Ruby could discern. He had been intercepting the reports from Matters of the Heart, and it didn't appear that Saint Valentine was aware that FriendNet was behind the low levels of love.

Agent Ruby didn't know how the halfling with demon blood had figured out the problem, which was why he'd enlisted a special spy. He'd learned that Paris and a student named Christine Welsh had taken it upon themselves to research FriendNet, figuring out much of what Dash had done to sabotage love. That wasn't all though, and the bonus information Agent Ruby learned was quite interesting, to say the least.

"What?" Agent Ruby said into the phone, accepting the call.

"We have a situation here at FriendNet," Dash informed him.

"What is it?"

"There are two people here from Happily Ever After College posing as consultants," Dash explained. "Did you send someone? Or are you aware of what they are doing here?"

"I didn't," Agent Ruby said through clenched teeth. "Who are they?"

"I only was able to identify one so far," Dash answered. "Are you familiar with a Paris Beaufont?"

Agent Ruby growled. "I am."

"Well, do you know what she's doing here?"

"She's trying to figure out what we're up to so she can invariably stop us."

"Well, I think it's highly unlikely that she'll be able to find anything of use." Dash uttered a conceited laugh. "I mean, she's a fairy, and I'm a genius programmer."

Agent Ruby's eyes swiveled to the large orange cat named Casanova, sitting next to him in the sitting room of the fairy godmothers' mansion. "Don't underestimate her. Does she have a squirrel with her?"

"Yeah, my buddy said it was her support squirrel before he introduced us," Dash answered. "I saw videos of her talking to it in various places."

"The squirrel talks," Agent Ruby said bitterly, having learned a great deal from the tattle cat.

"No way," Dash muttered.

"Way." Agent Ruby had trouble keeping his patience with the hipster. He glanced at Casanova, who explained about the squirrel named Faraday. "Where is Paris now?"

"Don't worry," Dash stated. "I left her in the community workspace."

"And the squirrel?" Agent Ruby asked.

"Oh, I haven't seen him," Dash answered.

"Go now and find them!" Agent Ruby yelled, turning off the phone and shaking his head. He had no idea that it would be a halfling that caused him problems, but he was still hopeful that his plans were far enough along that she couldn't ruin them.

CHAPTER FIFTY-NINE

"No one is shutting down FriendNet," Dash said, sliding into the doorway, a look of menace on his face.

Paris tensed at the sight of the hipster. "Hi. I'm not sure what you think you heard, but—"

"I heard you talking to that squirrel." Dash pointed at Faraday, who pulled his paw off a key and straightened. He tensed and gave Paris a look like he'd eaten a handful of nuts and was having an allergic reaction. "He was talking back to you."

Paris forced a laugh. "Talking back to me? That's ridiculous. Animals can't talk."

"I heard you talking to him," Dash stated.

"So you didn't hear him speak then?" Dash must have just arrived and heard the last part of her statement.

"I know who you are and what you're up to," Dash said, his eyes murderous.

"I'm sure you don't." Paris sensed that something had suddenly changed since he'd been gone. "I'm sure whatever you're thinking is a misunderstanding."

"So you're not Paris Beaufont? A student for Happily Ever After College—a fairy godmother in training?" He pointed at the squirrel, indiscreetly still pecking at keys, trying to finish the operation to end the program breaking up people at FriendNet. "That's not Faraday, a talking squirrel who is helping you to shut down the program that I have running to end relationships?"

Paris glanced at Faraday before looking back at the hipster. "That was strangely accurate."

"The gig is up," Dash stated. "You're going to leave here right now and as quickly as possible, not telling anyone anything as you go. No phone calls. No talking to Rosewater or whatever her name is. No nothing."

"Wait," Paris blinked, seeing Faraday press a key with his back foot, but ever so slightly so that Dash didn't notice. She needed to buy them time. "You're going to allow me to leave after all this?"

"Well," Dash said smugly. "It's not like it matters. Make a phone call, and I'll know about it. Talk to your friend, and I'll hear. Once you do, well, let's just say you'll regret it." He held up his mobile phone and shook it in the air, a threat in the gesture.

Of course. This programmer controlled everything. He probably had figured Paris out because he had spy software on everything. The moment she left here, he'd use his resources to watch her, do something to come after her if she didn't cooperate. He was probably coming after her regardless of what she did. Still, she had no intention of cooperating, even if it would keep her safe. She was shutting down FriendNet and getting love back on track. A stupid hipster wasn't destroying all the efforts of fairy godmothers.

"Fine, I'll leave and won't tell anyone," Paris began, knowing from reading Faraday's expression that he needed her to buy a little more time. He was very stealthily pressing keys unseen by Dash. "You wanted to break up relationships using FriendNet. Help me to understand why? Was this a scheme to get back at an ex-girlfriend that got out of control?"

"My reasons aren't your concern." He rolled up the sleeves of his flannel shirt.

"Was someone behind this?" Paris remembered that Handlebar

Mustache had mentioned another consultant in a black suit with a bowler hat.

His dark eyes skated to the side as a gust of wind trespassed into the open office, making his beard sway. Paris sensed his tension.

"If someone threatened you, we can protect you," Paris said. "I have people who can ensure that whoever forced you to do this doesn't get away with it."

"They didn't force me!" he exclaimed.

"But you aren't working alone," Paris guessed. "Look, I'm going to leave here as you asked. I won't say a thing to anyone. Just tell me who put you up to bringing down love?"

"My source is none of your concern," Dash stated bitterly.

So he was working for someone. Paris glanced down at Faraday, who was still trying to complete the sequence to stop the programming. She hadn't had a chance to get evidence about this. Since she didn't think that whipping out her phone right then to take pictures was a good idea, she hoped Saint Valentine took her word for it. Now she still needed to stall Dash a little longer.

Her eyes flickered to his diploma on the wall to correct for her looking at Faraday. "So your name…can you please enlighten me?"

He sighed. "I want you out of here!"

"Sure, but so I know, do I address you as raz-eight-period-dash? Is that right?"

Dash shook his head. "My name is raz8.dash."

"Is that a family name?" Paris asked.

"No," he grumbled. "My parents named me John. John…"

"The savages," Paris said sarcastically.

He nodded as if she were serious.

"So is raz the first name? Dash the last? Where does the eight fit in?"

The hipster looked close to losing his temper. "It's easy. My name is raz-eight and pause for the period and dash."

Paris scratched her head, strode over to the diploma, and pointed. "I don't really get it. It's raz-eight." She paused for a moment. "Dash."

"That's right," he said. "But the first initials aren't capitalized."

"Why?" Paris asked, still stalling and hoping that by moving, she'd taken any attention off Faraday.

"Because I don't want to inflate my self-importance," he answered.

"You have a number and punctuation in your name," Paris argued.

"That's so that I can set myself apart and help people to remember to pause between names," he stated.

"Right." Paris drew out the word. "Because nothing says high-maintenance like having to pause when saying a name."

"Do you think I'm stupid?" Dash's gaze was full of anger.

She shrugged. "Well, I wouldn't call you the smartest organic biscotti in the cookie jar."

He pointed in Faraday's direction. "I know that the squirrel thinks he's shutting down my program. It's not going to work. When you leave here, I'm certain that the bus you meet will keep you quiet."

Paris narrowed her gaze at him. That was a threat if ever she heard one. Dash was planning on mowing her down using his techno devices. Paris had just about enough of this guy.

She held up her hand, preparing a combat spell. "Two can play at that game, but only one of us has magic here."

Paris tried to throw a stunning spell at the hipster, but nothing happened. She glanced at her hand, wondering if it had cobwebs on it or whatever would prevent her magic from working.

Dash laughed wickedly. "I have wards on my office. Ever since the last magical creature was in here, I decided to protect myself, in case."

"Other magical creature." Paris still looked at her hand. She'd been able to use magic in the lobby, but it appeared it was blocked there, which was no good for her attempts to escape. She and Faraday might be screwed.

Dash rounded on her, pushing her back several feet. Faraday took this opportunity to jump off the desk and run out of the office. She hoped that meant he had what he needed. She also hoped he would grab Christine wherever she was, especially because Dash was marching forward, forcing Paris back toward the open wall that led to the ground below—twenty-six stories down to the pavement.

CHAPTER SIXTY

Paris realized that since she couldn't rely on magic, she would have to pull up her first defense—her fist. She balled up her fingers and charged up as she usually did before a fight. In a flash, Paris shot forward, throwing a punch through the air.

Having fought giants, gnomes, elves, and many other magical creatures, Paris had experienced a lot of reactions when she threw the first punch. However, she hadn't seen a grown man put his hands over his head and cower as he begged for mercy. "Please don't hit me in the face!"

Sidestepping, Paris exchanged places with Dash, staring at him in disbelief. "Dude, relax." She pulled back her hands. "I won't hurt you. I never wanted any trouble. I don't want you using FriendNet to break up relationships. Maybe we can come up with a deal?"

Dash straightened, shaking his head, a sinister look on this face. "Yeah, right."

This was one hot and cold psychotic piece of work, Paris observed, watching as a smile transformed his face. "I didn't want to get hit. I bruise easily. Now get out and walk slowly down the road or fast. Doesn't matter. You'll meet your death either way."

Paris sighed, realizing that she wouldn't be able to compromise with the guy in skinny jeans. Unfortunately, she was going to have to deliver his demise, but she definitely wasn't going to dirty her hands to do it.

She smiled at him, which put him on guard immediately. Pointing at his shirt, Paris said, "Hey, where did you get that lovely plaid shirt? I want one for my boyfriend."

"You don't have a boyfriend," he replied rudely.

"Not on FriendNet," she retorted. "You know, people can have a life not controlled by social media, and you can't do anything to them."

"I can," he threatened bitterly, standing in front of the open window wall, the wind making his beard move.

"So, the shirt? Was it at Gap? Or Nieman Marcus? Or Amazon?"

He scoffed. "I'd never shop at any of those places."

"Oh, a thrift shop then?" Paris teased, knowing that the best defense was to get under someone's skin and make them their own worst enemy.

"I'm not telling you where I got this. Or anyone else." Dash regarded her with evil eyes.

Paris shrugged. "That's fine. I can ask anyone on the street below. When we were coming in, I saw, like, ten people in the city wearing that same shirt."

His mouth fell open, total offense written on his face. "Shut up!"

"Oh, it's true." Paris pointed at a roll of mints on his desk. "I used to love those candies."

"Stop talking," Dash warned, grabbing the edges of his shirt, trying to pull it up.

"Of course," Paris continued like she hadn't heard him. "I don't have those mints anymore since I learned that they have so many preservatives in them."

"They don't!" Dash struggled with his shirt, trying to pull it over his shoulders and nearly tripping on his feet.

Paris nodded. "Oh, it's true. Too bad. But you know what song always makes me feel better?" She pulled out her phone and scrolled to her favorite playlist on Spotify, picking a song she knew would kill the hipster.

A moment later, and *Oops I Did it Again* by Brittany Spears started playing.

Dash gasped in pain. His hands tried to shoot for his ears as if they were suddenly bleeding, but they were still still tangled in his shirt. The effort sent him backward, and he stumbled on his feet and tripped. Paris realized what was going to happen and rushed forward, but it was too late. She wanted to subdue the guy until she had backup, but she never wanted him to die. However, as he fell over the side of the building, down twenty-six floors, she knew that the hipster's death was inevitable.

CHAPTER SIXTY-ONE

"That was intense." Christine sipped hot cocoa in the headmistress' office. "I had to stomach an entire conversation about suspenders for an hour."

"Christine." Headmistress Starr gave her a pointed look. "I think there are other things to attend to."

"An hour," Christine repeated, bringing the hot cocoa to her mouth.

"How are you doing?" Headmistress Starr asked Paris with a consoling look.

Before she could answer, Faraday cut in, bringing his doll-sized cup of cocoa to his mouth. "I'm okay. The pressure to perform was a lot. But I pulled through and got the results, saving the day as only I can do."

Paris sighed, realizing that with a bunch of divas around her, she was never going to get her moment in the limelight...not that she wanted it.

"Paris witnessed someone's death," Mae Ling stated calmly. "I think she deserves our attention right now."

"I'm okay," Paris urged, not wanting any extra attention. "I don't want to talk about it."

"Good, because it sounds gross." Christine winked at her friend, knowing she wanted her deflection.

"I didn't see anything," Paris admitted, looking at Willow and Mae Ling. "I didn't want to kill him."

"You didn't," Mae Ling stated.

"He killed himself," Willow added.

"Yeah, but although Faraday was able to stop the programming, we don't know who at FGA was behind it," Paris continued, having explained so much of what had happened during her time at FriendNet and what she'd learned.

"Not yet," Willow stated. "We should when the report from Bep comes back about the poison meant for Saint Valentine. That should tell us who was after him and sabotaging love from within."

"It's so weird that an agent would try and destroy love when that's the whole purpose of FGA," Christine related.

"The purpose of an organization isn't so straightforward," Faraday related, finishing his tiny cup of hot chocolate. "You see, it might behoove someone gunning for power to make the love meter plummet so the current administration looks bad. Then they are abolished, making room for good blood."

"Although I appreciate you as a squirrel and a programmer," Christine began, "please leave these matters of power to the humans with big pants."

"He's right," Mae Ling stated.

Everyone looked up at her. "Those who want power have the best chances of gaining it by discrediting those who have it."

"So someone is either trying to kill Saint Valentine or make his efforts look bad by sabotaging love with antics?" Christine asked.

Mae Ling nodded. "Our job is to explore and keep our eyes open. I don't think this one will be easily gunned down."

"'Gunned down' is a strong phrase for a fairy godmother," Christine observed.

"Shot with an arrow?" Mae Ling countered. "How is that one?"

"Either works for me," Christine stated. "I like my fairy godmothers with a bit of edge."

Mae Ling winked at her. "Me too."

CHAPTER SIXTY-TWO

"Wow, a full moon makes the Enchanted Grounds look different." Paris gazed out at the Bewilder Forest, realizing that she was stalling.

Hemingway gave her a reassuring look. "It's fine. I put up wards again to ensure that my...the ghost doesn't come near where we're going. Don't worry."

Paris swallowed and nodded. She didn't know how to tell him that she wasn't afraid of the ghost of his mother...well, she was...who wouldn't be. What Paris was really afraid of was losing her friend, Faraday. That was how this whole thing ended, and both she and the squirrel knew it. That's why he hadn't looked at her once since they'd set off on this mission from the mansion.

Everyone had worried that she was upset about witnessing the hipster's death or that there was a killer loose in the fairy godmother mansion who had tried to murder Saint Valentine. None of that bothered her as much as losing her very first friend.

Paris had her Uncle John her whole life. She'd been loved by her family even if they couldn't be there for her. It wasn't until Faraday that she'd felt lovable. He had loved her without obligation—or at least she thought. Later she learned it was a part of a deal, but she didn't know that at the time, and his companionship had been her strength during the hardest transition of her life. She felt as if she lost it now, that it would retroactively take away her power.

Paris tried to breathe through the pain in her chest and pretended to act strong. "Which way to the sharp bend in the river?" she asked Hemingway.

He pointed to the left of the Bewilder Forest. "Just a ways through here."

Paris nodded. "Let's get going and turn on these twinkle lights. I, for one, don't like to be left in the dark."

She started forward fast, feeling the guy and squirrel standing confused at her urgency behind her.

"Pare," Faraday said, hopping after her. A moment later she heard Hemingway trudging after her.

Paris didn't care. She didn't want to stop until this mission was over. It had gone on too long for her.

In the weight of her backpack, she felt the stones that Papa Creola had given her. They felt as if they carried her future of more loneliness and solitude, but Paris tried to remind herself that she had other friends now. She had Christine and Penny. Wilfred and Chef Ash. And there was Hemingway. Of course, always Uncle John. Most importantly, her parents and her family. Losing Faraday, well, it felt heavier than she would have thought.

Paris was charging forward when Hemingway caught up to her, almost breathless.

"Hey, I didn't realize you knew where you were going," he said to her, hurrying to keep up.

Paris pointed ahead. "It's up there."

"How do you know?" he asked.

"Because I can hear the water," she admitted and paused, surprised by her answer.

"That's true." He was also shocked. "Then why did you ask me along?"

"I don't know," she answered honestly. "Maybe I thought I needed you here. Maybe I wanted you here."

Hemingway let out a long breath. "I know you've been through a lot lately."

"Everyone keeps worrying about me," she began.

"But no one is allowed to care," he cut in.

"No." She continued to hike, getting closer to the stream. "They can…but I'm fine."

"I'm guessing Paris Beaufont is always fine," Hemingway stated. "She was born fine, and even when she sees death and her secrets are exposed and has her world turned upside down, she's always fine. My question is, when is Paris not fine?"

She halted, blinked at him, and swallowed. "I'm not sure. I haven't found what breaks me yet, and I hope never to."

He toughened himself from the inside out, the same as her. Hemingway nodded. "Yeah, let's hope you don't."

"Guys," Faraday said, capturing both of their attention.

Paris looked at the squirrel behind them and followed his gaze. It led ahead to a ray of moonlight in the clearing next to the babbling water where two majestic animals stood waiting.

CHAPTER SIXTY-THREE

Paris was the least reluctant to approach Edison and Curie, having met them both before. Hemingway had obvious hesitations, halting a safe distance away and watching as Paris closed the distance.

Faraday, on the other hand, seemed less hesitant and more perplexed, as if he couldn't remember the two animals.

"Hey." Paris took off her backpack when she neared the two animals. "I have the rocks, and it's a full moon. So it appears we have everything that we need. Well, if Curie is ready."

She gave the owl perched on a large boulder next to the creek an unsure look.

The owl hooted as if that was all the reply necessary. Paris took that as a yes, looking over her shoulder at Faraday still in the distance, her expression saying. "Are you freaking coming? I did this for you, Jerk Face."

The squirrel got her drift and hopped along, joining the other two.

"Hi." Faraday looked down at the ground.

"Can we get this over with?" Edison asked.

"I'm ready," Curie said stuffily.

Paris glanced among the three of them. "Wait. Weren't you all friends? Why is there no reunion?"

The stag huffed. "Of course not. We were associates, and that's all."

"Science and magic brought us together," Curie explained. "I found through my notebooks, things that Faraday and Edison had scribbled—"

"Same here," Faraday chimed.

"Yes, so I followed Curie's notes," Edison explained.

"Then you all time traveled as animals," Hemingway guessed, striding forward. "You intended to—"

"Make animals talk freely," Faraday supplied.

"Except we got stuck," Edison added.

"Now, here we are," Curie finished.

"Three scientific animals from different timelines, who had a good mission that went wrong," Paris summarized.

"We've been stuck as animals ever since," Edison confirmed.

"Lost from our lives," Curie continued.

"All against our will," Faraday muttered.

"Well, I'm here to help you fix that." Paris pulled the polished river rocks from the bag that Papa Creola gave her, laying them in front of each animal. She gave the owl a pointed look. "What happens next?"

Curie hooted once. "Your spell is one of transformation. That can't happen until we've time traveled. Can you help us, magician?" To Paris' surprise, the bird looked at Hemingway.

He nodded, a sturdy expression in his eyes. "I can do it. When you time travel, when the rocks are still glowing, I can transform you back to what you once were, when you're back in your timeline."

"We were human," Edison said stuffily.

"We were scientists," Curie informed him.

"We were trying something new," Faraday added shyly.

Hemingway glanced at Paris. "I can help. Once the time travel rocks are activated, I can use a transformation spell safely."

"Okay." The heaviness of the moment hit her. "Then I guess we have to activate the rocks."

She stood back, the moonlight making her feel like she was in the spotlight. "Are you all ready to do this?"

"Yes," Edison answered.

"Of course," Curie stated.

"Not at all," Faraday muttered.

CHAPTER SIXTY-FOUR

"What?" four voices asked at once.

All heads turned to look at Faraday.

"We need you," Edison stated.

"You can't stop us," Curie said.

"What?" Paris repeated.

The squirrel shook his head and hopped forward toward the stag and the owl. "You don't need me...not to time travel and transform. Because we did the original spell together, sharing each other's notes, we needed each other for this part. We have to be together. But I don't have to time travel or transform for you to be able to."

"You're not going back to your time?" Edison asked.

"It's complicated," Faraday answered.

"But if you don't go back..." Curie didn't finish the thought.

"I think you both still can," Faraday stated. "You need me here to complete the original spell."

Paris stepped forward. "Faraday, what are you saying?"

The squirrel turned and looked at her, and if she'd never felt love before, she knew it then. He lowered his chin and regarded her with such fondness.

"Pare, I don't want to go back," Faraday said. "I want to stay with you. This is my life now."

She was suddenly speechless. "But Faraday, you have this whole life to return to. You haven't been able to tell me about it, but it has to be better than sleeping in my sock drawer."

He shook his head. "That's what you don't understand because I could never tell you. I didn't have a life before you. Not really. I didn't have friends or a mission or anything like what I do now. I had science and my experiments, but I have that in this life too. Here I also have you and the college and your friends and things that make me feel excited. Why would I want to go back to the nothing that I had?"

"But..." Paris didn't know what to say, and she didn't have any words.

That's why when the *ding* on her phone echoed, she reached for it in her pocket.

No one seemed to mind when she retrieved the phone and read the message from Papa Creola. His message was simple and heartbreaking, and Paris had a hard time reading it aloud.

CHAPTER SIXTY-FIVE

"What does it say?" Faraday asked, as the one who knew it had to be important if it came through right then.

"It's from Father Time," Paris admitted, staring at her phone, the tears choking in her throat.

"He wants us back on our timelines," Faraday guessed.

Paris nodded.

"He won't let me stay, will he?" the squirrel asked.

"He will," she said, surprising everyone. "But there's a caveat if you do."

Paris looked directly at Faraday, suddenly feeling like they were the only two in the Bewilder Forest. She blocked out the others, knowing that it needed to be about her and him right then.

"Faraday, Papa Creola says you can stay in this timeline for a magician's lifespan, which you possessed," Paris explained, reciting the message the best she could. "But you have to remain a squirrel for that entirety. Never returning to being a man. Ever again."

She tensed, clenched her hands tightly, and prepared to lose her friend forever—something she'd been preparing for all this time.

To her surprise, Faraday smiled at her. "Then the decision is rather easy."

Paris nodded, swallowing down her remorse. "I figured. I understand. I'll miss—"

"The decision is easy. I'll remain a squirrel," he stated.

"What?" everyone echoed.

Faraday grinned. "I was never happy as a human." He looked at Paris intently. "The only thing that's ever made me happy was being a part of your world, Paris Beaufont. If you let me, I'd like to stay with you forevermore."

CHAPTER SIXTY-SIX

Paris simply could not believe it. She really couldn't...
Faraday was supposed to desert her. He was supposed to abandon her like everything else in her life. Instead, he was choosing to stick around after being given the choice of a body and a life.

Paris had a hard time believing it, but she did, and when she stepped back, she saw the most memorable sight of her entire life.

The time travel stones activated, hovering in front of Curie and Edison in the air. They shimmered and glowed and disappeared as bright as the glowing moon overhead. Then the whole thing was over, well, besides that Paris was face-to-face with a squirrel who had sacrificed his entire life to be with her.

That was a lot, she realized.

That was like marriage—except there was no diamond ring—and she got that this wasn't marriage.

Still, it felt like forever, although no one had ever proposed to her.

Yet, she wanted Faraday by her side always, and in many ways, she was glad he'd made the decision. Still, she had a squirrel friend forever, and it felt weird and right, and she was secretly very happy for it.

Her best friend had chosen her, and it made her feel unbelievably loved.

CHAPTER SIXTY-SEVEN

"It's such a relief." Headmistress Willow Starr looked proudly at the love meter. It had recovered. Not entirely, but it was at least over thirty percent, whereas before it was getting close to zero. Paris had worried that it would go into the negative, something that hadn't happened in a very long time. She hoped that one day, the love meter could be well over fifty percent and higher. Maybe over one hundred percent. What would a world like that be?

"It is nice to see the love meter recovering." Mae Ling stood beside the open window in the headmistress' office in the fairy godmothers' mansion—the spring breeze sweeping into the room. It suddenly reminded Paris of Dash falling from the twenty-sixth floor at Friend-Net, and she shuddered slightly.

As though sensing Paris' sudden tension connected to her trauma, Mae Ling shut the window and turned to the group. "You two did good work on this case."

Headmistress Starr nodded in appreciation, picking up her feathered quill. "Saint Valentine is very pleased and was very impressed with your work when I gave him the details that you've provided about the mission. He was shocked to learn that someone orchestrated this all with the motive to sabotage love."

"Someone who I think could be an agent for FGA." Paris glanced at Christine, who was back in her blue gown, her orange hair grayish once more.

Christine nodded. "Yeah, I tried to get more out of that handlebar mustache guy, but he didn't know anything. He said that the consultant who showed up at FriendNet talked only with Dash privately."

"He was wearing a black suit," Paris said. "Like the FGA agents."

"I'm afraid that's not enough for us to draw any conclusions," Willow stated with regret.

"Well, maybe now that Saint Valentine is involved with FriendNet he can get the security footage, and we can see who the guy was," Paris offered.

The leader of FGA had decided not to shut down the social media site, saying that he thought that although someone used it for evil, it could also bring good. Saint Valentine contended that it could as easily bring people together, creating love, as break them up. However, there would be strict company supervision from agents at the Matters of the Heart office only.

Willow frowned. "I asked about that. Unfortunately, it appears that whoever this consultant was, they used magic to ensure they didn't appear on any security cameras. There's no record of their visit."

"See, it has to be an FGA agent," Paris nearly exclaimed, adamant on the subject.

The headmistress shook her head. "I'm sorry, but we simply don't have enough information to support that conclusion. It could as easily be a magician or any of the other magical races."

"They don't have a motive to sabotage love," Paris argued.

Willow sighed. "An FGA agent has zero reasons to do so. They are in the business of creating matches."

"For the wealthy, famous, and elite." Paris was almost vibrating with frustration. She knew something was going on behind the scenes but couldn't figure out what it was—yet.

"Someone did try and murder Saint Valentine," Christine added. "So things aren't all hunky-dory at FGA."

"We don't know that was an agent," Headmistress Starr repeated. Her stress showed in her eyes.

"Actually, we do," Uncle John said from the doorway.

"Detective Nicholson." The headmistress stood and waved her feathered quill. Another poufy armchair appeared beside where Paris and Christine sat. "Please come in. You have an update on the case?"

"Yes." Uncle John held up a piece of paper. "I got the report back from Bep at the Rose Apothecary on the poison."

Headmistress Starr waved her quill again, and Paris recognized the silencing spell she'd used to ensure they weren't overhead in the hallway. She glanced at Paris and Christine. "I trust you'll not disclose anything we hear."

Before either girl could answer, Uncle John said, "It won't matter. This news will spread very fast. I've already called in my FLEA officers, and I'm here asking that you open a portal for them to enter Happily Ever After College."

"Your officers?" Willow asked. Paris knew why he'd dispatched the agents, but she knew that the fairy godmother was naïve about such things.

"To make an arrest," Uncle John informed her. "I've solved the murder, and I know without a doubt who created the poison that killed Agent Opal. All the evidence points to only one person."

"Who was it?" Willow's voice shook.

"The poison was confirmed as being made by a fairy," Uncle John began. "Furthermore, Bep was able to extract the magic used to create the binding of the deadly nightshade, a process that must happen for it to be odorless and tasteless. She found remnants of a certain gem in the potion."

"Remnants of a gem." Mae Ling's eyes narrowed. "The agents all channel their magic with instruments that possess gems."

Willow nodded. "Yes, it's how they brand their magic. A tracking device of sorts."

Uncle John drew in a breath. "I'm well aware. Remnants of topaz laced the poison."

Paris gulped suddenly.

Christine gasped. "I knew that guy was trouble."

"Agent Topaz," Headmistress Starr said in disbelief. "So it was an FGA agent then?"

"It appears there's more contention within Saint Valentine's ranks than we originally thought," Mae Ling offered wisely.

"I knew that the FGA agents and board didn't fully support everything that Saint Valentine has been doing, but murder?" Willow said, as though the act that she had witnessed was just setting in for her.

"There's a lot more at stake for FGA than love," Mae Ling stated. "The current Saint Valentine's administration has challenged traditions and ideology, and some hold onto that more than life itself."

"It would seem so if Agent Topaz was willing to murder someone," Willow murmured, her eyes distant as the shock hit her fully.

"I also think, after conducting the interviews and doing a full search of the campus," Uncle John began, "that Paris was supposed to take the fall for this." He gave his niece a sympathetic look. "I'm sorry, but I had to search your room."

Paris nodded, not at all put-off. "I understand."

The tension on his face deepened. "That's when I found this." Uncle John pulled a small clear pouch from his pocket. Inside and visible was something Paris recognized—deadly nightshade.

"Wait!" Paris exclaimed. "That's not mine!"

"Dum-dum-dum!" Christine sang. "The plot thickens."

CHAPTER SIXTY-EIGHT

"I didn't think it was yours," Uncle John said in a consoling voice. "I didn't think you'd take the deadly nightshade. I know that I'm biased, but I knew you wouldn't try and murder someone...well, on purpose."

He was alluding to Dash's death, which she didn't technically do, but his blood was sort of on her hands.

"How did that get in Paris' room?" Willow looked between Paris and her uncle.

"I don't know," the detective answered. "I believe someone planted it to indict Paris for the murder. However, a recent conversation with Hemingway about the deadly nightshade got me thinking. I did some research on demon blood and found something of particular interest."

"Demons can't touch deadly nightshade," Mae Ling cut in.

Uncle John nodded. "Yes, I found it interesting when Hemingway explained that Paris' demon blood had caused the deadly nightshade to start popping up. That's when I went to her father, Stefan, who is a demon hunter. He explained that before he could sense a demon to track them down, he would look for deadly nightshade, knowing that meant a demon was close by. However, ironically, the plant can be used to weaken the demons. He used to break down the plant and dip his weapons in it. Then he got bitten and couldn't touch the stuff because it also caused him pain. Most wouldn't know this information even if they knew Paris had demon blood since it's very specialized knowledge."

"Like someone who was trying to frame Paris by planting the deadly nightshade in her room," Christine interjected in sudden realization.

"Exactly," Uncle John confirmed. "Touching the plant doesn't harm others. It's only when they ingest it." He withdrew a black berry from the pouch and held it out in the palm of his hand. "If my suspicion is correct, Paris won't be able to touch this." He offered his niece a regretful look. "I'm sorry, Pare, but I need you to touch this."

She stood, nodding. "It's okay. It will only hurt, right?"

"Yes, Stefan said it wouldn't cause lasting damage." Uncle John answered.

Paris swallowed, extended her hand, and cautiously placed her fingertips on the berry. Immediately, her hand seared as if she'd suddenly touched fire. Smoke billowed up from the berry, and Paris yanked her hand back, hissing from the pain.

Uncle John also pulled his hand away, putting the deadly nightshade back into the bag. "I'm sorry, but that confirms my point. There's no way that Paris stole or created the poison."

"So Agent Topaz murdered someone and framed Paris for it," the headmistress said, shaking her head.

"I believe so, but we will have to try him before we can fully confirm it. I'll need to take him into custody with your permission," Uncle John stated with confidence.

Willow gave Mae Ling a sturdy expression. "Please open a portal for the FLEA officers. It appears that they need to make an arrest.

CHAPTER SIXTY-NINE

The entire school was gathered on the Enchanted Grounds when the officers from the Fairy Law Enforcement Agency led Agent Topaz out of the mansion and down the long walk.

They'd magically bound the fairy's hands behind his back, and his head was low as he strode for the portal in the distance. In the lead, with an air of authority, was Uncle John. In his hand was a clear plastic bag, and inside it was the silver pocket watch with the large purple topaz that Paris had seen the agent use when teaching Art of Love class.

Agent Topaz's magic was also locked so that he couldn't use it in an act of desperation to get away. However, the fairy wasn't resisting, although shame and regret spilled off his every move and expression.

Paris watched from the sidelines, her eyes more on the crowd than the alleged murderer the officers led away. Many seemed relieved that they'd caught the suspect. However, Paris still had a strange feeling on the matter. Her gut told her something wasn't right. Even though Willow had said they couldn't connect Agent Topaz to FriendNet, Paris firmly believed someone at FGA had to be involved in that devious scheme. Someone was trying to take down Saint Valentine, and what better way than to sabotage love, making the leader of the fairy godmothers look incompetent.

In the distance, split off from the crowd was a lone figure. One that Paris could easily see even though he was far away. Her father had explained that her demon blood made it so that her senses were heightened—something she'd never known, not knowing any differently. She could see farther and better than most.

Standing beside a tree and watching the murder suspect was Agent Ruby, his black bowler hat tucked down low over his eyes. From the inside of his suit jacket pocket, the agent withdrew an object. At first, Paris couldn't make out what it was because of the flash of light created by Agent Ruby's portal.

However, before he stepped through the portal, disappearing, Paris saw the instrument he used to channel his magic. It was a silver ballpoint pen that had a red heart-shaped gem on its end.

CHAPTER SEVENTY

"I knew it!" Faraday exclaimed from the sock drawer.

Paris sat up in her bed, thinking that she'd never go to sleep from the sudden revelation she'd discovered that day. "You knew that Agent Ruby was the one behind FriendNet? How?"

"The hat, of course," Faraday said. "The hipsters said the guy in the black suit had a bowler hat."

Paris sighed. "That's about as flimsy as my idea that it was an agent because the consultant was wearing a suit."

"How many people in this century sport bowler hats?" Faraday asked.

"Not many," she agreed. "Still, that wasn't enough. However, his magical instrument is a silver ballpoint pen with a red heart-shaped gem on its end, as the hipster described. That's pretty specific."

Paris had gone to Uncle John and Willow with the information immediately. However, neither said it was enough to connect Agent Ruby to the FriendNet debacle. Uncle John promised to keep an eye on it but didn't seem convinced. If anything, everything pointed at Agent Topaz being behind it because of the murder. They needed more evidence, they all agreed.

Paris hadn't liked Agent Topaz, who was uptight and judgmental, but she didn't think of him as a murderer. Agent Ruby though, that man was pure evil—announcing to everyone about her demon blood. He seemed like the one trying to frame her, but all the evidence for the murder pointed to Agent Topaz. Everything would hopefully come out when he went to trial.

"Do you think that Agents Topaz and Ruby were working together, possibly?" Faraday turned over in his makeshift bed, trying to get comfortable.

Paris laid back down, enjoying the waning moon's light streaking through her bedroom window. "I think anything is possible. It appears there's a lot of corruption in FGA. Who knows how many dirty agents there are trying to take Saint Valentine out."

"Well, they don't know that Paris Beaufont and her trusty sidekick are on the case," Faraday sang. "No one is getting away with destroying love and murder when we're around."

Paris smiled, her heart suddenly full of love. "That's right. We're going to ensure that love spreads and the fairy godmothers prosper—one way or another."

"You know what, Paris?"

"What?"

"I know you didn't want to come to Happily Ever After College at first, but I'm glad you did," he stated.

"Because you wanted to check out this anomaly that is Happily Ever After College?" Paris questioned in a teasing voice. She had worried before that Faraday had only helped her to fulfill his deal with Plato. However, in the end, he'd declined to be turned back and returned to his timeline. That's when it dawned on her that Faraday helped her because he wanted to. Also, because he was good at his core and he wanted to help Edison and Curie to get their lives back. There were few as noble as the squirrel getting ready for bed in her sock drawer.

"I'm glad that you came to fairy godmother college," he continued, "because it needs you. Mae Ling is right. You're the one who needs to change things the way only you can. If my hypothesis is correct, you're going to revolutionize this place."

"I don't know about all that." Paris suddenly felt a lot of pressure.

"You will, and you can tell me how I was right," he sang through a yawn.

Paris yawned too. "Hey, Faraday."

"Yes, Paris?"

"Will you tell me soon about your life before being a squirrel? Now that you can and all," she asked.

"Sure," he answered. "But it's not all that interesting. Not as interesting as my life with you, but I'll tell you anything you want to know now that I can."

"Deal." Paris smiled and closed her eyes. "Also, thanks for choosing me over your old life. I'm still shocked."

"You shouldn't be," he said fondly. "There was no choice. It was always going to be you."

There didn't seem any better way to end that long day than with those words, so Paris pulled up her covers and let out a long breath. "Good night, Faraday."

"Good night Paris."

Before too long, the squirrel's soft snores filled the room. They didn't disturb Paris at all. They reminded her that she had her best friend close by and wasn't alone—and hopefully never would be.

Paris quickly fell asleep too, joining Faraday, dreaming of all the adventures that they'd have and all the love they'd bring to the world.

SARAH'S AUTHOR NOTES
MAY 26, 2021

Thank you a ton for reading! Your support means more than I can ever say. Ever. But I will try. Thank you.

I always have so much to tell you about when it comes to the author notes. One might argue I tell you all too much. What can I say, my life is an open book.

Ohhhhh that reminds me that I used to journal...when I was a teenager. I don't anymore, unless this is considered journaling. But on the inside of all of my rose scented journals was a phrase I stole from a forgotten source. It read:

My life is an open book with the pages ripped out, pressed and dried between the folds of time, read by no one. There is a chapter there devoted to you.

I was quite the poet in my youth, now I prefer magic and fantasy and a little less Walt Whitman. I'm still a romantic at heart though.

Currently, I'm on my way to Scotland after almost two months apart to see the Scotsman. The United States still hasn't opened up so I do the traveling. I don't mind because I love adventure. And I have cats and they are easy to leave. Well, they get grumpy but they can, according to science, go longer than most without food and water.

SARAH'S AUTHOR NOTES

Don't worry, I set them out tons of food and water and people will be checking on them. I'm just saying, they are fine.

So, you all need a story full of gruesome blood at this point. The Paris series is more about strategy and romance and less about flesh wounds, so here's something bloody to get you going.

When I was working on book 4 in the Inscrutable Paris Beaufont series I was running straight up against the deadline with a boatload of words to do in a short period of time. I always do it. No matter what!

But that week, I had my annual doctor's appointment. I just needed her to sign off on my prescriptions which required a simple blood test. Then I could get back to my desk and write. So I kept saying to the doctor, "Let's get this over with! Chop! Chop!"

The doctor could see what a rush I was in but encouraged me to go to the lab for my blood work instead of doing it in the office right then. I was like, "Nope! Send the nurse in here. Chop! Chop!"

My doctor was super reluctant and she was like, "How are your veins?"

"Great! Send the nurse in here! Take my blood. I've got a book to write. Chop! Chop!"

I quickly learned why the doctor was hesitant. The nurse was brand new and not skilled at drawing blood yet. So this young girl was nervous and sweating, all preparing to take my blood. The conversation went like this.

Shaking, the nurse said, "Are you afraid of needles?"

Impatiently, I replied, "No, are you?"

Trying to make light of the situation and fearful for my good writing arm getting stabbed, I said, "Is this your first time doing this?"

She gave me a horrified look.

Newbie Nurse started to draw my blood after stabbing me a few times and she looked faint.

Still shaking, she said, "Do you feel dizzy?"

"No, do you?" I retorted.

The woman didn't laugh. Instead she said, "Do you need some juice?

Do you need to lie down?"

"No, do you?"

This nurse was so done with me after that. And that was fine because I survived and got back to write my words. However, I realize now that when I kept saying, "Let's do this! Chop! Chop!" The universe heard, "Stab! Stab!"

And that's all she wrote folks. Literally. I'm out! Here's Mr. Bird Killer.

Much love and Peace,
Tiny Ninja

MICHAEL'S AUTHOR NOTES
MAY 28, 2021

Thank you for reading this Paris Beaufont book and the author notes here in the back.

CHOP CHOP!

I can just visualize the little bitty blonde tiny ninja, feet dangling in the air off the Dr.'s painful bed (complete with paper protection that crinkles as you try to get comfortable), and Sarah making a tomahawk cutting motion when she says to get busy stabbing her.

(I am now sure Sarah doesn't think about the ramifications of her comments on the mortal world.)

Which, when you think about it, is why her characters do so well. Sarah doesn't need to create bogus situations to put her characters into to continue the story. She just needs her characters to do what SHE does in real life and <<redacted>> happens.

Story problem solved or created. One or the other. I guess it is author problem solved, character issue created.

So, I would like to recommend that everyone who likes the series and has the time or inclination to write a review to mention that while we vote Sarah Awesome Author, we suggest she never run for any government office which might need to interact with a foreign power or aliens.

MICHAEL'S AUTHOR NOTES

I'd hate to see Sarah rush an important first contact with 'Chop chop! I have to get some writing done, bitches!' and they decide to blow up our planet or worse. I have no problem imagining that the aliens grab her and take her into outer space, and she plays the Princess in the *Star Wars* scene where the aliens act like Darth Vader and blow up Earth like Aldaran.

"Huh," she would sigh. "I guess that book isn't due by tomorrow night now."

Peace Out, you Urban Fantasy fanatics!

SARAH FOR PRESIDENT 2024.

Ad Aeternitatem,

Michael Anderle

ACKNOWLEDGMENTS
SARAH NOFFKE

I have so many people to thank who make this all possible. Firstly, thanks to Mike, who really pushes me to be a better writer, coming up with the best ideas, not just the really good ones. We work together pretty well, I'd say. I wonder what he'd say... Anyway, MA gave me the opportunity to write with LBMPN a few years ago and it's been life changing. He's very supportive and really cares. Thanks Bird Killer.

A huge thank you to the LBMPN team who work tirelessly so that I have less stress. Thanks to Steve and Kelly for making my life easier and being on top of everything. Thanks to Tracey and Lynne for fixing all my editing mistakes. A big thank you to the JIT team whose feedback at the 11th hour before publishing is invaluable. Thank you to my alpha readers Juergen and Martin. Thank you to everyone who makes getting the books to the reader possible. I really can't do this without you. And you make it so much more fun.

Thank you to my daughter, Lydia, who inspires my stories over and over again. She's my muse and we are always discussing story. She's an avid reader and listens to the Liv Beaufont series at night and reads the Sophia Beaufont books with me before bed. She also reads other authors, which I guess is okay. But my point is that she's supportive of me in so many ways. I need to stay immersed in this universe and remember all the details. There are 12 book in each series so there's a lot to remember. And Lydia loves my stories and then also supports me by listening and reading them so I can keep crafting. But also, she puts up with me when I go all psycho pants during a big crunch of a deadline. I will be the first to admit that I'm pretty intense a day or two before a book is due. And she always just smiles and says, "Mommy, you can do it."

Thank you to my family, the Scotsman and all my friends. You all are always so supportive of me and for that, I'm infinitely grateful. I really couldn't do this without the encouragement of those I love. On the really tough writing days, the Scotsman points out all the things that I don't see, like my dedication to the craft or how much readers are enjoying the books. I don't know what I did to have the most loving and thoughtful people in the world in my corner, but I'm going to do everything to keep them and hopefully keep making them proud.

And finally, thank you to you the reader. Without you I wouldn't be able to do what I love. Your support means so much to me and my family. Thank you from the bottom of my heart.

Love,
Tiny Ninja

BOOKS BY SARAH NOFFKE

Sarah Noffke writes YA and NA science fiction, fantasy, paranormal and urban fantasy. In addition to being an author, she is a mother, podcaster and professor. Noffke holds a Masters of Management and teaches college business/writing courses. Most of her students have no idea that she toils away her hours crafting fictional characters. www.sarahnoffke.com

Check out other work by Sarah author here.

Ghost Squadron:

Formation #1:
   Kill the bad guys. Save the Galaxy. All in a hard day's work.
   After ten years of wandering the outer rim of the galaxy, Eddie Teach is a man without a purpose. He was one of the toughest pilots in the Federation, but now he's just a regular guy, getting into bar fights and making a difference wherever he can. It's not the same as flying a ship and saving colonies, but it'll have to do.
   That is, until General Lance Reynolds tracks Eddie down and offers him a job. There are bad people out there, plotting terrible

things, killing innocent people, and destroying entire colonies. **Someone has to stop them.**

Eddie, along with the genetically-enhanced combat pilot Julianna Fregin and her trusty E.I. named Pip, must recruit a diverse team of specialists, both human and alien. They'll need to master their new Q-Ship, one of the most powerful strike ships ever constructed. And finally, they'll have to stop a faceless enemy so powerful, it threatens to destroy the entire Federation.

All in a day's work, right?

Experience this exciting military sci-fi saga and the latest addition to the expanded Kurtherian Gambit Universe. If you're a fan of Mass Effect, Firefly, or Star Wars, you'll love this riveting new space opera.

NOTE: If cursing is a problem, then this might not be for you.

Check out the entire series here.

The Precious Galaxy Series:

Corruption #1

A new evil lurks in the darkness.

After an explosion, the crew of a battlecruiser mysteriously disappears.

Bailey and Lewis, complete strangers, find themselves suddenly onboard the damaged ship. Lewis hasn't worked a case in years, not since the final one broke his spirit and his bank account. The last thing Bailey remembers is preparing to take down a fugitive on Onyx Station.

Mysteries are harder to solve when there's no evidence left behind.

Bailey and Lewis don't know how they got onboard *Ricky Bobby* or why. However, they quickly learn that whatever was responsible for the explosion and disappearance of the crew is still on the ship.

Monsters are real and what this one can do changes everything.

The new team bands together to discover what happened and how to fight the monster lurking in the bottom of the battlecruiser.

Will they find the missing crew? Or will the monster end them all?

The Soul Stone Mage Series:

House of Enchanted #1:
The Kingdom of Virgo has lived in peace for thousands of years...until now.

The humans from Terran have always been real assholes to the witches of Virgo. Now a silent war is brewing, and the timing couldn't be worse. Princess Azure will soon be crowned queen of the Kingdom of Virgo.

In the Dark Forest a powerful potion-maker has been murdered.

Charmsgood was the only wizard who could stop a deadly virus plaguing Virgo. He also knew about the devastation the people from Terran had done to the forest.

Azure must protect her people. Mend the Dark Forest. Create alliances with savage beasts. No biggie, right?

But on coronation day everything changes. Princess Azure isn't who she thought she was and that's a big freaking problem.

Welcome to The Revelations of Oriceran. Check out the entire series here.

The Lucidites Series:

Awoken, #1:
Around the world humans are hallucinating after sleepless nights.

In a sterile, underground institute the forecasters keep reporting the same events.

And in the backwoods of Texas, a sixteen-year-old girl is about to be caught up in a fierce, ethereal battle.

Meet Roya Stark. She drowns every night in her dreams, spends her hours reading classic literature to avoid her family's ridicule, and is prone to premonitions—which are becoming more frequent. And now her dreams are filled with strangers offering to reveal what she has always wanted to know: Who is she? That's the question that haunts her, and she's about to find out. But will Roya live to regret learning the truth?

Stunned, #2

Revived, #3

The Reverians Series:

Defects, #1:

In the happy, clean community of Austin Valley, everything appears to be perfect. Seventeen-year-old Em Fuller, however, fears something is askew. Em is one of the new generation of Dream Travelers. For some reason, the gods have not seen fit to gift all of them with their expected special abilities. Em is a Defect—one of the unfortunate Dream Travelers not gifted with a psychic power. Desperate to do whatever it takes to earn her gift, she endures painful daily injections along with commands from her overbearing, loveless father. One of the few bright spots in her life is the return of a friend she had thought dead—but with his return comes the knowledge of a shocking, unforgivable truth. The society Em thought was protecting her has actually been betraying her, but she has no idea how to break away from its authority without hurting everyone she loves.

Rebels, #2

Warriors, #3

Vagabond Circus Series:

Suspended, #1:

When a stranger joins the cast of Vagabond Circus—a circus that is run by Dream Travelers and features real magic—mysterious events start happening. The once orderly grounds of the circus become riddled with hidden threats. And the ringmaster realizes not only are his circus and its magic at risk, but also his very life.

Vagabond Circus caters to the skeptics. Without skeptics, it would close its doors. This is because Vagabond Circus runs for two reasons and only two reasons: first and foremost to provide the lost and lonely Dream Travelers a place to be illustrious. And secondly, to show the nonbelievers that there's still magic in the world. If they believe, then they care, and if they care, then they don't destroy. They stop the small abuse that day-by-day breaks down humanity's spirit. If Vagabond Circus makes one skeptic believe in magic, then they halt the cycle, just a little bit. They allow a little more love into this world. That's Dr. Dave Raydon's mission. And that's why this ringmaster recruits. That's why he directs. That's why he puts on a show that makes people question their beliefs. He wants the world to believe in magic once again.

Paralyzed, #2
Released, #3

Ren Series:

Ren: The Man Behind the Monster, #1:

Born with the power to control minds, hypnotize others, and read thoughts, Ren Lewis, is certain of one thing: God made a mistake. No one should be born with so much power. A monster awoke in him the same year he received his gifts. At ten years old. A prepubescent boy with the ability to control others might merely abuse his powers, but Ren allowed it to corrupt him. And since he can have and do anything he wants, Ren should be happy. However, his journey teaches him that harboring so much power doesn't bring happiness, it steals it. Once this realization sets in, Ren makes up his mind to do the one thing that can bring his tortured soul some peace. He must kill the monster.

Note This book is NA and has strong language, violence and sexual references.

Ren: God's Little Monster, #2
Ren: The Monster Inside the Monster, #3
Ren: The Monster's Adventure, #3.5
Ren: The Monster's Death

BOOKS BY SARAH NOFFKE

Olento Research Series:

Alpha Wolf, #1:
Twelve men went missing.

Six months later they awake from drug-induced stupors to find themselves locked in a lab.

And on the night of a new moon, eleven of those men, possessed by new—and inhuman—powers, break out of their prison and race through the streets of Los Angeles until they disappear one by one into the night.

Olento Research wants its experiments back. Its CEO, Mika Lenna, will tear every city apart until he has his werewolves imprisoned once again. He didn't undertake a huge risk just to lose his would-be assassins.

However, the Lucidite Institute's main mission is to save the world from injustices. Now, it's Adelaide's job to find these mutated men and protect them and society, and fast. Already around the nation, wolflike men are being spotted. Attacks on innocent women are happening. And then, Adelaide realizes what her next step must be: She has to find the alpha wolf first. Only once she's located him can she stop whoever is behind this experiment to create wild beasts out of human beings.

Lone Wolf, #2
Rabid Wolf, #3
Bad Wolf, #4

CONNECT WITH THE AUTHORS

Connect with Sarah and sign up for her email list here:

http://www.sarahnoffke.com/connect/

Michael Anderle Social

Website: http://lmbpn.com

Email List: http://lmbpn.com/email/

Social Media:

https://www.facebook.com/LMBPNPublishing

https://twitter.com/MichaelAnderle

https://www.instagram.com/lmbpn_publishing/

https://www.bookbub.com/authors/michael-anderle

BOOKS BY MICHAEL ANDERLE

Sign up for the LMBPN email list to be notified of new releases and special deals!

https://lmbpn.com/email/

For a complete list of books by Michael Anderle, please visit:

www.lmbpn.com/ma-books/

www.ingramcontent.com/pod-product-compliance
Lightning Source LLC
LaVergne TN
LVHW041623060526
838200LV00040B/1415